TANGLED TRUTHS

DEATH BEFORE DRAGONS
BOOK THREE

LINDSAY BUROKER

Tangled Truths: Death Before Dragons Book 3
Copyright © 2020 Lindsay Buroker. All rights reserved.

www.lindsayburoker.com

No part of this book may be reproduced, scanned, or distributed in any printed or electronic form without permission. Please do not participate in or encourage piracy of copyrighted materials in violation of the author's rights. Thank you for respecting the hard work of this author.

This is a work of fiction. Names, characters, places and incidents are either the product of the author's imagination or used fictitiously. No reference to any real person, living or dead, should be inferred.

Edited by Shelley Holloway
Cover and interior design by Gene Mollica Studio, LLC.

ISBN: 978-1-951367-05-3

TANGLED TRUTHS

Foreword

Thank you, good reader, for picking up another installment in the Death Before Dragons series. I'm having a great time writing these characters, so I hope you're enjoying reading them.

This adventure takes Val (and Zav, of course) to the small town of Harrison, Idaho, on Lake Coeur d'Alene, where I've vacationed a couple of times. If you're ever in the area and enjoy bicycling or inline skating, you should check it out. The 72-mile paved trail follows lakes and rivers, and you almost *never* have to worry about dragons swooping down to eat your bike. I do remember seeing a moose, but they're not quite as pesky.

Before you jump into the story, please let me thank my editor, Shelley Holloway, and my beta readers: Rue Silver, Sarah Engelke, and Cindy Wilkinson. Also, my thanks to Gene Mollica for the cover art, Vivienne Leheny for the audiobook narration, and my typo hunters Cyd, Gen, and Jenna for screening an early copy.

Now, I hope you will enjoy the story!

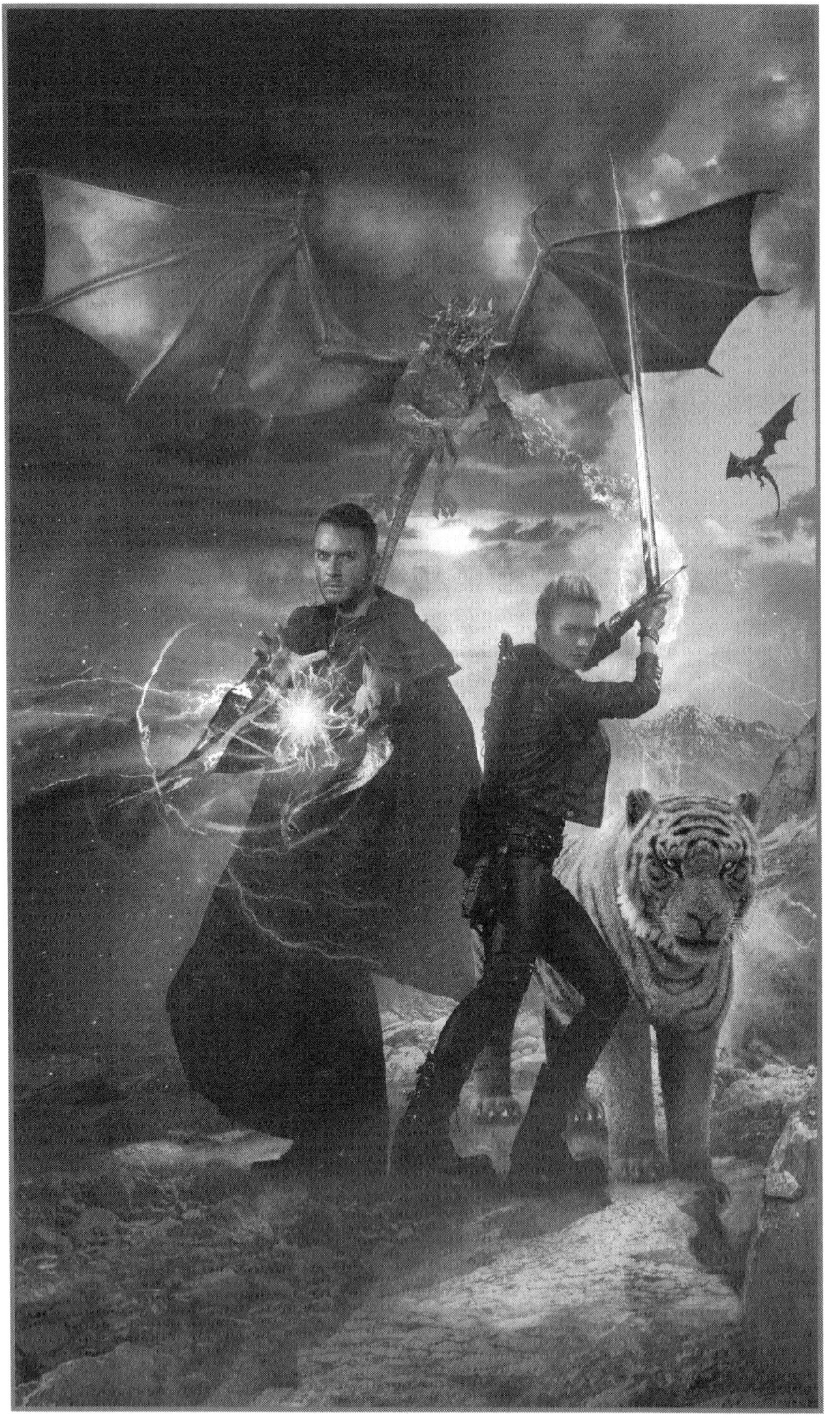

CHAPTER 1

The alien squeals, twangs, and buzzes that reverberated through the unmarked alley door sounded more like a wrecker flattening cars in a junkyard than music. Two dumpsters overflowing with bags of decomposing food, coffee filters, and used bathroom-cleaning supplies stood to either side of the entrance. A rat scurried out from behind one dumpster on its way to the other, dragging a rotting fish head in its mouth.

"Are you sure this is the right place?" I asked Nin, friend, food-truck owner, and the craftswoman who'd made the magical submachine pistol—Fezzik, I'd named it—that I carried in my thigh holster.

My finger wasn't far from the trigger now. On the way in, we'd spotted a massive clawed footprint in a dusting of spilled flour sticking to brown goo on the cracked pavement. I checked to make sure my magical longsword, Chopper, was loose in my back scabbard, the hilt within reach behind my shoulder.

Nin nodded, her blue pigtails flopping. "This is where I'm meeting my client. Did you not say you had been here before?"

Her soft precise English was barely audible over the music and the cars honking on the nearby Capitol Hill street. It was almost ten, but it was a warm rain-free summer night, and Seattle wasn't bedding down yet.

"Yeah," I said. "That's why I'm asking if you're *sure* it's the right place and really want to go in."

"I must go in. I was offered a handsome delivery fee to bring the ogre hunter in person." Nin patted a long package covered in the same brown paper she used to wrap the beef-and-rice dishes she sold from her truck. The shotgun inside, with explosive rounds designed to plow holes into the hardiest magical bad guy, oozed magic to my half-elven senses. "I need to earn every penny I can so I can help my family come to America. But you may wait outside if you're worried that you will not be welcome."

I snorted. I'd known I wouldn't be welcome the second she'd proposed this, but Nin made my magical ammunition and gave me free meals. She'd looked a little worried about being asked to come here for the drop-off, so I'd volunteered to come along. If I ended up in a bar fight—or worse—so be it. Having people regularly try to kill you keeps you sharp.

"Nah, I'll come in. This is the perfect place to test my new armor." I opened my duster, pushed my shirt up, and slid a hand over the sleek metal mesh vest. "It's like silk and almost as light. I love it already."

It truly would be good to try it in a low-key situation before relying on it during a mission. I needed to know it would stop magical bullets, swords, and fangs and claws. We'd fired a few rounds at it, but I would feel better once it had been battle-tested.

"I believe you can be arrested if you are caught touching yourself like that in public." Nin's dark eyes crinkled.

As the crafter of the armor, she was pleased by my reaction. After four years working with her, I could tell.

"I can't help it. If something feels nice under your fingers, it makes you want to rub it." An image flashed into my mind of the dragon Zav, shape-shifted into his handsome human form, with his chest bared and my fingers rubbing *it*.

I grimaced. It had been three weeks since an enemy dragon had compelled me to kiss Zav to distract him during an impending battle, and my dreams had been ridiculously lurid since then. They were pissing me off. No arrogant asshole of a dragon should be allowed to occupy my mind, even my sleeping mind, for that many hours. Ridiculous.

"I'll go first." I shoved the bare chest out of my thoughts and patted Nin on the shoulder. "*Way* first. You better wait a minute to come in, so any shrapnel flying off me doesn't hit you."

"I can simply stand behind you. You are a giant wall."

Nin was barely over five feet tall and would probably have to carry the "ogre hunter" on the scale with her to top a hundred pounds. Since I was six feet tall, that was possibly a fair thing to say, but...

"It's not polite to call a woman *giant* or *a wall* in this country. I'm tall, lithe, dangerous, and the appropriate weight for my height." No need to mention that I kept an inhaler in my pocket and bad air quality could take me down like a demolitions team imploding a skyscraper.

"Two of me could fit behind you."

"Ha ha. Just stay back." I braced myself to deal with the music—and a whole bunch of magical beings who wanted me dead—and walked through the door.

Armor-testing aside, I hoped there *wouldn't* be a fight. I got paid to assassinate vile criminals, not beat up magical beings in bar fights. I wished these people would figure out that I only hunted down their kin who committed crimes, not random members of their community. But I knew better than to expect anything had changed.

As I descended the stairs to the basement establishment that had neither a name, a website, nor a phone number, the smell of booze mingling with dozens of sweaty non-human patrons hit me as hard as the music. Orcs with tusks writhed and wiggled on the cement dance floor in the middle, and green-skinned goblins sat at indestructible plastic tables along the walls. Four hulking trolls claimed stools at the bar in the back, and shifters of all sorts congregated at the axe-throwing cage, hurling hatchets at a picture of a fanged vampire that had been pinned up over the plywood target. At least it wasn't a picture of me.

But everyone here could sense the auras of magical beings, including *half*-magical beings, and two dozen sets of eyes turned in my direction when I walked in.

The blue-skinned, white-haired troll owner squinted at me from the bar as he poured beer and sludge—a drink fermented from moss that orcs couldn't get enough of. Since the music kept playing, I couldn't hear the whispers of Ruin Bringer, Mythic Murderer, and Deathstalker, the nicknames the magical community had for me, but I could read them on their lips.

Coming here probably hadn't been a good idea. Nin might have been safer without me. Though if everyone was focused on me, maybe she wouldn't have to worry about being mugged while she waited for her buyer.

Two male shifters left the axe-throwing area, weaved through the orcs, and walked up to me with the predatory grace common for their kind. There was a lupine aspect to them, but that didn't mean they hadn't heard I'd recently taken out a bunch of lion and panther shifters from the Northern Pride.

One came to my right side and the other stopped in front of me, their proximity almost making me draw Fezzik. Dark-haired, yellow-eyed, and made of hard, sinewy muscle, the shifters were close enough that I could smell the mossy sludge on their breath.

The one in front reached for the flap of my duster, but I caught his wrist. Shifters were fast, but this guy's reflexes weren't up to par right now.

"It's not for sale," I said.

"What?" He looked at his buddy.

"The jacket." I pushed his arm back and let go. "I'm just here for a drink."

"This place doesn't serve the Ruin Bringer."

His buddy on the right was the one to lunge for me.

He was lightning fast, especially for a drunk guy, but I'd expected trouble. I sprang to the left, evading his grasp, and launched a side kick. The shifter was almost quick enough to dodge, but my heel clipped his hip and sent him spinning into two of the dancers.

An orc with saliva moistening his tusks whirled, grabbed him, and threw him onto one of the sturdy tables. The goblins around it leaped up, cursing at their spilled drinks.

The shifter in front of me started changing into a massive black wolf, his skin warping, blurring, and sprouting fur. Before he finished the transformation, I planted a front kick in his chest and sent him stumbling into the growing crowd of onlookers.

I grasped the cat-shaped figurine on my charm necklace. "Sindari," I whispered, summoning my ally.

One of the orc dancers charged toward me as two already-transformed lion shifters sprang toward me, their roars thundering over the music.

Sindari, a great silver tiger from another realm, solidified out of a mist and intercepted the big lions. A burly half-troll the orc had been dancing with charged after him, eager to join in against me.

They reached me, fists leading. I whipped up blocks to deflect their powerful blows and threw punches whenever I had an opening. Resisting the urge to draw my weapons, I put my back to the wall by the door so nobody could get behind me. I hadn't come to kill anybody, and I hoped the owner would break this up, if only to protect his establishment from damage.

As I traded blows with my two opponents, a part of me was exhilarated at the battle, but most of me stayed focused, gauging where the threats were in the room. Sindari was slashing and biting, keeping the lions busy, but the two wolf shifters had recovered from my kicks and were looking for an opening to lunge back in. I might have to draw Fezzik to get everyone to back off.

A click sounded, someone readying a switchblade. It was the half-troll. She rushed toward my side, knife jabbing.

Here was the opportunity to test my armor, but my instincts wouldn't let me take the hit when I had the power to deflect it. I knocked the blade high with a block to her forearm, then sprang in, hammering a palm strike into her broad chin. As her head snapped back, I kicked the blade out of her grip. It slammed into the wood doorframe and stuck, handle quivering.

I'd turned enough to move my back from the wall, and, sensing someone reaching for me from behind, I threw another kick, this one to the rear. An inhuman yowl sounded as it connected with an orc's nuts.

Are we killing these enemies? Sindari asked telepathically, his voice as calm as a tranquil lake as he slashed and bit, keeping the two lions from reaching me.

No, I replied in my mind. *This is a bar fight, not a mission.*

People are trying to kill you.

Someone across the room drew a pistol and aimed it in my direction. My opponents weren't tall enough to block his view, so I ducked low and grabbed the switchblade out of the doorframe. The gunman fired. As the bullet slammed into the door, I sensed a blur of an enchantment to it. I almost wished I'd let that one hit me so I could test the armor, but he'd been aiming at my head, not my chest.

It does seem that way, I admitted to Sindari and threw the switchblade.

The clunky weapon wasn't weighted for throwing, but enthusiasm and good aim did wonders. It thudded into the gunman's shoulder, and he dropped his pistol.

A meaty orc fist flashed in from the side as one of the wolves crept in from the other side. I whipped my head back as the blow breezed past my nose and caught my assailant's wrist. Gliding into him, I thrust with my hip and threw the orc over my shoulder. He smashed into the wolf.

As I readied myself for another opponent, a thunderous boom sounded just a few feet away—a weapon firing with the oomph of a howitzer. Everyone in the bar halted to stare at the gunman. The gun*woman*.

Nin had unwrapped her "ogre hunter" and fired it at the ceiling. The pump-action shotgun had left a sizable hole in the tin tiles and probably in the floor above. Hopefully the coffee shop and restaurant up there were closed for the night.

"It is time now to put an end to the fight," Nin said calmly but as loudly as her little voice could manage, "or I will blow your fucking heads off." She grinned and winked at me.

Cute, quirky Nin swearing was like a Disney character swearing, and it usually startled people into paying attention. It had that effect this time—or maybe the booming gunshot had.

"Enough," growled the troll owner, stepping out from behind the bar. Eight feet tall and half as wide, he waded toward us, pushing patrons aside with his meaty hands. "Go back to your drinks, everyone. I'll handle this."

He glared at me, glanced at the hole in the ceiling, and gave Nin an exasperated look.

"I bought indestructible tables for this place," he said in a voice like a bear's growl. "I didn't know I'd need the *ceiling* to be indestructible."

Even though Nin had fired, the troll continued to glare at me.

"What do you want here?" he demanded.

"I am here to meet a client and sell this fine weapon." Nin patted the big gun and nodded toward a back table where a hyena-headed gnoll dropped his face into his hand in a very human gesture.

"Go." The troll pointed Nin toward her contact, then pointed at me. "You came here to kill a werebear three years ago. I told you to stay out then."

"He was a murderer and a rapist."

"This is a safe place for our kind."

"This is a bar, not some holy sanctuary. Besides, no place should be safe for murderers."

"If the law guardians come, so be it, but you are an assassin. Mongrel scum." He spat on his own floor. Maybe someone else handled cleanup at the end of the night. "You're worse than the dark elves."

My ears would have perked up like a cat's if they could. Dark elves had been here? My employer, Colonel Willard, and I were looking for information on the dark elves hiding out somewhere in the city. Hiding out and plotting nefarious schemes and creating dangerous artifacts.

Sindari, his opponents having backed away after the gunshot, padded silently up behind the troll. *Shall I bite this hulk in the ass?*

No. I'm negotiating with him.

Are you sure? He looks like he's about to throw you out.

That's because I haven't turned on my charm yet. I smiled at the troll, raised my eyebrows in a friendly manner, and nudged my duster open enough to show the curve of my breasts.

"Dark elves, you say? Would you be interested in telling me what you know about them for a few dollars?"

He threw a punch at my face.

I hadn't expected it, and I barely dodged in time. His fist slammed into the doorframe, leaving it cracked and smashed.

When will you start turning on your charm? Sindari asked blandly.

I'll let you know.

As the troll pulled his fist out of the doorframe, I grabbed his wrist and looked into his stone-gray eyes, then said words sure to charm any business owner. "Tell me about your dark-elf visitors, and I'll pay a few dollars to have your ceiling fixed."

He glared at my presumptuous hand wrapped around his tree-trunk wrist, but Sindari growled from behind him, poised to take a bite out of his butt—or spring and snap his jaws around the troll's neck. I wasn't smiling now, and even though I was female, blonde, and not bad looking, few people dismissed me as a non-threat. I'd been in the business long enough to earn a lethal reputation.

The troll squinted as he considered Chopper, the hilt visible behind my shoulder, and then me. His eyes narrowed further in contemplation.

Of what? Something shifty?

"If you pay me a few *hundred* dollars for the ceiling and handle a problem the dark elves left me, I will consider letting you walk out of here alive."

I almost pointed out that he wasn't in a position to keep me from leaving, but his gaze flicked to the sides. The entire establishment was watching this confrontation, including the shifters and orcs I'd been fighting. They were poised to spring at me if I tried to walk out.

It didn't matter. This had started as a favor to Nin, but now I had a lead. I wouldn't leave before learning what I could about the dark elves.

"What *kind* of problem?" I couldn't imagine what an eight-foot-tall troll couldn't handle on his own.

He yanked his wrist out of my grip—with his strength, I couldn't have kept him from doing that even if I'd wanted to.

"Follow me."

Sindari stepped aside so the troll could head toward a corridor in the back. *I do not trust him, Val.*

I don't either.

You're still going to follow him, aren't you?

Yup.

Chapter 2

Sindari stuck close to my side as I followed the troll owner deeper into the establishment. Nin, who'd taken a seat with her gnoll client, watched me pass, her face tight with concern. I gave her a thumbs-up, even though I suspected the troll was leading me into trouble.

That feeling didn't go away as we entered a windowless cement hallway with rooms opening up to the sides full of couches littered with orcs, trolls, kobolds, goblins, and even a ten-foot-tall giant. The eclectic patrons were talking, making deals, or making out. Or all three.

I'd never seen this part of the establishment and wouldn't have guessed all this was under the Capitol Hill coffee shop where hipsters got their cold brews and avocado toast in the mornings.

Dull green and blue lightbulbs mounted on the walls glowed behind cages. Rather than creating some appealing ambiance, it turned everyone a sickly gray-green. The air smelled of mold. How mold could grow on cement walls, I didn't know, but my sensitive lungs objected to the scent, and I would need to use my inhaler if I was down here for too long. Just the kind of weakness I loved to show off in front of a basement full of enemies.

"What's your name, boss?" I asked my guide.

Maybe it wasn't too late to establish a rapport with him.

He glared daggers over his shoulder at me, his blue lips rippling back to show gold-capped teeth and fangs.

One of his staff called him Rupert, Sindari informed me.

A terror-inspiring name.

On their world, trolls are usually moss and peat farmers.

He has a lot of fangs for an herbivore.

They also battle and eat the alligator-like creatures that live in their swamps and prey on their people.

I don't want to meet the alligator large enough to prey on trolls.

They're smaller than dragons.

I don't want to meet any more dragons either.

Is that so? Why did Sindari sound so skeptical?

As the troll—Rupert—slowed down, Sindari murmured, *Familiar magic*, into my mind.

What do you mean? My senses were bombarded by the auras of so many magical beings in one establishment that I couldn't pick anything specific out of the miasma.

And a familiar door. Sindari's green eyes pointed toward the end of the hall.

Rupert had stopped, and it was hard to see much around his hulking form, but I could make out shiny steel in a thick metal frame set into the cement wall. When he stepped aside, the spinning circular latch of a bank vault door was visible.

My gut twisted. This vault door was identical to the one that had been under the panther shifters' house in Bothell.

You can sense magic through it? I asked Sindari. *The same as before?*

I hoped not.

Yes. The door is a magic sink and is muting it, but my senses are sublime. I detect something similar to that dark-elf orb.

Another time, I would have cracked a joke about his sublimeness, but memories of that night flooded my mind, and I relived my battle with the shifters and the dragon Dobsaurin. I'd been so proud to leap on Dob's chest, drive Chopper through his heart, and kill him before he could kill me—or force me to kill the injured Zav. Until Zav had gotten angry with me for slaying a dragon and warned me that there could be repercussions from the Dragon Justice Court. I hadn't seen him again since that night, but Dob's body had disappeared from its impromptu morgue, and I had little doubt Zav's people had come for it. For a burial or an investigation? Maybe both.

"This is the problem." Rupert spun the latch.

As soon as he pulled open the door, lavender light and tangible magic poured out. Familiar magic, as Sindari had promised.

Like a heavy mist, it flooded the hallway, wrapped around us and called to something deep inside me. More than one curious magical being came to the doors of the side rooms and peered toward the open door.

One of the wolf shifters I'd been fighting, now back in human form, strode down the hallway, his eyes glazed. He didn't see me, Sindari, or Rupert as he stepped through the doorway to be swallowed by the lavender light.

He was pulled by the magic, the promise of pleasure. As was I.

Once again, images flashed into my mind, a mixture of carnal pleasures—what would I have to do to keep *Zav* from featuring in these things?—and then less salacious desires, such as to hang out with my daughter on her trip over to Idaho this summer, and to share my home with friends and family, rather than living alone out of the fear that enemies would target people I cared about.

Val? Sindari bumped my hip.

I'm fine, I assured him.

You took two steps toward that door.

Rupert wants us to investigate it.

Let me go in alone. It has some magical allure for humans. Your face got blank there. Any enemy could have stabbed you in the back.

Not with you protecting me. But I took his point. It had been ridiculously hard to resist the allure of the first orb, and this one was just as strong, if not stronger. I drew Chopper, willing the blade to help me push the invading presence out of my mind. *It's not just humans. The shifters under the house were really into this thing.*

Moans drifted out of the room.

Yes, but they're human too. From what I'm seeing, the other races here are curious but not as drawn. Sindari glanced back down the hall. A human woman wandered out of a side room and walked past us and through the open door, but the goblins, orcs, and other beings had returned to what they'd been doing.

That's interesting. But shifters aren't really human, are they? They're from—Asgash…something. What's the name of their world?

Osgashandril.

Right. Flows right off the tongue. They're not originally from Earth. They've come as refugees, the same as the others.

It is true they came back recently as refugees, but their ancestors were originally taken from Earth.

Before I could ask for clarification, Rupert pointed into the room. "Go investigate my problem. That sword will not help you."

Actually, it would. Chopper didn't make me immune to mental compulsion or attacks, but it lent some protection from them.

"Swords are handy. You never know when you'll need to scratch between your shoulder blades." *Watch my back, please, Sindari.*

Always.

Rupert gestured me to go in instead of leading me in himself. I imagined him locking the door, chortling, and running off, but I sensed many other people—his patrons, presumably—inside.

I stepped across the threshold and squinted, willing my eyes to adjust so I could pick out details. The room smelled even more strongly of mold. What a lovely place to install a magical pleasure orb.

A lavender sphere identical to the one I'd destroyed in Bothell floated in the air in the center of a large storage room filled with people. As Sindari had suggested, they were all humans and shifters, not any other species, and they didn't glance my way. They were transfixed by the orb, which pulsed like a beating heart, darker purple veins running along its glassy lavender surface.

I could barely see those veins because so many humans and shifters had their chests and faces plastered to the artifact, arms spread to embrace it, not seeming to notice that they were hip to hip and face to face with each other. Other people were barely touching the orb, instead pressed against the backs of those who were closer to it, with only their hands touching the pulsing surface. Some of the mesmerized souls stood still while others writhed and groaned against the orb. Still more people lay on the cement floor where it appeared they'd passed out after sating themselves on the pleasure-inducing mental magic.

A faint hint of semen and urine mingled with the mold, and my gut clenched. Weren't these people even leaving to pee?

"What's the problem?" I asked—Rupert was watching me intently from the hallway, and I had a feeling he hoped I'd plaster myself against the orb too. "Other than that your clients don't know when to leave to use a toilet?"

His stone-gray eyes narrowed, his blocky face twisting in disappointment. By my lack of a reaction?

Oh, I was reacting—I felt the pull keenly—but I'd resisted the other orb, and I would resist this one.

"That's part of the problem," Rupert growled. "The other is this." He stepped inside and used one of his size-twenty boots to nudge a woman sleeping on the floor.

No, not sleeping, I realized. Even though magic bombarded my senses and muddled everything, she was close enough that I could tell she no longer had an aura. She was dead.

"Some people have their fun and leave," Rupert said, "but some aren't smart enough to. They fall down and die from sensory overload or something." He shrugged. He didn't know the science.

I couldn't guess at it either. Someone on Willard's forensics team should be sent to study this, but if all humans were affected...

Sindari, what do you mean shifters came from Earth? And am I not completely pulled in because I'm half elven? Would elves be affected by this, or do you think it was designed to target humans specifically?

I thought about the dark-elf alchemist's notebook that I'd recovered from their lair. Willard had it locked in a vault in her office now, but I'd seen the translation. It was a recipe book on how to make "poisonous pleasure orbs." The Pardus brothers had said they'd been given their orb because it was a prototype with a few problems. Maybe the dark elves had refined the recipe and were distributing more of these around the city, to lure in humans and cause this result. People dying. How many could they create? How many had they *already* created?

That would be my guess as to why you can resist it, yes, Sindari replied.

I thought it was Chopper and my superior willpower.

Sindari didn't comment on that. *As far as the shifters, some thirty thousand of your years ago, humans were taken from this world and deposited on Osgashandril, a world full of unstable magic. Plants and animals there warp and shift with the tidal fluctuations from its three moons. Dragons of the time wanted to know if the world would be safe for colonization, so they dropped off humans and animals from Earth to see what would happen to them. They adapted to Osgashandril but were altered by it, gaining the ability to shift forms.*

A large meaty hand landed on my shoulder. Rupert.

I tensed, thinking it an attack, and almost whipped my sword up to drive him back. But Rupert gazed down at me with hooded eyes.

"If you are not drawn to the orb, perhaps we can go to my office," he murmured in a low rumble, "and discuss the repair of my ceiling."

I glanced at Sindari. *Is this troll making a pass at me?*

I believe so, but I am not an expert in this area. I thought you were flirting with Lord Zavryd when you assured me you were not.

Ugh. Trolls didn't fall for humans as a general rule. *Rupie here must be affected at least somewhat by the orb too.*

Yes.

"Let's go to your office, yes." I assumed Rupert's ardor would fade once we shut that door, and my lungs were growing tight from exposure to the damn mold. The idea of me losing my mind and then dying in this chamber because I wasn't aware of my body's need for medicine made me shudder.

Rupert didn't close the door as he walked out, so I did. Firmly. I felt guilty leaving people to possibly die in there, but if I drove them away, wouldn't they simply come back? Assuming they budged in the first place if I swatted them on their butts with my sword.

By the time we reached Rupert's office, his sexual interest had faded—thankfully. The idea of pushing away the advances of an eight-foot troll was alarming.

"What do you want me to do?" I asked. "Destroy it?"

Nin's magical grenades—or maybe the ceiling collapsing—had destroyed the last one, so I knew it was possible. But I couldn't collapse the ceiling under an eight-story building full of restaurants, retail shops, and apartments.

"I can't destroy it," Rupert said. "I'm being paid to have it here."

"By whom?"

"A dark elf. Yemeli-lor."

I froze. That was one of the two dark elves Zav had been sent to retrieve for "punishment and rehabilitation" from the Dragon Justice Court. I'd never seen either of them when I'd been in the dark-elf lair—or if I had, I hadn't known it—and Zav was, as far as I knew, still looking for them.

"Her mate, Baklinor-ten, comes sometimes and watches and makes notes," Rupert said.

"Watches? From where? The doorway?"

"No." Rupert opened a hidden door in the cement wall between two stacks of kegs and led me into a narrow, dark tunnel.

We came to a small room with a window that overlooked the orb chamber, a window that hadn't been visible from the other side. The wall insulated us from the magic, but I once again felt some of the orb's pull. Proximity made it stronger. With the bank vault door closed, the people inside were more vigorous, and a threesome had paired up—threed up—and was having sex under the orb itself.

"Why do you have a two-way mirror in your pub?" I couldn't keep from sneering in disapproval and looking away from the scene.

Rupert didn't seem that interested in watching the display either. "The dark elves put it in for scientific observation, they said." He pointed to a table and chair. "Baklinor-ten sits there and takes notes."

Sindari padded into the room, sniffing around the area and lowering his head to peer under the table.

"I was told those two dark elves were a high priestess and a warrior, not scientists." I was fairly certain that was how Zav had described them.

Rupert shrugged. "They are both. Their society values academics, and most of them study some branch of science."

"They must be paying you well if you let them alter your establishment."

"They paid well, but..." Rupert eyed me. "I didn't know people would be killed by this thing. I've carted out several bodies now. But dark elves are dangerous. It wasn't just about the money. I worried there would be repercussions if I refused to do business with them."

It dawned on me that he was confessing, laying the groundwork for being more victim than perpetrator. Maybe his original plan had been for me to grow so enraptured that he or someone else could stick a dagger between my shoulder blades, but since that hadn't happened, he was now worried I'd report this to my boss. And be sent to assassinate him because he was facilitating the deaths of shifters *and* humans. Not everybody in that room had been magical.

"I get it," I said. "They're not fun to deal with."

He nodded, relieved.

I suspected I could have walked out without paying him, but I still hoped that one day the magical community would realize I wasn't their enemy, as long as they didn't commit horrible crimes. It would be great if they realized they would be better off helping me than attacking me at every turn. At the least, I would love to gain their indifference.

Val. Sindari came over with something in his mouth.

I held out my hand, and he dropped something that reminded me of a brass cufflink into it.

Is this a magical artifact that will help me defend the world from evil?

I think it holds up the dark-elf's pants.

What, they don't have elastic?

I do not believe so.

You said his. You think this is Baklinor-ten's? Are you sure?

It has the scent of a dark elf about it. I've never met him, so I don't know if it's his specifically, but…

"Is Baklinor-ten the only dark elf that's been here?" I asked Rupert, trying not to think about why the supposed scientist would have been messing around with his pants in here.

"His mate came when they installed the orb and threatened me into cooperation." Rupert was emphasizing that now, that he'd been coerced. He wanted to make sure I didn't fault him. "But only he has come to observe."

"Thanks." I slipped the piece of metal into a zippered pocket, then pulled out the cash I carried for when I needed to bribe people into talking. I counted out five hundred dollars and handed it to Rupert. "For the ceiling repairs."

His thick eyebrows rose. "I didn't think you would pay."

"No matter what rumors are trending about me in the magical community, I'm not a villain."

The skeptical twist of his face shouldn't have stung—it wasn't as if it was a new reaction—but I did wish I could change these people's minds.

My phone buzzed. Willard.

"Yeah?" I left the weird viewing room and headed for the exit.

"We've got a new problem, Thorvald," Willard said, her southern drawl more terse than usual.

"Are you sure? I'm still working on our old problem."

"I'm sure. Your ex-husband and daughter may be in danger."

Chapter 3

I waited until I'd reached the relative isolation of the alley before asking Willard for details. "What do you mean Amber and Thad are in danger? They're not even in the city right now."

Thanks to a call from my mother, I knew that Thad and Amber had gone on a summer trip over to Northern Idaho. Mom was going with them. They hadn't invited me, but I hadn't expected them to. I hadn't spoken to Thad—or, sadly, Amber—in years. For their own good, I'd told myself many, many times.

"They're vacationing at Lake Coeur d'Alene, right?" Willard asked.

"How do you know that? I only know because my mom told me."

"It's on your daughter's social-media page. We keep tabs on them in case someone finds out they're a lever that can be used against you."

I gritted my teeth. As much as I appreciated that Willard didn't want anything to happen to my family, the idea of the military spying on them disturbed me. I'd taken great care to keep anyone from knowing that Thad and Amber were linked to me in any way. It wasn't surprising that Willard's office knew about them—I'd met Thad when we'd both been in the army, after all—but if the soldiers there knew, how many others might know?

"Something's going on in a little town on the east side of the lake," Willard said. "There haven't been any murders or anything incredibly troubling yet, so I would usually send one of my salaried soldiers instead of calling you, especially since we're researching this dark-elf threat right now. But I'll make an exception if you want. I'm not sure where exactly your family is staying, but there aren't that many towns around the lake. If it's possible they're in the problem area, I thought you might want to take this assignment yourself."

"What problem area? What's going on?"

"So far, there have been several reports to the sheriff in Harrison, Idaho, of damage done to parked cars and buildings and also of things going missing. Everything from garage tools to trailers and boats. Goblins have been spotted in the area, and there have also been a lot more sasquatch sightings than usual."

"Than *usual*? How many sasquatch sightings are a normal amount?"

"A couple a year in that area. We actually have more here west of the Cascades."

I digested that. Unlike goblins, orcs, trolls, and the other magical beings that originated on other worlds and had come here periodically throughout history via portals, sasquatch were, as far as I knew, a local myth without much basis in fact.

"We've been called out a couple of times to look at footprints," Willard added. "Large plantigrade footprints."

"Like those of a bear?"

"I don't know. We have our agent take a casting, and then it disappears into the evidence vault under the office. Have you been down there? It's an interesting place."

"I'm sure. I'll check it out next time I'm holiday shopping. Why would my family be in danger from goblins or sasquatch, assuming the latter exist?"

"It's possible they aren't, and it's possible this is nothing more than a few goblins looting a town for something they're building, but they don't usually vandalize property when they go scrounging for goods. It's possible there's something bigger going on. Do you want the assignment?"

When I'd first learned about their trip, I'd been tempted to show up, but I'd talked myself out of that. I was positive they would be more alarmed than excited if I walked into their lives after years without contact. But if I happened to run into them while I was on a mission... that wasn't weird, right?

Not if I was a creepy stalker.

I grimaced. I would email Thad before going over. If he had some warning, maybe it wouldn't be quite so awkward.

"Dream on," I muttered.

"What?" Willard asked.

"Nothing. Yeah, I'll go."

"At this point, I'm not asking you to take anyone out, and I'm not offering a combat bonus—"

"You don't think goblins stealing boats are a dreadful threat to humanity?"

"—but I'll arrange per-diem pay while you investigate. If things escalate, that may change. I'll send over the sheriff's reports and videos and photos that have been posted on local social-media accounts."

"I assume the newspapers don't cover goblins or sasquatch?"

"The *Coeur d'Alene Press* has not reported on the subject and has likely been instructed not to," Willard said.

"Remember the good old days when newspapers were independently owned and didn't take squelch orders from the government or corporations?"

"The world leaders got together years ago and decided that magical refugees from other worlds wouldn't be reported or acknowledged. There's not much we can do about it."

With more and more refugees showing up every year, especially these last few, I wondered how long that position could last. But as long as the government paid my salary, I wouldn't rock the boat.

I told Willard about the orb and the names of the dark elves. She promised to send agents to stake out the bar and watch for the duo while I was gone.

"Maybe when you get back," Willard added, "I'll send you on a mission to steal that orb so we can study it."

That sounded like a challenging mission. How could I remove the orb when shifters were plastered all over it like bacon on a filet mignon?

"It's not going to fit in a purse."

"You're clever. You'll think of something."

"Have you ever noticed that you only praise me when you want something?" I asked.

"No."

As I said goodbye and hung up, the door opened, and Nin walked into the alley. She no longer carried the shotgun, and she didn't look worried, so I trusted she'd made her deal without trouble. Funny that *she'd* been the one who'd wanted me to come along and watch her back.

"There is powerful magic in that place, isn't there?" Nin asked. "I felt a huge surge where you were and this strange feeling like I should go check it out. That I would enjoy myself if I did." Her forehead wrinkled. "Then it disappeared again."

"I'll explain it later. Do me a favor, and don't do any more deliveries here for a while, huh?" I pulled up my phone contacts and called my mother. It was after ten, so she ought to be at home.

"Hello?" Her old-fashioned rotary phone didn't have caller ID.

"Hi, Mom. I have a question."

"Normal people don't call this late."

I thought about mentioning that my boss had called me *this late* just to give me an assignment, but Willard was dedicated to her job, and we regularly exchanged information outside of work hours. I doubted anyone would call either of us normal.

"I know," I said. "Are you still planning to drive out and join Thad and Amber for their vacation?"

"Yes. I finished packing earlier, and I'm leaving early in the morning. Did you change your mind about going? Have you talked to them?"

"Not… exactly. But I may be in the area for an assignment. What's the name of the town where they're staying?"

"I haven't plugged it into the car's map program yet." She actually *used* the technology that had come with her SUV? Shocking. "Let me find the address."

While I waited, I pulled up a map of Lake Coeur d'Alene on my phone. The main city in the area, Coeur d'Alene itself, was on the northern end. The town Willard had mentioned, Harrison, was down on the southeast side, population two hundred and three. That was definitely a small enough place that some goblins might think they could get away with swiping things. It probably had a lot of vacation homes.

With luck, Thad had opted for the excitement of the larger city. It was hard for me to imagine teenage Amber wanting to sit on a dock and fish.

"Got it," Mom said. "They've got a rental house on the lake for a week in Harrison."

I leaned back against one of the alley's dumpsters and groaned.

"Is that a problem?" Mom asked.

Yes.

What I said was, "I'll make sure it isn't."

Chapter 4

I left early in the morning, but it was noon by the time I passed through Coeur d'Alene and turned off the interstate to follow a road south along the lake to Harrison. I hoped I would get there before my mother, since Seattle was a more direct route than coming from Bend, but I doubted I could solve all the problems and wrap everything up simply by arriving two hours earlier.

Besides, Mom could take care of herself. She probably had her Glock in the glove box and Rocket riding shotgun. I was more worried about Amber and Thad.

The night before, I'd emailed him for the first time in years, letting him know I'd be in the area and trying not to feel silly talking about goblins and sasquatch. We'd been married for two years, and he'd never quite seemed to believe that magical beings existed or that I was half-elven, despite my mother sharing the tale of how she had met my pointy-eared father in the woods, and despite Thad knowing what my job had been in the army. He'd seemed to find my mother delightfully quirky and me... I'm still not sure what he saw in me, other than that he'd approved of my fantasy-novel collection. He was a good guy, and he'd been my attempt to settle down with someone nice and stable, to have a normal life and forget about being an assassin. That hadn't lasted long.

The tree-lined road grew windy quickly, and I had to concentrate on the drive. In spots, a cliff rose steeply on the left and the lake fell sharply away to the right.

There wasn't much traffic, so I didn't have any warning when I came to a spot where the road had been washed out. No, *more* than washed out. It looked like sky giants had come down and ripped up the blacktop and land around it, sending it all tumbling down into the water. Logs lay scattered along the slope, further blocking the way. The roots were freshly uprooted, dirt still dangling from them.

I stared dumbfounded. There hadn't been any warning of a road closure on the GPS, nor were there any cones or barriers set up to keep drivers from careening off down the slope and into the lake. This had *just* happened.

"Coincidence? Or does someone want to keep me from getting there?" It seemed hubris to believe this might have been done because of me, but in the past, magical beings had shot up neighborhoods, attempted to bomb a yoga studio, and *successfully* bombed a parking garage, all in an attempt to kill me.

I rolled down the Jeep's window and stuck my head out, looking at the pale blue sky as I reached out with my senses. This could have been done by lesser magical beings than dragons, but for a dragon, it would have been easy. But Dob was dead, Zav wouldn't tear up a highway, and I didn't sense the powerful auras of any other dragons around. Nor did I sense the lesser auras of other magical beings, neither in the sky, nor in the woods upslope from the destroyed road.

Movement caught my eye in the distance between two evergreens. Something dark and furry and standing on two legs. As soon as I tried to focus on it, it disappeared into the undergrowth.

"A bear?" That was my guess, but I couldn't help but add, "A *sasquatch?*"

I tapped the charms on the oft-repaired leather thong around my neck, tempted to summon Sindari to try to chase the creature down, but it had been at least a half mile away. The magic of his charm only allowed him to get a mile away from it before he snapped back to his own realm. If that furry critter could run quickly, it would be out of range before he could catch it.

Besides, I would need Sindari's help with the investigation in Harrison. This wasn't the only road into town. I would have to backtrack and go around.

As I turned my Jeep around to head back to I-90 and over to the next major road heading south, I wished I could call Mom to warn her. But she hadn't entered the twenty-first century and didn't own a cell phone. I'd have better luck telepathically communicating with her dog, Rocket, than leaving her a message. Nonetheless, I sent her a quick email in case she stopped somewhere with computer access along the way.

While I was in my inbox, I noticed that Thad hadn't responded to my email from the night before. I also noticed I only had one bar of cell reception. Hopefully, there would be coverage in Harrison.

Before I'd driven more than a mile back north, the powerful magical aura of a dragon washed over me.

I groaned. "I knew it."

It wasn't Zav.

I couldn't think of any benign reasons for another dragon to be following me. Uneasy, I drove faster than was wise on the windy two-lane road, hoping in vain to get back to the highway before it showed up. As much as I would have liked to believe this was a coincidence, I highly doubted it.

Unfortunately, I didn't make it back to the highway before a dark shadow fell across the gray pavement behind the Jeep. With trees hemming in the road on either side, there was nowhere else to go.

I stuck my head out the window again for a look. The dragon was huge, wings spanning wider than the road, and flying in the same direction I was going. And it was silver. Just like Dob.

For a moment, I thought it *was* Dob, somehow healed by his people and returned from the dead to avenge himself on me. But even if this dragon was the same silver color and looked similar, my senses told me the aura was different. This was a new dragon.

"Like that makes anything better."

The shadow increased speed, quickly going from behind the Jeep to in front of it. A bend in the road forced me to slow down, but as soon as I was around it, I floored the accelerator.

Getting back to the interstate might not do anything to help me, but I had a delusional hope that the dragon wouldn't attack if there were lots of witnesses, such as the drivers of semi-trucks barreling by on their way to the pass.

The dragon landed on the road dead ahead.

An unwise urge to keep my foot on the accelerator and plow into him came over me, but I quashed it and threw on the brakes. I couldn't crash another vehicle this year. This Jeep wasn't even mine.

The tires squealed, and the dragon didn't move an inch or show a sign that it was worried. The Jeep halted two feet from its forelegs. The dragon was crouching on muscled rear legs and smaller forelegs, sleek silver scales gleaming in the sun. Yellow eyes glowed as it lowered its head to regard me through the windshield.

Zav had once warned me that his eyes glowed as a warning or when he was calling upon his magic. In other words, never for a reason conducive to the health of the person looking at them.

I gave in to my second unwise urge of the minute and honked the horn. If the dragon was new to Earth, maybe the noise would startle it into jumping out of the way. But if a Jeep careening toward it with the tires squealing hadn't scared it, the horn wouldn't likely help. In my experience, it didn't even work on cattle.

Get out, a male voice spoke into my mind, the dragon not flinching at the noise.

"You forgot to say *please*," I called out the window.

Get out now. This time, a mental compulsion laced the command, and I almost flung open the door and prostrated myself on the pavement before I caught myself.

Growling, I grabbed my gun and sword from the passenger seat. Only Chopper had ever done anything against a dragon, and even then, only when the dragon had been so wounded that his magical shields had been down. Unfortunately, this big fellow did not appear wounded. He radiated the same kind of intense crackling energy that Zav did, and my skin crawled as I stepped outside and fully into his influence.

"What can I do for you?" I closed the door and leaned casually against it, wondering if any of the gear in the vehicle could help me if he picked a fight.

The only other things I had brought along were a tent, sleeping bag, hatchet, and my travel kit, with shampoo, soap, clothes, and extra ammunition for Fezzik. None of the contents would be useful, though I amused myself briefly imagining squirting toothpaste out of the tube and into his eyes. A heinous attack certain to debilitate him.

You are insolent for a lesser species. I am Lord Shaygorthian of the Silverclaw Clan. You will address me as your lord or master.

Ugh, Dob had been from the Silverclaw Clan. If this was some vengeful relative... I was in trouble.

"Your master," I said. "Got it. What can I do for you? You're blocking traffic."

Not that there'd been much traffic, but a yellow pickup truck was heading this direction. Maybe Shaygor here would be less likely to kill me if there was a witness.

Shaygor looked back, his fangs on display as his serpentine neck bent over his shoulder.

Tires squealed as the truck braked, drove off the road and around trees, knocking off one of its mirrors, and then back onto the road in the other direction. At top speed.

So much for my witness.

The great scaled head turned back toward me. *I have been appointed as inquisitor by the Dragon Justice Court to investigate the death of my son, Dobsaurin.*

His son? I kept my face as neutral as I could, but inside, it was hard not to tremble in fear. As soon as this guy figured out I'd killed his offspring, he would slaughter me.

"That's not a conflict of interest?" My fingers strayed to the flame-shaped charm on my necklace. It would protect me somewhat if the dragon breathed fire at me, but he could kill me with magic as easily as with heat.

Lord Zavryd'nokquetal has stated before the court that he killed my son in self-defense, but he is a poor liar, and he refused to open his mind to the arbiters for a telepathic scouring.

"Huh." My mouth was dry. What happened if this guy did a telepathic scouring on *me*? Why else would he have come?

It is extremely suspicious. That is why I am here. To find the truth and make certain, if he slew my son as part of a premeditated plan or out of sheer malice, that he will be properly punished. Or killed. To kill a dragon is the ultimate crime, but sometimes, punishment and rehabilitation are deemed too lenient. I hope that will be the case on this occasion. His voice pierced like ice in my mind, making me shiver with cold. And fear.

I didn't know when I'd started to be afraid *for* Zav instead of afraid *of* him, but it worried me that he had enemies among his kind.

It also bothered me that he'd tried to take the fall for me. He wouldn't have killed Dob. He would have done the noble thing and, after defeating him in battle, dragged him back to his Justice Court for judgment. Even though he'd openly admitted to me that Dob's family would have been able to get him out of punishment.

It is clear you have spent time with him, Shaygor continued. *I believe you may have seen the battle in which my son was slain.*

"I don't know who you've been talking to—" how had Shaygor even found me? "—but I'm known as the Mythic Murderer to the magical beings in this world. I don't spend time with them. I certainly wouldn't go to some pit fight between dragons and munch popcorn while waiting to see the outcome."

Do not lie to me! His yellow eyes glowed brighter. *I am not stupid, mongrel. His aura is all over you. It is clear you have been holding his tail for some time.*

"His aura is still on me? Damn, I've done everything I could to get rid of it. Hang on a moment. I need your opinion on something." I held up a finger and grabbed my travel kit out of the Jeep, even as I scrambled for something to say to get out of this situation. The dragon didn't realize I'd been the one to kill Dob, but if he could forcibly read my thoughts—which was what that telepathic scouring sounded like—he'd learn the truth. And there was nobody here to keep him from killing me.

"You're a dragon, right? How do people usually get rid of the telltale signs or whatever you call it when you leave your aura on people?" I pulled out my bathroom kit, unzipped it, and tossed my soaps and the three loofahs I'd been experimenting with onto the pavement. "Would any of these implements be better than another?"

I would send him off on a wild goose chase, I decided while he stared at me and the junk on the ground. I'd tell him I hadn't seen the battle but I knew who had. Maybe that would buy me time. And maybe Zav would come back to Earth in that time and I'd get a chance to ask him what the hell to do about his Dragon Justice Court.

You are attempting to stall me, Shaygor stated.

"No, I'm not." Yes, I was. "I'm genuinely curious. Those two loofahs have nice firm fibers and are organic and non-GMO and farm-grown. That tool there is a silicone body brush that gives a better scrub to the skin, and then I also have an exfoliating pumice stone. Do you think—"

Pain erupted in my head as if my brains were being blown out.

I gasped, grabbing my skull, and collapsed onto the pavement, the hard gritty surface digging through my jeans and into my knees. I barely noticed it as I sucked in air, trying to push away the mental attack and the pure agony. I wrapped a shaking hand around Chopper's hilt and tried to wall off my mind, but the attack only intensified. Blackness crept into my vision. What would he do if I blacked out? Kill me? *Eat* me?

The pain disappeared abruptly, but the blackness almost swallowed my vision before I managed to blink it away and focus on him.

There is a price for disobedience and for not showing proper respect for a superior being, Shaygor stated. *You will not defy or lie to an inquisitor of the Dragon Justice Court. Tell me what you saw the night my son died.*

"Look, I'm not trying to interfere with your inquisition. But I know less than you think I know. You should check with a couple of panther-shifter brothers named Pardus." I pointed toward the west. "Back in Seattle. They were there that night. The fight happened right at their house."

All that was true. Never mind that the brothers were dead now and the house was flattened. If it took Shaygor a couple of days to learn that, maybe I could figure out something else in the meantime. Like how to find a portal that would take me to a world dragons didn't know about.

Shaygor shifted into human form—no, *elven* form. Like his son, he preferred pointed ears. As a silver-haired elf of indeterminate age, clad in black leather with lots of silver rivets that gave him a biker look, he strode toward me.

"Already you have wasted too much of my time," he stated, lifting a hand as he approached. "I will find the answers in your mind."

I scrambled to my feet, refusing to face him from my knees, but that was the last movement I managed. His power wrapped around me, locking me in place, and I couldn't budge a muscle.

His cold hand came up to my face, fingers touching my temple. I couldn't spit at him, yell at him, or kick him in the balls. I was screwed.

Chapter 5

Even though he'd shape-shifted into elven form, the dragon's aura made all the hair on my body stand up, and my skin ached all over from the charge of electricity battering it. But that was nothing compared to his presence in my mind. Shaygor's touch on my temple was light, but mental talons raked through my head, eliciting pain as they stirred up my thoughts, digging trenches into my meager barriers.

I still gripped Chopper, but it didn't matter. I couldn't move that hand, couldn't move any part of my rigid body. The mental protection the magical blade gave me was too little to be of help against a dragon. My thoughts were all I could attempt to use to thwart him.

I pictured ponies, childhood carnival rides, and grass growing up through cracks in a sidewalk. I thought of boring PBS specials I'd watched… Anything but the night I'd battled Dob.

But Shaygor kept pushing Dob's image into my head, trying to stimulate the reaction, the memories, he wanted. He sifted through my mind, my resistance insignificant to him, and even though I kept pushing my thoughts in other directions, it would only be a matter of time before he got what he wanted.

Shaygor forced Zav's image into my mind, and I reacted more strongly to that. I couldn't keep from remembering our conversations at the water-treatment facility—and that lurid kiss.

Shaygor grunted in what might have been disgust. Would seeing me entwined with human-form Zav make him want to avoid touching my mind? In that case... I let myself dwell on that moment, on all the things a couple of humans—or a mongrel half-elf and a shape-shifted dragon—could do together, at least according to the naughty dreams that had been plaguing my sleep for the last three weeks.

Shaygor's eyes narrowed, but he didn't pull away from me. *He has claimed you as a mate? No wonder you fight to protect him. Foolish mongrel. You are not good enough for a dragon, but if you were, you would want one whose family is on the rise in power, not on the wane. Your precious Zav will not be anything much longer, especially if he insists on supporting his mother instead of coming over to the side of those who will take power next. Those who know it's time to strip lesser beings from the worlds they're destroying with their taint and to claim those worlds for ourselves.*

Shaygor's fingers shifted into talons that dug into my temple, and he pushed aside my sexual thoughts, using pain to keep me from letting my mind stray. Zaps of agony assaulted me until the correct thoughts flooded my mind. I wanted to continue to resist, but with no end in sight, it was hard. My mind weakened and let in memories of the battle, of Dob and Zav fighting over the rooftops of houses in that neighborhood, of the trees and homes burning all around.

Yes, Shaygor purred into my mind, leaning in so close that I could see his silver eyelashes. *Show me what happened. Show me—*

He dropped his taloned hand and spun away from me.

My knees gave way as control of my body returned. I would have collapsed, but I stumbled to the Jeep and used it for support.

Shaygor glared toward the sky, and then I sensed what he sensed. Zav's aura. He was flying in our direction.

At first, I thought I was saved, but Shaygor turned his glare over his shoulder onto me.

Isn't that telling? That your master has shown up in time to keep me from learning the truth?

"He's not my master," I said. It was supposed to come out as a defiant snarl, but my weakened body could only manage pained gasps.

If a dragon claims you for a mate, you will do whatever he wishes. And consider yourself the luckiest and most honored wench in the Cosmic Realms.

"Yeah, sure. And I'll keep experimenting with loofahs until I find one that can scrub off dragon aura."

You are truly stupid. Clearly, he mounts you because of your looks. Though it is hard to imagine why any dragon would lower himself to shape-shift into some beast form to have sex with animals.

"Says the dragon doing time as an elf right now."

If Sindari had been here, he would have reminded me not to push a dragon's buttons, but I'd unwisely not thought to summon him. I shouldn't feel braver because Zav was coming—it was clear he was in as much trouble as I was, if not more, but a giddy ebullience filled me. Only because I'd survived, at least for the moment, not because I was delighted to see Zav again.

Elves are the most distinguished of the lesser species. They are not beasts.

I thought about asking Shaygor if being half-elf made me only half a beast and therefore more appealing, but Zav's sleek black form appeared as he flew over the trees.

Zav landed on the road in dragon form, his eyes glowing violet as he stared at Shaygor. He didn't acknowledge me at all.

The last time we'd spoken, he'd been pissed at me. He was protecting me, but it had been clear I'd put him in a bad position by needing to be protected. And by forcing him to lie. At the time, I hadn't realized any of that or understood why he was so mad that I'd killed our mutual enemy, but now I got it. I didn't regret killing Dob and still thought I had been right to do it, but I deeply regretted that Zav was in trouble with his people now because of it.

Shaygor folded his arms over his chest and stared indifferently at him.

Leave her alone, Zav's telepathic words boomed in my mind. In both our minds. *If you wish to question someone, I am here. To bring a lesser being into your inquisition is ludicrous and demeaning for your entire clan. Dragons handle their affairs with each other, without leaning on defenseless creatures.*

Normally, I would object to being called a defenseless creature, but this seemed like a good time to shut up and back out of the way. It occurred to me that I was holding Chopper and Shaygor's back was to me, only a few feet away, but attacking a dragon was what had landed me in hot water to start with.

You think to question my *honor?* Shaygor answered telepathically, again broadcasting so I could hear the words, but he laughed out loud. *I expected you to claim protection for her since she's your mate. Under* Tlavar'vareous.

Under what?

She is not my mate. She is nothing.

Thanks, Zav.

Your aura is all over her. At the least, she is your accomplice, but she has some interesting memories of you two rutting in some cement structure. Are you sure she is not your new tail holder?

"Uh." I lifted a finger, trying not to sound as embarrassed as I felt. Why was he bringing *that* up? "It was only kissing. Humans take their clothes off to rut."

Zav didn't look at me. Neither did Shaygor. I wondered if either of them would notice if I hopped in the Jeep and drove off.

If that is what she showed you, she merely demonstrated the treachery of your son, who thought to use her against me as a distraction. Zav stalked forward, his wings spread, his powerful muscles flexing under the scales of his chest and forelegs. *Dobsaurin came here to distract me from the sessions at the court and to kill me if at all possible. Do you deny that?*

Of course I deny that. My son was not the aggressor nor was he the one at fault. He was sent here to observe you and see if you were completing your task.

He had no authority to spy on me. Your son came to kill me. Zav's eyes flared even brighter. *Maybe you are the one who sent him. Maybe the Dragon Justice Court should question* you.

I am an elder and not responsible for the death of another dragon. They will not question me. They trust me. Even your mother trusts me. Shaygor lifted his elven head in haughty defiance and showed no fear that Zav was now scant feet away from him. *You couldn't even capture the dark elves and other criminals you were sent to find. You are vermin dung right now in the eyes of the court. You should be on your belly, confessing to the murder of my son, and groveling and begging for my lenience.*

If you believe I murdered your son, then why are you standing in front of me, here in this world with no witnesses, and irritating me? Zav opened his maw, his long fangs gleaming in the sunlight.

Even though he wasn't looking at me, instinctual terror rushed into me, and I had to fight the urge to scurry away. These dragons were the consummate predators and powers in the Realms, and my body knew that even if my sarcastic mouth forgot at times. The air around them crackled with a sun's power, and my heart raced and my mouth went dry. Either one of them might fling magic and kill me by accident.

You would not dare attack an elder.

Who would know?

Shaygor glanced at me, his haughty demeanor fading for a moment, but he snarled and reaffixed his mask, glaring again at Zav. *Attack if you wish. I am not afraid of you. I will defend myself, and if I must do so, I will be within my rights to use deadly force on you.*

Dobsaurin tried to use deadly force on me, and I am still here. Are you stronger than your son was, elder?

They stared at each other, seconds passing with neither moving, neither blinking. I didn't know if they'd switched to communicating without projecting their words to me, or if they were simply past words, but power fluctuated all around me, as if they were magically testing each other's shields.

Sweat dampened my palm where I gripped Chopper's hilt. If Zav attacked, I would help him, but what if that only made things worse? Much, much worse.

Zav took a step back, and I feared he'd lost the battle of wills, but then Shaygor transformed into his dragon form, almost knocking my Jeep over as his massive silver bulk filled the road.

I lifted Chopper, half expecting him to whirl and attack me. But he didn't look at me. He sprang into the air, his wings beating so hard that the current whipped my braid about, and he flew off to the south. In the direction of Harrison. Wonderful.

Shaygor sent one more telepathic message for both of us: *Know this, Zavryd'nokquetal. A formal investigation has begun. If you maliciously killed my son, I will find out about it, one way or another. And your disgrace will be all that's needed to get your mother to step down from power. Other dragons will not stand with your family any longer.*

I wasn't angry with Zav, but he was the only one left in front of me, so he got my exasperated look, along with, "Are there any dragons in the galaxy who *aren't* assholes?"

Too late to retract the words, I reminded myself that he was just as powerful and dangerous as Shaygor, and that I shouldn't assume we were friends and that he would tolerate my irreverence. Especially if he was having a bad day. Or a bad month.

Zav shifted into his familiar human form, his robe once again clean and free of holes, his short, curly black hair fastidious, his beard and mustache perfectly trimmed. But his violet eyes somehow conveyed tiredness. They hadn't when he'd been in dragon form glowering at Shaygor, but maybe this form revealed more. Or maybe he'd been hiding it. He didn't have bags under his eyes—surely, he wouldn't let such a feature tarnish his handsome face—but I had a feeling he'd had a rough few weeks, and I felt bad for my outburst.

"Sorry," I said. "You're not an asshole."

"No?" He smiled faintly.

That smile, that hint of humanity, made my insides get mushy. Not that I would acknowledge it.

"You're irritatingly haughty and pompous, but I'm starting to like you a little," was all I said.

"Oh? How do you treat people you *don't* like?" Zav waved to the longsword I still held up.

I'd been pointing it at Shaygor, but with him gone, it pointed vaguely in Zav's direction.

"I chop off their toes and curse their ancestors." I sheathed Chopper and stepped toward him, lifting an arm, thinking of offering him a hug, but I paused mid-motion as uncertainty encroached.

Weeks earlier, when I'd reached up to brush a leaf off his shoulder, he'd stopped me, as if believing I'd been about to grab his throat. And he eyed my arm warily now.

It surprised me that he would consider me a threat, though it was possible he thought I meant to make a pass at him and objected to *that*. We'd shared a moment, after the battle at the water-treatment plant, where he'd touched his forehead to mine, and it'd almost seemed like he might kiss me, but he hadn't. Then he'd left without another word. I still had no idea what to make of it.

Not that I *wanted* him to kiss me. My life was easier when dragons weren't in it.

"Thank you for showing up to keep him out of my head." I wriggled my fingers on my outspread hand, then lowered my arm. "I was going to hug you, but I remembered how prickly and standoffish you are."

Zav arched his eyebrows. "You are no different. Every time I've healed you, you've bristled and been offended."

"That's because you don't ask first." Admittedly, I hadn't intended to ask to hug him either. "Generally, when a guy sticks his hands in a girl's jacket, it's to grope her boob. That's why women get bristly at that kind of presumptuousness."

"I have no interest in your boobs."

"Thanks for clearing that up. Because you rubbed your forehead against mine at the water-treatment plant. That's had me confused." This time, I arched *my* eyebrows.

This wasn't the conversation I'd intended to have with him—I'd genuinely wanted to show gratitude for his help—but nothing was ever easy with a dragon.

Zav hesitated before responding. I didn't think I'd ever seen him hesitate.

"I was pleased that you survived and chopped off Dobsaurin's toe to vex him. Forehead-to-forehead contact is how elves demonstrate the bond they feel for those they survive battles and grueling travails with. It has nothing to do with mating desires. Is this gesture not also done among humans?"

I squinted at him. I couldn't tell if he truly believed it was or if he was covering for something I had taken as more intimate. Probably the former. This was the guy who'd been confused about what a dick was.

"No, you're thinking of hand-to-hand contact. Also known as a high five." I lifted my palm, then nodded for him to do the same. Because he looked puzzled, I explained further. "It's a high five because there are five digits and they're up in the air."

He squinted suspiciously at me—it was silly, but it made me glum that he didn't trust me after the battles we'd been through—but he slowly mirrored the gesture. I leaned in to swat my palm to his. He didn't react. Still, it amused me that the fierce dragon who'd been radiating power like a supernova minutes before allowed it.

"That kind of contact is safest for us," I said.

The brief touch hadn't given me much time to think about the way Zav's power made my body tingle in a different way from the power of the other dragons. A more appealing way. It also didn't give me time to have flashbacks to our previous kiss or my lurid dreams.

"And it conveys approval and a battle bond?" Zav sounded dubious.

"Yes. Athletes on sports teams give each other high fives all the time. We can be like jocks working together to defeat common enemies."

Though I was concerned that our common enemy might now be this

Dragon Justice Court, or at least all the dragons on it that didn't like his family. How many *was* that exactly? Maybe I was better off not knowing.

"The high five is engaged in at the completion of defeating of enemies?" he asked.

"Yeah. You should have given me a high five after we defeated Dob. Instead, you gave me a lecture. That's not cool."

He winced, and I regretted mentioning Dob. Idiot, Val. The last thing I wanted was to remind him that I'd screwed up his life.

I lifted an apologetic hand. "I don't regret that I killed that bastard, especially since he wanted to use me to kill *you*, but I'm sorry it's made so much trouble for you."

The urge to hug him returned, and I wished he would allow it. I didn't often feel like hugging people—it wasn't as if I got that from my mom, who'd always insisted that nods and handshakes were acceptable ways to greet old friends—but I felt a tangle of guilt and appreciation for Zav that would be easier to express with a physical gesture. I was horrible at conveying feelings with words.

"I'll understand if you tell your court what really happened," I said. "It's not right that you should be blamed. If they come after me... I'll deal with it." How I would deal with it, I didn't know, but keeping my cloaking charm activated all the time came to mind. Too bad the magic faded and had to be renewed every hour or so. I would have to set the alarm to wake myself up multiple times every night.

"You are not powerful enough to *deal with it*."

Even though I wanted to bristle and point out that I could handle myself, we both knew I couldn't. Not when it came to dragons. I resented that, but what could I do to change it?

"You're right, but it's my problem, not yours."

Zav opened his mouth, but his nostrils twitched, and his gaze slid from my face down to my groin. No, I corrected. To my pocket. Surely, my groin did not excite him.

Remembering the pants fastener I suspected belonged to the male dark elf, I fished it out. Had Zav sensed it? I hadn't detected magic about it. Maybe he recognized the dark elf's scent and had caught a whiff. If so, he had a bloodhound's nose.

Zav stepped closer to look down at the brass fastener in my palm. His powerful, electrifying aura increased as he drew closer, making my skin tingle and putting thoughts of more than high fives in my head. I ruthlessly shoved them aside and made a mental note to pick up my loofahs and shower belongings before driving away, so I could thoroughly scrub my skin that night. Maybe the vampire alchemist Zoltan could make a magical cleanser guaranteed to remove dragon aura. Too bad his rates were exorbitant.

"One of your dark elves showed up at a pub in Seattle," I said.

"Baklinor-ten."

"His mate was supposedly there once too. They installed a pleasure orb that's got people so into it that it's killing them."

Zav nodded, not reacting with the surprise I expected.

"Their science experiments are part of the reason I was sent to retrieve them. They killed three islands' worth of shapeshifters on Osgashandril."

"How many people is that?"

"About thirty thousand."

I rocked back. "They did that with those orbs?"

"I have not seen the orbs specifically, but on Osgashandril, they created artifacts that killed people slowly over time and from a distance, so there was no possibility the shifters would detect them and retaliate. At first, I thought the dark elves came here to escape the court's wrath, but it's possible this was their destination all along, to reunite with their kin who've always lived hidden in the Underworld here and to do something to the inhabitants of your planet."

"Something like killing them?" I had been disturbed by but not worried about the dead woman on the floor in Rupert's pub, but if those artifacts could kill thousands of people... that was definitely something to worry about. I needed to get this new information to Willard.

"Yes."

"You said that's part of the reason you're after those two. What was the other part? That they stole your artifact?"

"Yes. They might have gotten away with the rest if not for that. I was affronted by the blatant crimes, but in general, my kind think little of the animal shifters of Osgashandril and might not have investigated their deaths."

"Why are you different?" I didn't doubt that he was, now that I'd met two dragons that fell firmly into the asshole camp, but I was curious.

"I was raised to be honorable and believe it is our right to maintain order in the Cosmic Realms. Crimes among the lesser species can have repercussions that affect all." He plucked the fastener from my hand. "I may be able to use this to find him."

"You're welcome." I thought about objecting to him taking it, but it wasn't as if I knew anyone else who could sniff a button and find a dark elf.

"In addition to being interrogated by the court, including my own mother, I've had my competence questioned—mostly by the Silverclaw Clan but also by others—because I haven't retrieved those two criminals yet." He closed his fist around the fastener. "I will now make finding them my priority. You will come with me."

"I see you haven't learned how to say please yet. I'm on my own mission."

"You must stay with me for protection. Shaygorthian will find you again, and he will learn the truth if I'm not close enough to stop him from probing your thoughts."

"*You've* never been able to read my thoughts. Or so you've said."

"I've only attempted to skim your surface thoughts, not do a *vayushnarak*."

"And that is what?"

"A forced reading. It's painful for the recipient."

"Tell me about it."

Zav opened his mouth, but I lifted a hand.

"No, that was sarcasm. I know all about it. Trust me. He was digging in for a few minutes there before you arrived." I touched my temple and winced. It was sore, and my fingers found dried blood.

Zav leaned over to see the side of my head and his jaw clenched, a muscle high in his cheek tensing.

"You *will* stay with me," he growled, his tone sending a little shiver down my spine, "and I will protect you."

"How about you stay with *me* and I'll educate you in the ways of human hand gestures. Next, we can cover fist bumps."

"I have a mission to complete." He rubbed the fastener between his thumb and forefinger and looked toward the west, toward Seattle.

"So do I. *Here*. In Idaho. Goblins are stealing from a town on this lake."

Zav stared at me. "Goblins *always* steal. That's not a crime; it's a cultural manifestation of their inner feelings of insignificance and lack."

I was positive he'd feel differently if a goblin stole some vaunted dragon artifact. "There could be more to it than the stealing. Also, my family is here, so I have to make sure they're not in danger."

"You have family." Was that a question or a statement? Zav sounded puzzled.

Maybe he couldn't imagine me and my sharp tongue attracting a husband.

"My daughter and ex-husband and mother are all in the area for a vacation. I have to make sure they're safe."

"*You* will not be safe." Zav flicked a hand toward the sky in the direction Shaygor had gone.

"I never am, but that's the job. When I finish here, I'll come back to Seattle and help you with the dark elves."

Willard would likely have an assignment related to them for me as soon as I returned. She'd been on the verge of giving me one for weeks, and now she had more data about the orbs.

Zav scrutinized me in that haughty way of his, that way that made me feel like he found me exceedingly strange and a pain in the ass—insomuch as dragons had asses—and I hoped he wasn't thinking about magically compelling me to come with him. We'd had a deal for my last mission, and he'd agreed not to do that, but Dob was dead and that mission complete. Zav might go back to his old ways.

"They may be in more danger because of your presence," Zav said, his tone surprisingly reasonable and without—as far as I could tell—magical manipulation. "It will be better for you and them if you come with me. Goblins are not a concern. Dragons are."

The argument struck me harder than others would have because it was so close to my existing fears. But…

"I can't be sure the goblins are the only problem." I pointed my thumb over my shoulder. "Someone knocked the road into the lake back there. I doubt it was goblins."

"It could have been. They make mechanical contraptions with what they steal."

"I have to find out." I took a step back to stand beside the driver's side door. "Thank you for coming to help me, Zav. I'll do my best to avoid this new dragon." I tapped my cloaking charm to activate it. It couldn't make my Jeep disappear, but it would make me fade from sight, smell, and magical senses, though he would continue to see me at this close a range. "If you want, you could stay and help me investigate Harrison. With you, I could probably finish more quickly and then go assist you with the dark elves."

His chin rose. "I do not need a mongrel's *assistance*."

"I didn't say you *needed* it." It drove me nuts when he called me that instead of using my name. "Just that we could both assist each other and maybe finish our tasks more quickly that way."

"My task is of paramount importance."

"I already told you why I don't agree with that," I said.

"I cannot help it if you do not acknowledge the wisdom of dragons."

"Can you help being so exasperating?"

His eyes narrowed, reminding me of the icy look he'd leveled at Shaygor. The very dangerous icy look.

"If you do not come with me," he said, "I will not be able to protect you from other dragons."

"I understand. We've already covered that." I tapped my charm. "I won't let him find me."

Zav was probably worried that Shaygor would catch up with me again, scour my mind, and find out the truth. Then he would be in hot water for having lied to his people. What if he forced me to go with him to prevent that?

After a long moment—I refused to look away or back down from his stare—Zav stepped back and transformed into his dragon form.

He will be able to smell your blood in your offspring, Zav warned telepathically as he sprang into the air. *Do not draw his attention to your kin.*

I slumped against the Jeep. I hadn't needed anything else to worry about.

Chapter 6

The other road leading to Harrison was also destroyed.

I was inland now, the area dotted with as many farm fields as stands of evergreens, with the lake out of sight to the west. The pavement was buckled and even pulverized in places, and the land to either side torn up, as if giant tunneling worms had burst up all over the place.

I sat in the Jeep and stared at the mess. This time, there were other cars around, but their drivers were in the process of turning around and heading out.

My phone struggled to get enough reception to pull up a map, and I ground my teeth at the delay. Two destroyed roads could not be a coincidence. Someone didn't want outsiders—or maybe me specifically—arriving in Harrison. But my family had traveled over yesterday and was already there. Only Mom was stuck on the road somewhere, like me.

The map showed another possible route, but it involved going all the way back to Coeur d'Alene, down the far side of the lake and beyond before swinging around. There was nothing direct about it.

"And what happens when that road is destroyed too?"

When the last of the cars sped off, I put the Jeep into four-wheel drive and rolled into the mess. There wasn't a possibility of falling into a lake this time, so unless I encountered a sinkhole, I should be fine.

"Nothing like thinking about sinkholes to make them pop into existence," I muttered, voice rattling as the Jeep bumped and ground over the broken asphalt and chewed-up terrain.

It occurred to me that Shaygor would be able to spot me easily from the sky. Even though I'd activated my charm, he had seen my vehicle, and *it* wouldn't be camouflaged.

I touched Sindari's cat figurine and summoned him. His dragon-detecting range reached farther than mine, and once I got to town, he would more easily spot goblins or other magical beings lurking about.

Sindari materialized in the back where I always left the seats down so he had more room, though he was too tall to stand up fully.

The tires dipped into a pit, and he braced his forelegs.

Are we being attacked? Sindari looked toward the side windows.

"No, I'm driving."

The Jeep crawled out of the pit and over the next obstacle.

I do not believe you're doing it correctly.

"This is called off-roading. It's fun."

His head bumped the hard ceiling. *It was not necessary for you to bring me to experience this* fun.

"Were you busy hunting again?"

No, I was napping. Peacefully. The Jeep pitched sideways, and he growled.

I opened the back windows so he would have more air and could smell our surroundings. "We're almost out. Someone destroyed the road and doesn't want us to reach town. Also, one of Dob's relatives is here on Earth, and he tried to tear the truth about Dob's death out of my mind. Zav showed up in time to stop him, but he's not sticking around. He's after those dark-elf scientists back in Seattle."

We reached the far side and rolled onto the undisturbed pavement. I put the vehicle back into two-wheel drive and sped toward town as fast as I could, worry knotting my stomach.

I assume that means Lord Zavryd did not tell the truth to the Dragon Justice Court?

"He covered for me, but he wouldn't let them read his mind, so they're skeptical he was telling the truth." I glanced back at Sindari. "They doubt him because of me, and that sucks. I'm tempted to tell that inquisitor dragon that I was responsible, but I'm pretty sure he'll kill me instantly if he finds out."

You are in a difficult situation.

"No kidding."

Is that the reason your cloaking charm is activated?

"Yeah. I'm hoping he won't be able to find me and that he'll go harass Zav instead. Or better yet, go back to his world." I didn't mention my new concern that Shaygor would be able to tell Amber was my daughter if they crossed paths. My fantasy of walking up and chatting with her and Thad while I was here on my mission dissolved. Maybe it was for the best. Maybe I should accept that my life was too dangerous and the only people I could hang out with without worrying for their safety were Sindari and Zav.

A depressing thought. Did I even consider Zav a friend? He still wanted to order me around, but at least he was more interested in protecting me than using me now. Or at least *equally* interested.

Inquisitors are tenacious. And you said he is a relative?

"Dob's father, yes."

He will not give up easily then.

"I know." The turnoff for Harrison came into view, and I took it, butterflies battering the sides of my stomach with their wings. What if the town was on fire? What if it had been pushed into the lake? What if the earth had swallowed it whole?

But as the first houses came into view, nothing appeared amiss. I drove in to the little tourist town perched on the slope of a hill overlooking the lake. Shops lined the single main street, and a grassy green park overlooked a marina and campground on a flat piece of land jutting into the water. A railroad-turned-bike-trail meandered along the lake.

"Do you sense goblins or anyone else magical about?"

Like a dragon.

Not at this time. Sindari peered out the window opposite the park, toward evergreens carpeting the hill above the town. It was easy to envision hidden goblin dwellings in that direction.

"Huh. Maybe they're doing their thieving at night."

Two kids standing on the sidewalk with ice cream cones saw Sindari's head and shrieked and pointed.

"Maybe you should activate your own magical stealth." I parked under a tree. A car rolling around without a driver, as it would seem to anyone looking toward me, was just as strange as one with a silver tiger hanging out the window.

The denizens of this town should witness what a magnificent predator has come to visit them, Sindari said.

"If kids see you, they'll want to come over and pet you. You know how you feel about people with presumptuous hands." With my meager cell coverage, I did a slow search for local hotels.

This is true. I will camouflage myself.

I thought you might.

Sindari stealthed himself before opening the door—how did he manage that without thumbs?—and letting himself out onto the grass of the park.

A bed and breakfast and a lodge were my only options, other than the campground by the marina. I did have camping gear in the back, since missions out of town sometimes took me far from civilization, but it wasn't my preferred lodging option when enemies were nearby. When I was sleeping, I liked stout bulletproof walls around me and a roof over my head. That was doubly true if dragons were nearby, though I'd seen Zav flatten houses, so roofs did not guarantee safety.

While I made calls, Sindari rubbed his scent all over the trees and peed in carefully selected spots in the grass. Probably covering up some poor dog's attempt to mark territory.

You're my weirdest friend, Sindari.

Sindari rubbed his side on a picnic table. *I assure you I'm completely normal for a Zhinevarii.*

On the far side of the park, a Dachshund sharing a picnic blanket with her people looked in Sindari's direction and barked uproariously.

Does that dog see you or just smell what you're laying down?

The latter. Such an inferior predator couldn't see her own tail if she were spinning in circles.

The two hotels were booked. Not surprising since this was summer, the height of the tourist season. Droves of three-wheel rental bicycles with orange flags on the backs meandered past on the trail below. Reluctantly, I called the campground, but I could see from above it that all the RV lots were filled.

We may end up sleeping in the Jeep alongside the road, Sindari. I refused to call Thad and ask if I could stay with them, especially after that parting warning from Zav.

You may end up sleeping there. I sleep in my homeland in a comfortable den.

Lucky you.

The campground had a cancellation and an available tent spot.

"Well, that's slightly better than sleeping in the rig."

As I drove down the hill toward the marina, two Coeur D'Alene Police Department boats docked. A couple of unmarked SUVs drove down behind me, heading straight for the dock and parking in a no-parking area.

Curious, I left my Jeep near the tent-camping area and trotted over with my camouflage still activated. This had to have something to do with the destroyed roads. Hopefully, it had nothing to do with dragons.

Uniformed men stood on the boat while men in plainclothes carried boxes out of a hold. I half-expected crates of guns and ammunition, but there were tomatoes and cartons of orange juice pictured on the sides. They loaded the groceries into the backs of the SUVs.

A woman in a skirt and blouse got out of one and walked over to talk to the senior police officer. I wandered close so I could hear the conversation. Sindari checked out trees and benches beside the bike trail while children played at the nearby beach.

"...repair the roads?" the woman was asking as I came within hearing range.

"Teams are heading down to work on them, Mayor Aspen. We're just now getting reports that the road from St. Maries has also been destroyed—that happened within the hour. Nobody saw how it was done or saw anyone suspicious in the area. As with the others, the road was destroyed in an area without houses around. For now, boat is the only way in and out of town."

The woman—Mayor Aspen—rubbed her face. "This is crazy. Things like this don't happen to Harrison."

This week, they do, I thought grimly.

"We've heard you've had a number of, ah, sasquatch sightings," the police officer said.

Aspen gave him an exasperated look. "Somebody must be messing around out there. I'm sure it's a hoax."

"Hm." Maybe the officer was a believer in magical beings. "But there were houses broken into and ransacked?"

"Yes, but not by sasquatch."

"Did you see who did it?"

"No, but they made horrible messes. You should see the place up on Cliff Way. The owners live out of state. I don't know when it'll get fixed up. We just rely on the county sheriff's office here, so it's hard to police the neighborhoods. Are any of your men here to stay and help out?"

He nodded. "I'm leaving a couple of officers, and the county will repair the damaged roads." He lowered his voice. "It's up to you what you want to tell people, but the word will get out quickly, and your locals and tourists could become difficult to manage, especially if they believe they're trapped."

I tapped *Cliff Way* into the notes app on my phone, then pulled it up on a map of town. Maybe I would take a look later. It was a short dead-end road, so finding the house should be easy, if it was in as poor of a condition as the mayor implied.

"I know. I'll deal with it. At least we're not completely cut off." Aspen waved to the lake and the boats.

Val? Sindari sat next to a park bench a few yards from a group of bicyclists who'd gotten off the trail. *You may want to hear this.*

I hesitated, not wanting to miss anything important between these two, but they'd wound down, and the mayor started helping the men load groceries into the SUV.

"It was a bear, not a sasquatch," one biker, a fit man with short gray hair, said to what was probably his wife and three kids. "Sasquatch are just stories."

"I saw four of them. There's no way they were bears." That was a boy of eleven or ten. He pointed toward the south. "And you all heard that roar."

"A *bear's* roar," the father said.

The two older siblings, twin sisters, I guessed, exchanged long looks with each other. The mother appeared dubious too.

"There's all kind of wildlife out there," the father continued. "The bike-rental lady even said to look for moose and bears."

"She neglected to mention sasquatch," the mother murmured.

Her husband frowned at her. "You're not helping."

"I'm glad we're not sleeping in one of those flimsy tents tonight." She waved to my new home in the campground.

Remembering that I was camouflaged, I kept myself from snorting. The family headed up the hill to turn in their bikes.

"You want to go for a ride down that trail, Sindari?" I asked quietly.

Will it be as rough as the ride down here?

Probably not, unless a herd of sasquatch rushes out of the trees to chase us.
A herd connotes herbivores, rather than predators. They should not be dangerous.
I'm not sure if herd is the right word. Sasquatch are supposed to be mythological.
Like dragons?
We'll find out.

It was about two o'clock. I had plenty of time to rent a bicycle and get back to pitch my tent before dark. My tent with the flimsy walls. I was more concerned about dragons trashing those walls than sasquatch, at least for now. When I thought of the way the roads had been destroyed, I decided that dismissing them might be unwise.

Chapter 7

When you suggested a ride, I didn't know you would be in that ridiculous contraption and I would be expected to lope alongside.

I grinned over at Sindari from the rather comfortable seat of my rented three-wheel reclining bicycle. We were about two miles south of town, with the lake stretching to my right and houses perched in the trees to the left. I'd never ridden a bike with a back rest before, and it made perusing the shadows to either side of the paved trail comfortable and easy.

Sindari, who only had to trot to keep up—the bicycle was definitely not designed for covering great distances at a racing speed—was complaining for no reason. It was sunny, beautiful, and tigers needed to exercise as much as people did.

"There's a basket if you want to see if you can fit in." I patted the little crate behind the seat.

Very funny. I'm larger than that entire contraption.

"I'd offer you a spot in my lap, but then I couldn't see. I should have gotten a smaller tiger."

Your foot is in danger of being chewed off today.

"I bet a service animal could fit in my lap."

Both feet.

"So grouchy."

I'm hot.

I extended a hand toward the water, surprised he hadn't already jumped in.

He grunted, leaped over a log, and bounded into the shallows. He didn't linger for long though. Maybe he thought I needed protection and that he shouldn't let me out of his sight.

Tigers aren't supposed to be small. We're apex predators, both here in this world and at home in Del'noth.

"Apex predators shouldn't mind jogging a few miles. I remember looking up tigers shortly after I met you. The article said they travel up to thirty miles a day in search of food."

In search of food, yes. Not in search of goblins. Have you tasted a goblin? They're stringy and less flavorful than scat. I'm convinced that's why they've survived over the generations despite being so puny. Nobody wants to eat them.

"Maybe sasquatch are tastier."

You implied they don't exist.

I remembered the furry, two-legged creature I'd seen in the woods on the way here. "I'm not sure about that anymore. We're getting into a more wooded area. Keep your eyes open."

My eyes are always open, as are my ears and nostrils.

"That doesn't make sleeping difficult?"

No.

Two bicyclists appeared around a bend up ahead, pedaling in our direction. I reached for my cloaking charm—I'd been removing the spell whenever we saw someone, so they wouldn't gape and fall over at the sight of a bicycle moving with no bicyclist—but Sindari halted me with a word.

Don't.

Dragon?

Dragon.

I couldn't sense him—Shaygor, I assumed—but one of the reasons I'd summoned Sindari was because of his greater range.

The bicyclists did indeed gape at what, to them, appeared to be an empty bike coming toward them. They stopped and got off the trail. *Way* off.

Let me know if he's heading this way, please. I switched to silent speech, on the off chance that a dragon miles away could hear my voice.

He's flying over the south end of the lake. He may be fishing.

Fishing? I imagined a silver dragon lounging on the end of one of the docks we were passing, sunning his belly while his pole extended out over the water.

More like an osprey, Sindari informed me dryly.

I scanned the wooded slope, hoping to see the sasquatch the family of bicyclists had seen—or maybe goblins. Was it possible goblins were behind a hoax? Using their magic and maybe some gadgetry to convince people that sasquatch were rampant around the town? If so, to what end? To scare the inhabitants away so they could loot the houses here?

For a town with a population of two hundred, there were a lot of houses. Vacation properties and rentals, I supposed. Everything from mansions with great wrap-around decks to log cabins to rickety old shacks that looked like they'd been temporary homes for loggers back when the bike path had been a railroad.

As the trail headed out into the open, the lake on one side and marshy pools on the other, I caught sight of the silver dragon. It *was* Shaygor.

As Sindari had suggested, he was flying over the lake. As we watched, he pulled his wings in close and dove down toward the water. At the end of his dive, he tilted his head up, turning the descent into a skimming of the surface with his maw open. He closed it, and even from a mile away, I imagined I heard the clack of those jaws snapping together. If he'd gotten a fish—or a dozen—I couldn't tell, but he rose back up, wings unfurling and flapping again.

I stopped pedaling. The trail continued in the open right beside the lake, and he was sure to notice the bicycle steering itself along the bank. Dragons, I was positive, had sharp eyesight.

The hair on the back of my neck rose as Shaygor flew a little closer, entering the range of my senses. It seemed strange that my eyes had spotted him first, but I could see for miles up and down the open lake.

Shaygor flew lazily north, heading in our direction, but not *directly* in our direction. His yellow eyes glowed slightly as they perused the shoreline. Looking for me? He shouldn't have known I had come here, but maybe something he'd plucked from my thoughts had hinted of this town as my final destination.

I don't think he's aware of us. Sindari sat in the grass beside the trail, alternately eyeing the dragon and a log in the marsh that was full of turtles sunning themselves. Maybe turtles tasted better than goblins.

Let's keep it that way. I was tempted to backtrack, but turning the wide-framed bike on this tight stretch of the trail would take some doing. And he was sure to catch any movement. It didn't help that the bike had a bright yellow frame.

His scan of the lake ended, and his gaze locked on me. Or, more likely, on the bike. I could feel the faint magic from my cloaking charm and knew it was still activated.

Did a dragon know enough about bikes to think it strange for one to be sitting out by itself on a trail? I hoped not.

You may want to move, Sindari suggested as Shaygor banked and sailed toward us.

Damn it. He was coming to check out the bike.

I eased off it, glad the three-wheeler would stay upright without me doing anything to it. The dragon pulled in his wings again for another dive, but I doubted he had fish in mind.

I scooted away from the bike and backed up the trail far enough that I wouldn't be close enough for him to see through my charm's magic if he landed. Shaygor picked up speed, coming in as fast as he had in the fishing maneuver. But it wasn't trout that he plucked up this time.

He swooped down, his massive maw locking around the bike frame, and back up with it in his mouth. Metal wrenched as he snapped his jaws together, and pieces flew in dozens of directions. The turtles on the log scattered, disappearing into the water. Shaygor shook his head as his flight carried him over the marsh, and the remaining bike pieces plunked down, disappearing under the surface as the turtles had. The orange flag that had been sticking out of the back on a pole fluttered down to land on the trail.

The dragon banked and circled back. Had he smelled my scent on the bike? The charm would keep someone from smelling *me*, but I doubted it could mask my entire route.

Get off the path, Sindari warned me. He waded quietly and slowly into the closest pool.

Good idea. It was a quarter mile back to the trees and more cover. If I ran, Shaygor would hear my footsteps.

As he dove to skim along above the pavement, nostrils quivering with his sniffs, I slipped carefully off the trail and into the water. Moving far more slowly than I wanted—I didn't dare go fast enough to leave ripples on the surface of the water—I waded out toward some of the logs wedged in the mud and reeds on the far side of the pool. The water might help hide any scent I was leaving behind. But I might also end up being snapped up next.

Shaygor flew past in front of me, sniffing as he glided three feet above the trail.

I drew Chopper, expecting him to catch my scent on the ground and veer toward me. Fighting when I was waist-deep in water wouldn't be ideal, but the water had been my only hope of hiding my trail.

Shaygor kept coasting along, flapping his wings when he reached the trees, but only enough to rise up over them. He continued to follow the trail back toward town, his gaze locked on the pavement below.

Soon, he soared out of sight and out of my range, but I waited a long time before leaving the water. I kept expecting him to come back and hunt down the trail in the other direction.

The reeds rustled behind me, and I jumped. But it was only Sindari. He'd found something of interest and was climbing out of the water and heading into the woods.

I waded the other way and scrambled up the slope and back onto the trail. All that remained of the bike were a few bent, broken pieces of the frame and the little flag. I walked over to pick it up. Even it was damaged, with a distinct fang mark through it.

I rubbed my face, wondering how much the bike cost—and how I would explain its utter destruction to the rental shop owners. Would they believe a horde of roving sasquatch had come out and ripped it piece from piece?

Val? I caught sight of a goblin. I'm seeing if I can catch him.

Good.

Maybe something positive would come out of this.

Never mind. He disappeared.

Disappeared? From your superb tracking abilities?

I think he has the goblin version of your charm. He was definitely here, up in the branches watching the dragon incident.

The dragon incident. Maybe I would put that down on whatever form the rental owners asked me to fill out in regard to their destroyed bike. There was a "dragon incident." That hadn't worked with the car insurance company when I'd reported my demolished Jeep, but maybe they were less stringent out here.

There's sign of more goblins back here, Sindari added. *Lots of footprints.*

They're gone now, but they were here.

Any sign of sasquatch or maybe sasquatch costumes or robots designed to look like sasquatch?

Not that I can find. Just the goblin footprints.

All right. Thanks for looking.

Even though I'd been sent to investigate the goblins, I was more worried about the dragon. Had I made a mistake in not going with Zav so he could protect me? Maybe, but I couldn't spend my life hiding behind his tail. And I couldn't leave here, knowing my family was in danger.

Chapter 8

The five-plus miles I'd biked from town were a lot slower walking, and I was getting a headache from straining my senses, trying to guess where Shaygor had gone. Hopefully, he hadn't been able to follow my scent all the way back to the campground and to my Jeep. If I arrived and found it smashed and up in a tree, I was retiring. To hell with this job.

Sindari was still with me, but searching the woods off to the side of the trail, hunting for more signs of goblins.

As I walked between two vertical rock walls, I eyed the tops, imagining a dragon or other predator jumping down onto me. I was so focused on the terrain that I almost missed the familiar green Subaru driving across the trail ahead.

I blinked and stared. Had that been… my mother's SUV?

There was a driveway that crossed the trail there, heading out to a house on a point. I grabbed my phone and pulled up the address of the vacation house Thad had rented. And almost fell over. I was right next to it.

For a moment, I stood there, completely flummoxed and indecisive. Should I go say hello? Or run past and hope nobody saw me?

"Yeah," I muttered. "Let's act like a seven-year-old. Always a good plan."

Val? Sindari asked.

Sensing him nearby, I looked up toward one of the rock walls. He stood on the top, gazing down at me.

Yes?

Who are you talking to?

Myself. Don't act like you haven't seen that before.

Occasionally. I found more goblin tracks in the wooded areas between the human domiciles.

We call those houses.

They do not exist on Del'noth. We live in dens.

Is it hard to get cable internet run to those?

He gazed down at me, too confused—or too mature—to answer.

Never mind. You say there are a lot of goblin tracks?

Yes. Either a dozen goblins who've been extremely busy or dozens of goblins who've been moderately busy.

Dozens?

Maybe hundreds.

I didn't realize that many goblins had come to Earth.

Because they're all located here.

I heard my mom's voice and then a voice I hadn't heard in years. Thad.

Anxiety stampeded into my gut. Why was the prospect of this meeting so much worse than the prospect of being killed by a dragon? Or having to battle impossible odds in a shifter's secret basement compound? There was definitely something wrong with me. Maybe I should have called my therapist before leaving Seattle. Mary wouldn't be pleased when I canceled the coming week's session because I'd be out of town. She thought I needed help. A *lot* of help.

Keep looking for interesting things, will you? I'm going to go see my mom and… my ex-husband. Amber was the one I most wanted to see and the one I most dreaded being rejected by.

But I braced my shoulders, turned off my cloaking charm, and continued to where the rock walls ended and the driveway crossed the trail. The pavement meandered out to a solitary property on the point, the lake on three sides and the rocks providing privacy to the east. Mom's Subaru was parked next to a BMW on the north end, her door still open. She had gotten out and was talking to Thad, who stood on the huge wrap-around deck of a beautiful two-story Victorian house that probably had a view of the lake from every window. I knew it was a rental, but the nightly fee had to be exorbitant. Thad did well for himself, as the BMW attested.

Rocket woofed from the grassy bank next to a tire swing, and Thad and Mom turned to face me, Mom with a grave nod, Thad with a gape. Maybe he hadn't checked his email since I'd sent it. It had said I would be in the area, but he was looking at me like he'd believed I'd been on Mars and was beaming down from my spaceship.

I glanced back to make sure there wasn't a dragon looming behind me, but the trail was empty. Even Sindari was out of sight.

"Hi," I said, and waved like an idiot. "I was, uhm, walking down the trail." I waved behind me, not even tempted to explain the bicycle and the dragon. Thad wouldn't believe it, and Mom would worry. "I tried to get a room at one of the hotels—the two *small* hotels in town—but they didn't have anything, so I'm staying at the campground."

Thad looked me up and down. At first, I thought his gaze lingered on my chest and he was checking me out, but it quickly drifted lower. My jeans were still damp and marsh grass draped my combat boots.

I bent and plucked it off. "There were puddles along the way. Did it rain here yesterday?"

"Are you all right?" Mom squinted at me as Thad looked toward the blue sky over the lake.

"Yeah. I'll give you some details of my work later." Did Shaygor count as *my work*? It wasn't as if I wanted anything to do with him. "How'd you get here, Mom? All the roads are washed out." I wouldn't have guessed the Subaru, SUV or not, could replicate the feat my Jeep had accomplished.

"I actually took the scenic route and came up from the south, through Plummer and over to St. Maries. I'm just now learning about the destruction to the other roads." She waved to Thad.

She must have just missed the destruction that had happened along her route. The police officer had mentioned it being recent. Maybe she'd stopped in town for provisions before finding this place.

"Did you see anything peculiar on the way in?" I resisted mentioning goblins and sasquatch.

"Not until you walked down the driveway." Mom smiled, but there was tension around her blue eyes.

Maybe she expected this meeting to go poorly. I wished I could reassure her it wouldn't.

"Funny," I said as Rocket bounded up and nuzzled my hand.

I patted him on the head.

The dog's arrival stirred Thad from whatever startled thoughts my appearance had prompted. He came forward to greet me. He'd gotten older, some gray at the temples of his short black hair, but he was still lean, almost skinny, so he probably still got wrapped up in work and forgot to eat. He wore khaki shorts and a black T-shirt with a flowchart of tips for "debugging your code."

"I'm sorry, Val. I was just—wow, you really haven't changed. You look good." He lifted his arms, leaned in for a hug, but then paused and lowered one arm as if to offer a handshake. Then he shook his head and lifted them again, his face screwed up with uncertainty.

It was as bad as me trying to figure out how to greet Zav. I hoped I wasn't that intimidating to Thad. I stepped in and gave him a hug. That he was greeting me with one instead of flinty hostility put some relief in my heart. I hadn't truly expected hostility—he'd only lost his temper a handful of times in all the years I'd known him, and it had never been at a person, just at some software that was vexing him—but I'd always wondered if he'd resented me for leaving. He'd never truly understood my work—or why I felt compelled to choose it over them—so I'd let my doubts run rampant.

The hug was awkward and brief, though it was sadly the best one I'd had in a long time. Before letting go fully, Thad gripped my arms and studied my face.

"You really haven't changed. Amazing."

I'd explained the elven blood before and that it might cause me to live longer—if I could keep from being chomped on by a dragon—so I didn't bring it up.

"You haven't changed that much either. Same wardrobe." I smirked and plucked at his T-shirt.

He grinned, then glanced toward the deck and hastily dropped his hands and stepped back. A woman had come out of the house, curly red hair, curvy, and in her mid-thirties. A new girlfriend?

Thanks to keeping tabs on Amber's social-media pages, I knew there had been a few over the years but Thad hadn't remarried. If he worked as many hours a week as he had when I'd known him, that wasn't surprising. Even if he didn't realize it, he'd always put his career first too. I'd worried—and felt guilty—from time to time that Amber didn't have a parent around that much, but I'd always believed she'd been better off with Thad than with me. At least he came home every night, and covered in printer ink, not blood.

"Hey, honey." Thad lifted a hand and waved for the woman to come down. "This is Val. Val, this is Shauna. We're, uhm, seeing each other."

Shauna looked me up and down a lot more brazenly than Thad had, then gave me a scathing smile as she walked up and slid a possessive arm around his waist. I'd gotten similar looks from women before, whether I was standing next to their boyfriends or not, so I didn't immediately dismiss her as a bitch, but I couldn't manage a cordial return smile. I had zero interest in interacting with her.

"That's nice. Is Amber here?"

Thad looked out toward the water. "She's out there with her friend Myung-sook from their swim team. The house has kayaks and a paddleboat. They're doing the paddleboat, so they shouldn't be far, but, uhm…" He frowned uncertainly back at me.

Did that mean he'd told Amber we might meet this week and that Amber had said she didn't want to see me? My heart shriveled.

"Should I take my stuff inside?" Mom asked into what was turning into an awkward silence.

"Oh, yes. Please, Sigrid." Thad waved her toward the door. "I'll help you in a minute, but there are a bunch of unclaimed bedrooms upstairs. Take whichever one you like." He looked at me again. "Did you say you're stuck at the campground? We have room if—"

"No, thanks," I hurried to say, anticipating Shauna's rejection and not wanting to impose, regardless. If Amber didn't want to see me, I didn't want to force my way into their vacation.

Red heat flushed Shauna's cheeks. Her mouth was open—she'd definitely been on the verge of objecting.

She turned it into a whisper that I might not have heard if my ears weren't sharper than average.

"You didn't say she was coming *here*."

"I didn't know," Thad murmured back.

"It was good to see you." I lifted my hands and stepped back, not wanting to intrude, but I couldn't keep from looking out to the lake, to where a blue paddleboat bobbed along near the shoreline. All I could see were the backs of Amber's blonde head and her friend's black-haired head, but longing and regret and more emotions I struggled to name wrestled for dominance in my heart. "I'll get back to my walk."

"Wait," Thad blurted as I backed up the driveway and turned toward the trail. He extricated himself from Shauna.

"Don't go *after* her." This time, Shauna's whisper wasn't that soft, and there was a note of warning in it.

Despite my vow to reserve judgment—I was sure she saw me as the Other Woman and some kind of threat—I found myself hoping their relationship didn't last and that Amber didn't get a new step-mother inflicted on her. Not this woman, anyway. If Thad found Carol Brady or June Cleaver to love and support him and Amber, I'd cheer for the wedding.

"I'll only be a minute," Thad called. "I just want to make sure she's all right."

"She's *fine*," Shauna said in exasperation.

Thad caught me at the trail. I stuck my hands in my pockets so Shauna, who, standing with her arms over her chest and clearly intending to watch, wouldn't have any fodder to misinterpret.

"Are you really okay staying in a tent?" Thad's brow furrowed. "Or do you have an RV or something?"

The last thing I needed was another vehicle for a dragon to destroy.

"It's a tent, but it's fine. It's summer. I camp out all the time on missions."

His forehead furrow didn't go away. "And that's really what you're here for? Don't take this the wrong way, but when I got your email… Well, I thought it was a little, er, weird that you were going to be on an assignment in the same place we're taking our vacation." He glanced back at Shauna, who would start tapping her foot like a cartoon virago any second, and I wondered if she'd read that email over his shoulder and pointed out the unlikely coincidence. "I mean, it's not a problem that you're here. I just… if you want to see Amber, you could say so. She said she doesn't want to see you, but I think she's just… I don't know. She's fourteen now. I don't understand much of what motivates her these days." His fleeting smile seemed more genuine than forced, and I read between the lines that their relationship was probably fine and the problem was more me. "But maybe she would come along if we arranged to have lunch in town. If you want to." He raised his eyebrows uncertainly.

"I don't want to get in the way of your vacation. If she doesn't want to see me, it's okay." The tightness in my throat would have told me that was a lie even if I lacked the perception to realize it. "And I hope *you* won't take this the wrong way, but the government keeps an eye on you because of me. Colonel Willard—I'm a contractor for her office—asked if I wanted this mission because she knew you'd be here." I spoke rapidly, well aware how Big Brother this sounded. "It's always possible one of my many, *many* enemies could find out about you guys and that I care about you and try to use you against me. The fact that weird stuff happened to be going on in the town where you're taking your vacation worried me."

His expression changed at least five times while I spoke—he'd never been one to don a mask and hide his feelings. It settled on thoughtful concern. "I guess I'm encouraged to hear you admit you still care."

I opened my mouth to say of course I cared and what kind of monster would I be if I didn't, but I caught myself. The years of silence didn't hint of someone who cared.

My therapist was right. I should have at least emailed over the years. I could have been careful and deleted the *sent* messages. It wasn't as if the dark elves, orcs, and trolls that broke into my apartment were typically tech-savvy enough to hack into my computer and get all my contacts. But no contact had always seemed safer. Amber and Thad were still alive, but would they have been if I'd been in their lives?

Granted, I couldn't truly know that they *wouldn't* have been if I'd been there all those years. And that gnawed at me like a dog worrying a bone.

"I do care," I said and left it at that. My voice was threatening to tighten up and betray how *much* I cared. Even my lungs were tight. How could they work fine when a dragon was eating my bicycle but squeeze up when I got the tiniest bit emotional? "Do me a favor and don't go on any hikes in the woods, okay?"

"Because of the sasquatch?" Thad raised his brows.

Rocket wandered past, his nose to the ground. He was probably on the trail of a magical silver tiger.

"Someone's plotting something against this town." I thought about asking him to cancel his trip and go home, but a selfish part of me made me keep my mouth shut. Thad, at least, was open to having lunch somewhere, and if he could talk Amber into coming, it would be good to see her and talk for a minute. Even if she sat in sulky silence, I would have the opportunity to let her know that if she wanted to talk one day, I would figure out a way to make it work. And I would.

"We're going to relax and stay on the property," Thad said. "That's it. Maybe go to dinner in town a couple of times. Shauna and Amber both said I work too much and that I need a tan."

"You do and you do." I smiled and glanced at the still glaring Shauna. I resolved to wrap this up so it wouldn't put a strain between them, but curiosity rooted me to the pavement to ask, "Do they get along? Is everything good with you?"

Thad hesitated. "Amber hasn't gotten along with anyone I've dated since she hit puberty—not that this represents a large number of women—" he smiled ruefully, "—but I think we're doing okay. I know Shauna can be a little… jealous sometimes, and I'm not sure why, because it's not like… well, you're the first woman I've talked with for more than two minutes that wasn't her, but anyway, they get along okay. And Shauna is nice one on one."

What did that mean? That he couldn't take her out in public?

"We're still getting to know each other, but it's good. We're good."

"Good." *Definitely* an awkward conversation. I resisted the urge to advise him on a prenuptial agreement if things got serious. I was the last person who should give advice on relationships, but I hoped Shauna was into the geeky things he liked and not looking to bag a senior programmer with money socked away.

"Seriously, Val. How is it that you don't look any different? I'm getting…" He grimaced and rubbed his graying temples. "Older."

"The dragon aura keeps me young."

He blinked. "What?"

"It's a skin moisturizer. I think there's a lot of Vitamin E in it. I better go. Email me if you and Amber want to do lunch, but no pressure. Have a good trip."

"Thanks. You too."

That was unlikely to happen, but I smiled as if I was sure I'd have a great time here, then lifted a hand in parting. His fingers twitched, as if he might raise his arms for another hug, but I hurried down the trail before the thought could come to fruition. In case Shauna *was* a good match for him, I didn't want to do anything to jeopardize that.

As I hustled away at a speed-walking pace, I prayed that dragon wasn't still hunting by scent and that he couldn't truly tell someone was my offspring by smell. If he could, Chopper and Sindari and I would pitch our tent on the top of one of those cliffs and keep an eye out for Amber.

Chapter 9

The Jeep hadn't been destroyed. Maybe my luck was turning.

Since the core of town was so small, I left it in the campground parking spot I'd been lucky enough to get and walked up the hill to Cliff Way. The street the mayor had named as having a house that had been ransacked, it looked down on the handful of restaurants and shops in town and had a view of the lake between the trees.

Sindari caught up with me as I walked along the street, looking for a vandalized home.

That odious hound insisted on following me and barking at me halfway back to town, he informed me.

"Rocket? He's pretty friendly. Even Maggie the-cat-who-loathes-everybody didn't find him odious."

Didn't your mother say she threw books at him?

"Yes, but I assumed that was a sign of affection. She wanted to play."

Abusively. I do not regret scent-marking your colonel's new apartment. The small feline must learn to respect larger, stronger predators.

"I *knew* you weren't just scratching an itch on that exercise bike." I stopped at an empty driveway covered in shattered glass. The front windows of the house looked like someone had put fists through them. Large fists. "I have a hunch this is the place."

I headed to the front door, intending to walk right in. Nobody was around, and I doubted there was anything valuable left inside. Who would object?

The door was locked. I almost laughed. All the glass in the window next to it had been knocked inward, and toppled furniture, bookcases, and an umbrella stand were visible.

I could have gone through the window, but as long as I had a lock-picking charm...

You sense anyone magical inside? I asked before getting started.

Magical? No. There's a dubious animal scent wafting out, and I can hear rats scurrying around in a back room. They are gorging themselves on food.

We can probably handle rats. Do tigers mouse?

Mouse?

Hunt for and catch mice. Like a cat.

Sindari snorted. Or maybe that was a tiger version of a haughty sniff. *I do not hunt such weak and meager prey.*

I guess we can't do the homeowners a favor, then, and get rid of the pest problem. I rested my palm against the door and willed the lock to open.

You may get rid of them if you wish. Should we encounter dakyar *or dual-horned wildebeests, then I will take care of them.*

The lock clicked open immediately. This mundane door was nothing compared to what I'd asked the charm to handle lately.

When I stepped inside, glass crunched under my boots. The place smelled like an animal den and also decaying vegetable matter, like fermented foods that had gone bad. Was that even possible? The stench permeated everything.

Sindari slid past me, going first even though we didn't sense a threat. *I do not believe the rats are the primary problem for these homeowners.*

You could be right. I wandered in after him, more glass crunching. There was so much of it that I couldn't avoid stepping on it.

It was as if a horde of goblins had surrounded the house and fired slingshots at the windows. And stink bombs. Though I didn't actually see any signs of projectiles thrown through the windows. That was surprising. Maybe someone had used a baseball bat.

The rats are in the kitchen, as are numerous boxes of partially devoured crackers and cereal, Sindari said.

Cereal and crackers wouldn't account for that stench.

There is also rat feces.

I curled a skeptical lip. Unpleasant, but whatever the smell was, it wasn't dried scat.

The odor is present all over the house. I believe it is the smell of an animal, like a muskrat but stronger.

"*Much* stronger." I had to fight not to gag.

I crossed from the tiled entryway to the carpeted living room. Great chunks of drywall covered with textured popcorn paint were scattered on the floor. There were holes all over the ceiling, as if someone had been throwing basketballs at it. Hard. One side of an overhead light fixture was broken off, a bulb shattered below, and a dark clump of hair—or was that fur?—had caught on the jagged corner.

"That doesn't look like goblin hair." I was tall enough to reach the clump and pull it down. It was coarse and dark brown, the strands five or six inches long. "Bear fur?"

I held it to my nose, gagged, and almost pitched it out the window. Or pitched *myself* out the window.

Sindari padded in from the kitchen to find me clutching a hand to my nose and wobbling, uncharacteristically off-balance.

Problem? he asked.

"I found the source of the stench." I held up the tuft of fur, then pulled out my phone to run a search for *sasquatch + odor*. "Don't tell me this isn't searing off the insides of your sensitive nostrils. It's worse than an open sewer."

I realized it was unlikely the stench in the entire house was coming from one tuft of fur. The creature—no way did goblins smell like this—had to have been oozing an odor of its own. Like a muskrat, indeed. Maybe it had slept in the house after breaking in.

My nostrils are sensitive but perhaps more accustomed to gamey scents than yours.

"This is more than gamey. This is… I feel like I should bag it and take it back to Zoltan in case he's willing to pay for it. This has to be an ingredient called for in some potion or another."

That is very possible. Malodorous substances seem to figure prominently in his craft.

"According to this, er, reputable online source—" the website was called *Finding Your First Bigfoot*, "—ten percent of sasquatch sightings involve someone remarking on a strong animal stench." I lowered my phone. "Strong is an understatement." I needed to get my nose and my stomach out of the house, but we'd barely searched it. "Why don't we check outside for giant footprints that might go with this?" I waved the tuft of hair.

I'll do that.

I almost followed him out, but on the chance that Zoltan truly would find this valuable, I wandered into the kitchen to look for a zip baggie. Maybe ten of them. Then I could zip this up like a Russian nesting doll and hope that would dull the odor. Even so, I would tape it to the bumper of my Jeep so it could ride on the outside on the way back to Seattle. If he didn't want it, Willard might take it for the evidence room.

As I finished wrapping it up, my phone buzzed. Thad's name popped up with an incoming text. Even though I never called him, I hadn't taken him off my contacts list. I'd always wanted to be able to call him—call *them*—if there was trouble.

Hey, Val. Good to see you today. I asked Amber about lunch, but she doesn't want to meet with you. Don't take this the wrong way—I'd forgotten that was his catchphrase—*but she was really curious about you a few years ago. That would have been a better time for this. Since she hit middle school, she's been more, well, teenage, and now that she's in high school it's even more pronounced. You know how it is. Sorry.*

Actually, I didn't. Other than a vague sense from hearing other mothers talk about their kids. I'd missed seeing Amber grow up and grow into being a rebellious teenager.

"My choice," I muttered and walked outside, needing fresh air more than ever.

Sindari must have still been checking the property. I sank down on the stoop and rubbed my face. The rejection was expected, and surely being rejected over an impersonal text message was better than in person, but it still depressed me. Maybe because Thad had been so reasonable, even friendly. He hadn't seemed bitter and jaded. Maybe he never had been.

I took my charm necklace off and looked at the mixture of bone, silver, and ivory trinkets, all emanating magic of one kind or another. Over the years, I'd sought them all out, and I knew what they did, all save one. A silver heart. I'd found it in a bear shifter's woodworking shop out near Forks in the dark, mossy Olympic National Park. He'd been killed by his crazy vampire lover, a woman who'd murdered ten other lovers before him. After I'd killed her, per my orders, I'd sent the location of the shifter's shop to Willard, to have the office do with it what it wanted—he'd had no next of kin that we'd been able to find—but I'd found the little heart charm sitting in a treasured spot on the hearth.

Usually, I wasn't sentimental, and I didn't collect useless things, but it had called to me, so I'd taken it. There was some magic about it, but I'd never figured out what it did. I'd always thought that someday I would and maybe it would put to rest the spirit of a man who'd been killed by the woman he loved.

I sense you.

The voice reverberated in my mind, and I dropped the charm necklace even as I swore at my stupid mistake. By taking it off, I'd deactivated the cloaking charm. I lunged at it and started to tug the leather thong over my head again, but my brain caught up to my instincts. That was Zav, not Shaygor.

A momentary lapse of judgment, I replied, deciding not to explain that my emotions were getting the best of me today and that maybe I'd been unwise to accept this mission. Maybe Thad and Amber would have been safer if I'd never come. I would most certainly be safer standing in the same city as Zav, even if it galled me to admit that. I hated to admit to needing anyone's protection or even help. *Where are you?*

Waiting until dark so that I may hunt the dark elves. In the meantime, I captured a roc in your town called Mountain Vernon.

Mt. Vernon, I corrected, not that he would care what our cities were called.

Yes. The roc had a nest and was feeding its young, but it was feeding them young humans plucked up from nearby farms. Before it fled to your world, it did the same thing with elves. It has a taste for the flesh of sentient beings.

I grimaced, surprised Willard hadn't heard about it and sent me up to deal with it. *If it was eating humans, thank you for capturing it. What will happen to its young?*

I have already delivered the mother and young to the Dragon Justice Court. The female will be punished and rehabilitated. A suitable non-murderous surrogate will be found for the young.

Someday, I would ask him what exactly punishment and rehabilitation involved. But the fact that the dragons would consider me a candidate for it if they found out the truth about Dob made me not want to know.

Good, I told Zav. *Are you able to speak with me all the way from Seattle then?*

Yes. I am near your domicile waiting for it to get dark.

I eyed the sky. It had been a long day, but that was how summer was at a northern latitude. The sun wouldn't set for a few more hours. Maybe that was why Zav was checking on me. He was bored crouching on my rooftop, flattening the deck chairs that had been replaced after the last time he flattened them.

You think my domicile is likely to be ravaged by dark elves again?

Has it not happened before?

Unfortunately, yes.

There will be no moon tonight. They may be active.

I don't suppose you'd like to scare away any dark elf that comes to ransack the place? I just got it cleaned up after the last time. Oh, and if you go inside, don't ask about your poster. I didn't do that.

Why would I go inside your domicile?

To catch the dark elf? Or to rummage through my panties drawer like a creeper? I don't know what motivates you.

Catching criminals *motivates me.* He sounded affronted. Maybe he knew about panties drawers. *Has Shaygorthian returned to search for you?*

I hesitated. Zav was on a mission to help his standing with his people, and that mission would also help *my* people. If the two dark-elf scientists were taken from Earth, maybe the rest of the dark elves would go back to being only a minor problem instead of plotting to take over the world or whatever they intended to do with those orbs.

And all that aside, I didn't want to ask Zav to come back and help me. Maybe it would be the death of me, but I didn't think my pride would allow me to beg for assistance from a dragon—from anyone. If I died because of that stubbornness, so be it.

He has *been searching for you,* Zav responded to my silence, his words like a growl in my mind. *When I am done here, I will come protect you.*

Thank you for wanting to do that, Zav, but you should worry about your own mission. I'm used to taking care of myself.

You cannot take care of yourself against a dragon. He will pluck the truth from your mind and either kill you outright or take you for punishment and rehabilitation.

What exactly does that involve?

Seven-hundred and thirty-four days of physical and mental pain inflicted by a magical device that keeps you alive while restraining you, followed by a mind wipe that steals your personality and inserts a new one.

Seven-hundred and thirty-four days. Was that a randomly chosen number? *So basically, it's like death. With a lot of pain beforehand.*

It is for the good of the societies of the Cosmic Realms. It is our duty as dragons to create order and vanquish criminals, one way or another. But I do not wish this to happen to you. When I first met you, I did, but I believe now that you are ignorant and misguided, not willfully criminal.

Wow, with words of praise like that, women must be eager to jump into bed with you.

That must not have been the response he expected because there was a pause before he replied. *All females of lesser species will jump into the nest of a male dragon if he wishes it. As will all males seek to satisfy the desires of female dragons.*

Voluntarily or because they're compelled to do so?

Most *will voluntarily do it. Only foolishly stubborn ones need to be compelled.*

I almost told him I didn't believe him, but that wasn't true. He was damn magnificent when he was a dragon, and he was hot as a human—even Dob and Shaygor had been hunks in their elven forms. A lot of people probably *would* ignore their haughty, arrogant insults for a chance to ride a dragon.

"People with low standards," I muttered.

I do not know why we are discussing this. Zav sounded exasperated. *Shaygor seeks you, so in the morning, I will fly back there to ensure he cannot put his talons in your mind again. Wear your charm and do not do anything foolish tonight.*

I sensed his presence fading from my mind and felt a sadness. For a moment, I'd forgotten my other problems.

Val. Sindari came around to the front of the house to sit in front of me. *Your charm is not activated.*

I know. I was talking to Zav.

He is here and will help us?

Not until tomorrow.

That is unfortunate because I sense the silver dragon is in the area.

I dropped my forehead into my hand.

I also found some footprints to match that fur.

Oh? Do you have time to show me?

I believe so, but activate your charm.

I did, then stood, expecting him to lead me around to the back yard or into the trees to the side of the house. Instead, he crouched and sprang twenty-odd feet into the air to land on the roof.

The footprints are up there?

It is easiest to see the story they tell from above.

If I had to climb onto a roof, the story had better be a scintillating drama with romantic elements.

Grumbling, I found a drainpipe to scurry up. My grumbles turned to curses as my weight caused it to pull away from the house. My agility let me compensate, and I ended up twisting in the air like a high-jumper and vaulting onto the rooftop, barely making it over the edge and landing on my feet.

"Thieves have a much easier time of this in fantasy novels," I muttered.

It probably helped that they were usually lightweight starved orphan children.

Over here. Sindari was on the far side, looking down at the back yard.

When I crouched beside him, I didn't see anything at first—unlike the house, the grassy yard was well kept, trimmed and green. But he was looking past it toward a bed of soft dirt and rose bushes that edged the back before the yard sloped down into trees and eventually the main street through town. We could see the tops of many of the buildings from here, along with people walking on sidewalks to the restaurants and shops, but it was the footprints in the rose beds that riveted my attention.

They were giant. The plantigrade prints had five toes, but each deep print was well over a foot long. Some were closer to two feet. Whoever had made them had been heavy enough that the prints were deep in the soft dirt. A few significantly smaller prints were also scattered about.

"Goblin?" I asked.

Yes. It looks like they were here around the same time.

"Could you tell if the sasquatch were real or maybe some mechanical contraptions the goblins made?"

Their scent seems authentic.

"True. So are they working together? Are the goblins somehow convincing them to tear up the town? And to what end?"

I do not know. Sindari shifted on the roof, his gaze turned to the south.

"Let me guess."

The silver dragon is coming here.

"You didn't let me guess."

It wasn't necessary. You knew.

At least I wasn't riding something that would stand out to a dragon this time. With my charm activated, he shouldn't see me up here on the roof. And if Zav *did* come back in the morning, maybe he could keep Shaygor away while Sindari and I clue-hunted.

As the dragon neared, coming into my range, I eyed the pedestrians on the streets below. If Shaygor soared over the park, anyone with a recent magical ancestor should be able to see him. A lot of people were out, enjoying the summer evening.

Including Amber and her friend. I swore, gaped at them, and swore some more.

They were walking up from the bike trail toward the ice cream shop. Why hadn't Thad told her to stay away from town?

Maybe nothing would happen. Maybe Shaygor would fly past without glancing down. He was looking for *me*, not random human tourists. Right?

The great silver dragon came into view, soaring over the road leading into town. Amber and her friend had turned onto that same road, heading down the sidewalk toward the shop. Maybe they would go inside and the dragon wouldn't notice them. There were dozens of people wandering the sidewalks, eating at outdoor tables, and picnicking in the park.

Amber glanced up as Shaygor flew toward them. An instant before she shrieked, I realized that her quarter-elven blood would allow her to see the dragon.

I heard her scream from the rooftop up the hill. She threw a hand over her mouth and clamped it off immediately, but Shaygor looked down, looked right at her. Maybe people screamed all the time when they saw him. Maybe he wouldn't care…

I couldn't take that chance. Drawing Chopper, I ran off the edge of the roof and landed with a roll in the grass below. I came up running, charging down the steep slope instead of going the long way down the curving road.

What are you doing? Sindari asked.

Helping my daughter.

Chapter 10

More shrieks echoed up from the main street as I charged off the slope and through a side yard between two houses. They didn't sound like Amber, but other people could have seen the dragon by now. I'd lost sight of him through the evergreens, but I could sense him. He'd stopped moving. Had he landed in the street?

No. He was on the rooftop of the building with the ice cream shop. Amber was running back the way she'd come, but her friend was still on the sidewalk, gaping in confusion. No magical blood there. Like most of the bewildered people looking around, she couldn't see the dragon. But a few could. They were either pointing and shouting or sprinting away.

With Chopper in hand, I raced after Amber. I was camouflaged, so Shaygor didn't glance in my direction. He was focused on… Damn it, he was looking at Amber.

So far, he wasn't chasing her, but his nostrils twitched, and I thought of Zav's warning that Shaygor would be able to identify my daughter by scent.

As Amber rounded the corner to run back down to the trail—ugh, it would be better if she stayed in town, not that this dragon necessarily cared about witnesses or making a scene—Shaygor sprang off the rooftop. He flew after her.

I barely avoided being hit by a car as I charged across the street, invisible to everyone here, and sprinted after her. Sindari caught up and passed me.

Amber ran, glancing back and swearing as she spotted Shaygor barreling after her. She veered into the park and ducked behind a tree with a stout trunk.

Judging by Shaygor's dive, he would go right through it.

No, he hurled magic at the tree before he reached it and blew the trunk off its roots. With reflexes that had come from her elven grandfather, Amber sprang to the side an instant before it would have smashed her. She rolled and ran toward another tree. Shaygor was almost on her. She wasn't going to make it.

Lungs straining, legs burning, and my gaze locked on the dragon, I prayed I'd make it in time. I was close, so close, but he dove right for her, talons outstretched.

Sindari smashed into Amber a split second before Shaygor would have struck her. They tumbled to the ground, and Shaygor's talons flexed around empty air as he flew past.

Instead of flying back up, he landed on the other side of the grassy park. Amber scrambled to her feet as Sindari placed himself in front of her. Shaygor spun and leaped into the air again, wings flapping as he arrowed toward them.

This time, I was close enough to do something. Focused on his prey—on my *daughter*—Shaygor didn't sense me until the last instant. He flexed his talons, preparing to go through Sindari to get to Amber. But I darted in from the side. He was low enough to reach with Chopper, and I swiped at one of those outstretched legs, willing all of my anger—all the power Zav claimed I had—to funnel energy into the magical blade.

Chopper flared with blue light as it sank through Shaygor's scales and into his flesh. My fantasy of the blade lopping off his foreleg completely did not materialize, but he screeched like a falcon. He jerked that limb away and landed ungracefully as he whirled toward me.

"Run!" I barked to Amber, who was gaping at us—I was close enough that she could see me through my charm's magic. "Sindari, get her out of here."

You presume to raise a weapon in the presence of a dragon! Shaygor boomed telepathically into my mind.

"Hell, yeah, I presume."

Since he'd landed on the ground, I rushed toward him, aiming for a more vital target this time. His belly.

But now that he knew I was there, he prepared his magical defenses. Chopper's blade struck an invisible shield as hard as a stone wall, and pain reverberated up my arms at the jolt of contact.

At least Amber was running out of the park and back toward the bike trail. Shaygor was focused on me.

He opened his great fanged maw, and I saw the fire coming before the first yellow flames curled out of his throat. I dove to the side, rolling behind a picnic table.

Unfortunately, he had no trouble moving his head to track me. A gout of dancing yellow and orange flames spewed after me and engulfed me.

The fire-protection charm I wore kept me from charring like a hot dog dropped into the coals of a grill, but barely. The wooden picnic table burst into flames.

I sprinted out of the fire and toward the main street, wanting to lead Shaygor in the opposite direction from Amber.

People were standing and gawking when I reached it. They might not be able to see the dragon, but they had seen a tree be destroyed and a fire spontaneously start.

"Get inside!" I yelled at them and spun, expecting Shaygor to give chase.

He watched me from behind the fire he'd started, studying me. He lifted his foreleg, blood visible where I'd cut into it, and looked at it. Then he gazed off to the west, put his limb down, and spread his wings.

You have a sword that can hurt dragons, he spoke into my mind.

Yes, I do.

And you presumed to use it on me. You have attacked a dragon and an inquisitor of the Dragon Justice Court. His words were as cool as ice. *There will be repercussions.*

You attacked my daughter, you pompous ass. She has nothing to do with any of this.

She would not be in danger if you were not cowering behind those stolen magical charms. How did you get them? Such things are not made on this world. I will bring up your thieving with the court, after I've pulled the truth from your mind.

Come on up here and try. I brandished Chopper, though as soon as I thought the words, I mentally kicked myself. As Sindari would point out, goading a dragon was foolish. But as long as he was focused on me, he couldn't go after Amber.

Later, you will not be prepared with your stolen gewgaws, and I will have your thoughts. But for now, I have new research to do. Shaygor sprang into the air and flew south again, disappearing over the rooftops.

I stared after him, my mouth dangling open in surprise. Even though I'd cut him, it wasn't as if it had been a grievous blow, and once he'd known I was there, he'd had no trouble keeping my blade from hitting him again.

I am down the hill with your daughter in a cement structure by the marina, Sindari informed me. *She opted for this instead of running out in the open along the trail.*

Probably a good idea.

I have revealed myself to her. I believe she sees me as a threat.

You are large and largely fanged. I'll be right there. Shaygor left. I have no idea why. You don't think he's scared of Chopper, do you? I eyed my blade. The blue light had faded, but a few drops of blood remained. If I'd had a vial, I would have tried to collect them for Zoltan. Something valuable to trade with the next time I needed his services.

It's possible. Sindari sounded skeptical. *It's also possible that Zav threatened him from wherever he is.*

True. If Zav had spoken to me telepathically from Seattle, he would also be able to contact Shaygor. Had he somehow known the other dragon was attacking me?

I thought of how he'd known I'd helped the goblins in the forest outside of Duvall even though he hadn't arrived until several minutes after they'd disappeared.

It's also possible he wants to consider what may be a new revelation to him, Sindari added as I cleaned Chopper and sheathed the blade.

What revelation?

People were staring at me—the dragon's attack must have knocked out my cloaking magic—and a fire engine was wheeling down the main road toward the park. A good time to leave. I trotted toward the marina.

That you have a weapon capable of piercing dragon scales.

He did fixate on that. An eerie chill licked at my spine. *Do you think he's considering the possibility that I could have killed Dob? He said he had to go off and do research.*

What if he found witnesses from that night by the river? The werewolves I'd hired to be a distraction might have still been close enough to see me kill Dob. And some of the Pardus brothers' shifter buddies could also have been in the area. And then there was Dimitri. He'd been there. But Shaygor couldn't possibly know about Dimitri, could he?

I think, Sindari replied, taking long enough to mull over his response that I worried I'd been right, *you need to come up with a way to convince the Dragon Justice Court to leave you alone.*

How am I going to do that? Even if I could somehow kill Shaygor, I would only end up incurring *more* wrath from the rest of the dragons.

I don't know.

Chapter 11

The cement structure Sindari had mentioned was the bathroom facility for the campground. I walked in and found Sindari sitting calmly in front of the sinks. The sound of scared breathing came from the handicap stall in the back.

"Amber?"

There was a long pause before her uncertain voice said, "Yeah?"

The single word prompted a pang of emotion that almost had me trembling. Facing off against a dragon hadn't made me shake, but coming face to face with my daughter after... shit, it had been almost ten years since I'd dared visit them in person. I wouldn't have even recognized her voice if I hadn't watched a few video diary entries she'd shared on her social-media page.

"It's Val." I meant to say more, but my words got stuck on my tongue.

"I know."

I was half-surprised she did. Maybe Thad had a picture of me somewhere. As he'd pointed out, I hadn't changed much.

"You can come out. The dragon is gone for now."

"You can see it?"

"Yes."

"My friend couldn't. She thought I was nuts."

"You're not. You have one-quarter elven blood, which gives you some extra strength, agility, longevity, and most likely, the ability to sense magical items and magical beings." I assumed her abilities were less than mine so I wasn't sure what the world was like to her, but Nin and Dimitri could both work with magic, so I trusted I was right. I almost said that she could meet them and talk to them someday if she wanted, but nothing had changed. I couldn't get her involved in my life. Today had only reinforced that. "You can come out," was all I added.

"There's a murderous tiger out there somewhere."

"He's actually in here, his tail in a puddle of soapy water and toilet paper stuck to his paw."

Sindari gave me a dark look.

"He's my friend," I added. "He wasn't trying to murder you. He knocked you out of the way so the dragon wouldn't get you."

Another pause as she digested that. "He's *huge*."

I am well and regally proportioned for a Zhinevarii tiger from the Tangled Tundra Nation on Del'noth, Sindari informed me.

I know.

You must educate her. Huge and murderous. Really, Val. I'm not an ogre.

I wondered if bribing a fourteen-year-old with ice cream so she would come out could work. Was the shop still open or had everything closed down while the fire truck put out the flames in the park? The shouts of people working on that mess drifted down the hill.

Finally, the stall lock slid aside, and Amber walked out, tall and lanky. Her long blonde hair had fallen out of the ponytail it had been in before the dragon showed up. She looked a lot like me except for the cute nose and freckles. I'd never had freckles, and I'd always thought of my nose as sharp, like my tongue.

She was so tall, just a hair shorter than my own six feet, that I almost forgot she was still a kid. A teenager, yes, but a kid. Her green eyes were wide and scared. Understandably so. I was positive my own eyes had looked the same way the day I'd met Zav and he'd been trying to incinerate me.

As Amber stepped forward, Sindari came into her view. He didn't move, but she braced herself with a hand to the wall and spat out a startled, "Shit!"

I resisted the urge to make some stupid parental comment like, *Does your dad let you swear?*

Besides, sarcasm was more my way of dealing with awkward situations.

"I think she finds you more impressive than the dragon," I told Sindari.

Naturally. I am a sleek and magnificent predator who must rely on fang and sinew to bring down prey, rather than ridiculously overpowered magic.

"I just didn't realize tigers were that big," Amber mumbled, then seemed to find her courage. She lifted her chin and stood straight as she looked me up and down, her gaze lingering on Fezzik in my thigh holster and Chopper poking up over my shoulder. "Huh. It's really true, isn't it?"

"That I'm a maniac who hunts magical bad guys and totes big weapons around?"

"Dad said you're an assassin for the army."

"An assassin of magical bad guys for the army. I don't kill humans." I felt it important that she know that.

"I thought you were a druggie or a deadbeat and Dad was trying to be polite. That's what he does. He should run for office or something. He never says anything bad about anyone, even that— never mind."

Her broken sentence roused my curiosity, as I immediately wondered if she'd started to say something about the girlfriend, but I highly doubted Amber wanted to share confidences with me. With a tiger watching on. In the nasty bathroom at the campground with damp toilet paper shreds all over the floor.

"No. I work hard and don't consume anything more mind-altering than hard cider. I'm sure other nouns apply, but druggie and deadbeat aren't among them." I couldn't even remember the last time I'd had a vacation. Willard seemed to think any time I traveled out of town counted, but camping out to hunt sasquatch while being stalked by dragons was not relaxing or rejuvenating.

"Can I go?" Amber eyed the door behind me, and I had a feeling she was only asking permission because I was armed and standing in the way. "Is that thing—was it really a dragon?—going to attack me again? What's it *doing* here?"

"You can go. The dragon is…" I wanted to lie. I wanted to pretend it was here for something unrelated to me and that I'd just happened to show up to heroically save the day. Or at least stab it in the elbow. "He's after me."

"Then why did he chase *me*? We don't look *anything* alike."

Actually, we looked a lot alike, but judging from the dismissive look she gave my duster, combat boots, and weapons, it was more our fashion styles that she was dismissing as similar. She was in a pale blue summer blouse with artistically rolled up sleeves and cut-off denim shorts with pink and yellow flower-shaped patches on the butt pockets.

"Apparently, we smell alike."

"What? Gross." Amber wrinkled her nose. "You stink."

I started to object, but then I remembered the sasquatch fur in a baggie—in ten baggies—in my pocket. It was fragrant enough that I could smell it through all the wrapping.

She's not wrong, Sindari observed. *Perhaps you should store that somewhere for the time being.*

"Our *blood* smells alike," I clarified. "To a dragon. They have noses like Rocket." Probably *better* than Rocket.

"That's so weird. Can I go?" Amber shifted, as if to go around me, but eyed Sindari warily.

He hadn't made a threatening move. He was simply large, and she would have to squeeze between us to get out.

A thousand things I longed to say threatened to burble out, and an ill-advised part of me wanted to block the door, to force her to stay and listen to me apologize for being an asshole of a mother who'd brought her into the world and then ditched her. I should have known way back then that I couldn't change my career, and that things wouldn't work out with Thad, but I'd been in denial.

If I *had* realized those things, she wouldn't exist. Could I truly apologize for giving birth to her? I barely knew her, but it was surely wrong to wish she weren't here in the world. I just wished she were completely safe and that she'd had a mother. Maybe that Shauna was better than I believed and would fill the role, if Amber still wanted someone in that role. Did she? Maybe it was too late.

Looking at her now, at the stubborn and belligerent set to her mouth, I couldn't manage to voice any of the thoughts spinning in my mind. I stepped aside so she could leave.

Without a goodbye, or a thanks for helping, she stalked for the door.

"Wait." I jerked my hand up, realizing nothing had changed. Shaygor might go after her again as she headed back to the rental, and if she was walking, it might be dark before she got back. Predators loved to hunt at night…

"What?" She twisted to avoid my hand, even though I'd stopped myself from grabbing her arm.

"I want you to take my charm."

Her forehead wrinkled as I reached for the trinket-filled thong around my neck.

"A specific one." I pulled it off so I could untie the knot and remove the camouflage charm.

Val, Sindari warned, *you need that. Shaygor will be on you faster than a hawk on a titmouse if you aren't hidden.*

We'll see. It's been off for the last ten minutes, and he's not back.

He will be.

Amber watched me warily, her hand on the door, appearing torn between wanting to get out of there and curiosity. Or maybe wondering if I was going to give her something useful.

"What do they do?" she asked.

"Each one is different. This one kept me from bursting into flames when the dragon spewed fire at me. This cat-shaped one summons Sindari." I nodded to him—he was in the middle of trying to shake a nasty piece of damp toilet paper off his tail. "And this one camouflages the person wearing it. There's no activation command, but you have to touch it and envision it making you disappear." I handed it to her. "This is a loaner charm, so don't lose it, please."

"I'm not an idiot."

"It's saved my life a lot of times. It won't work if the dragon is right on top of you, but if you see him coming or *sense* him coming—" I didn't know if she could do that or how large her range would be if she could, "—activate it. You have to keep it on you for it to work."

"'Kay." Amber pushed open the door, looking warily outside, but paused before leaving. "What do you mean I'm part elven?"

"Mom—your grandmother—never told you about that?"

Amber hesitated. "Maybe once when I was little, but Dad pulled her aside, and she didn't bring it up again. I don't remember what she said very well."

"Well, ask her about it now. She knows a lot more about it than I do. She's the one who got horizontal with an elf."

A horrified expression twisted Amber's face. "Horizon... Shit, lady, she's *old*. That's gross."

Lady? Did she not even know my name? "It's Val, not lady, and I'm sure she was a hot nubile vixen at the time."

The horrified expression only intensified. Amber fled, the door banging shut behind her.

I scratched my cheek. "That didn't go as badly as I feared."

She's abrasive, finds me murderous, and I predict she'll lose your most valuable charm before she gets back to her lodgings.

"I was abrasive at that age too."

You're still abrasive. There's just more wit underlying it.

Was that a compliment?

I will compliment you if you assist me. This wet paper is like glue. He'd succeeded in removing the piece from his tail, but now it was stuck to his paw. The scathing look he gave me conveyed his thorough distaste for all things human. *Why can your people not urinate in the grass like every other normal* species?

It's a mystery. I plucked the toilet paper off his paw and debated if there was a point to setting up my tent or if a dragon would inevitably show up and light it on fire.

Chapter 12

I yawned and rubbed my eyes, acknowledging that this had been an incredibly long day. There was about an hour of daylight left as I finished setting up my tent. Up the hill, the fire in the park was out, but the fire engine remained parked along the curb, as if the team expected more trouble before the day ended.

Given the way things were going for the town, I wouldn't be surprised if that turned out to be true. Shaygor hadn't yet returned, but as I unzipped the door of the tent, intending to put my sleeping bag in there, I sensed a familiar powerful aura.

Your cloaking charm is not activated, Zav spoke into my mind before I could see him in the sky, flying in over the lake.

I decided to court danger tonight. It's stimulating. I decided not to mention that I'd given my charm to Amber.

Zav didn't respond with words, but stern disapproval oozed into my mind.

By the time I'd laid out my sleeping bag—the tag said fire-retardant, but I was positive it hadn't been rated against dragons—his great black form soared into view. Powerful wings carried him over the marina to land next to my Jeep, his size dwarfing it.

Only a few campers were outside, and nobody seemed to have the ability to see him. Or they were looking the other way if they did. A pall of wariness had descended over the town, and a few of the RVs had pulled out after the fire. They must not have heard the news that all the roads out of the area had been destroyed.

"Were you, by chance, responsible for Shaygor leaving me alone earlier?" I glanced at the time on my phone. "About a half hour ago?"

I instructed him to come and speak with me if he has questions and to leave you alone or another dragon would die in this forsaken world. Zav shape-shifted into his human form, the silver-trimmed black robe and silver slippers not fitting in here in Harrison—or anywhere outside the set for *The Hobbit*.

"You threatened him again? Will you get in trouble for that?" I grimaced, not wanting to be the reason Zav got kicked out of his Dragon Court or his mother dethroned from it or whatever would happen. If he mouthed off to the wrong dragons, was it possible *he* would be subjected to the punishment and rehabilitation he had described?

"Likely," he said, walking toward me, "but he seemed distracted. He told me I had better watch out because *you* have a sword capable of harming dragons." He stopped in front of me, his gaze flicking toward Chopper's hilt.

His cool face was hard to read. I couldn't tell if he was only stating facts or if he was irritated because I'd tipped my hand. Shaygor might be off in the woods, putting two and two together and realizing it was possible I'd killed his son.

"Did you poke him in the butt with it?" Zav raised his eyebrows. The faintest hint of a smile tugged at the corners of his mouth.

He wasn't mad. Maybe he was even a little pleased that I'd vexed another of his enemies? Either way, I was relieved he wasn't angry. I didn't want to fight with him.

"No, the foreleg. If you'd prefer the butt, I can try to sneak up behind him next time."

"He would feel intense indignation and embarrassment if some mongrel stabbed him in the backside."

I decided not to be offended at being called a mongrel again. "So I should definitely aim for that target."

His lips twitched. "Definitely."

"I'm happy to see you, but what are you doing here so soon? I thought you were staking out my apartment for the new moon tonight. The preferred time of month for dark-elf activities."

"I believed you were in danger so I flew back."

I grimaced. "I'm sorry. I didn't mean for you to delay your criminal-hunting for my sake. I thought when you left earlier today you'd decided to prioritize that."

"Yes." He didn't expound.

"Did you fly all the way here both times? Can't you poof a portal open and travel from state to state or across the world?"

He'd flown the time I'd ridden on his back down to Oregon, but I'd watched him disappear through portals twice. That had always been when he was going back to his own world.

"Portals are openings onto magical pathways that were established by dragon scientists long ago. They allow us to travel between the main planets in the Cosmic Realms and also a few dozen others that have life and have been useful hunting places for our kind. I am not a scientist and have learned only enough to access the pathways, not enough to understand how they work, but each time you jump on to one, it takes you to another star system. You cannot open a portal from one side of a planet to another. You could travel from here, to my world, and back to here and arrive on a different continent, but though portal travel is fast, it is not instantaneous. In most cases, it is faster to fly."

"You don't mind flying? I assume it's a lot of work and burns a lot of calories."

"It does, but flying is glorious. Do you not agree? You've ridden on my back." He tilted his head. "Few have ever been given this honor."

"I do like flying. More so in an airplane and when I'm in control."

"Airplane. I've seen your metal tubes with stationary wings." Zav curled his lip. "That is not flying. You do not feel the wind caressing your scales."

"The wind is frigid at thirty thousand feet and the air isn't breathable."

"Dragons do not fly so high. We wish to see the ground, so we can swoop down to hunt if we spot a tasty morsel."

"Like what? A cow?"

"Cows are acceptable. Sheep are delicious."

"The wool doesn't get in your teeth?"

His eyes narrowed. "Are you mocking me?"

"No."

"Your tone is irreverent."

"Isn't it always?"

"It is *never* suitably respectful and appropriate for speaking with a dragon."

"That's what I thought. But I do appreciate you coming. Can I buy you dinner? Or did you fill up on sheep on the way over? How about an ice cream?"

He was still squinting at me. Suspicious. I truly wasn't mocking him, but I didn't know how to make my tone appropriately respectful for dragons. Maybe because I refused to acknowledge them as superior just because they were big, strong, and had lots of magic. Though if they had mastered space travel, that was pretty amazing. After talking to the likes of Dob and Shaygor, it was hard to imagine brilliant dragon scientists, but then, one could have the same experience with humans. Some smart ones. Lots of idiots.

"What is ice cream?" Zav asked.

"It comes from cows. You'll love it. Especially if you're hot. Do you get hot flying?"

"Occasionally. I dipped myself in the lake on the way here."

"Then ice cream is definitely appropriate. I'll buy yours since you came all this way. And also because you've said before that you don't have money." I zipped up my tent, trusting nobody would steal my twenty-year-old military sleeping bag.

"Because dragons hunt for their food and take what little else they need from the environment, not because I am weak or a pauper." Zav looked at me as we headed for the street leading up the hill and in to town. "If I wished to possess great wealth, I could have it. Such things are not important to dragons."

"I believe you. Your blood is worth half a million dollars a vial, I understand. The best I can get is a couple of grand for donating plasma."

Zav halted. "You *sold* my blood?"

"No. I found out its value when I gave it to Zoltan—the vampire alchemist. That was part of the deal to get him to heal my boss." I decided not to mention that *Zoltan* might sell it. Zav looked affronted and disgusted at the notion.

To change the subject, and because he might have some insight into what was going on here, I told him about the goblins and the sasquatch. Several people made wide circles to avoid Zav as we walked past. When he shape-shifted into human form, he was visible to all. I didn't know if that was a conscious choice, or something inherent in changing forms, but he retained much of his powerful aura, and even people without magical blood sensed that he was dangerous.

"I am unfamiliar with your sasquatch, but goblins are notorious schemers and tricksters," Zav said. "Like kobolds, but they're better at it. They build great cities on their world with all manner of mechanical monstrosities. If they were more organized, they might be as deleterious to their world as the vermin here are to yours."

I paused, my hand on the door to the ice cream parlor. "You mean as bad as humans are for Earth?"

"That is what I said, yes. Your technology has allowed you to overpopulate your world to the detriment of the other species."

"I'm not going to argue against that, but… is that what the rest of the magical beings out there think? Are they aware of what goes on on Earth? This isn't one of your Cosmic Realms, is it?"

"No. It was deemed unsuitable long ago, but yes, most of the other intelligent races are aware of it and you. Many do not approve of what is considered the overpopulation problem here."

"Do the dark elves have strong feelings about humans?" I remembered his words about the dark-elf scientists having killed tens of thousands of shifters, possibly as a *test* for their devices. And now those dark elves were here on Earth, tinkering with more magical devices.

"Likely so. I have not spoken to many dark elves. I will question Yemeli-lor and Baklinor-ten when I capture them."

A big man with a Yosemite Sam mustache hanging to his collar, a ten-gallon hat, and snakeskin boots strode out with two ice cream cones, frowning at me for blocking the door. I stepped aside. Zav eyed him, not moving, so the guy was forced to go around him. Nobody was getting very close to Zav. Only foolish Val, whose brain was as unwise as her tongue.

"Nice dress, buddy," the cowboy growled under his breath as he stalked away with his ice cream cones, the greatest defiance he dared risk.

"To what does he refer?" Zav asked me.

"Nothing. Why don't you snag that empty table over there before someone else gets it, and I'll go inside to pick out cones. Do you have any preference on flavors?"

"Flavors?"

"Yeah. There's probably not a sheep flavor. But chocolate and vanilla are popular."

His lip curled slightly again. My plan to make him fall in love with human creations and realize the vermin of this world could make cool things might not be working.

"I'll pick something." I waved him to the table.

There was a line inside, but the staff was efficient, so only a couple of minutes passed before I came out again. Even so, the tables around the one I'd pointed Zav to were oddly empty now. Two couples had shifted over to sit on the curb.

Zav wasn't doing anything overtly menacing, just sitting there with his aura oozing from him. I'd have to spend quality time with all three of my loofahs and hope for the best after this date.

I snorted as I walked toward him. This wasn't a date. This was… Hell, I didn't know what it was. Admittedly, he was probably the only guy in the world I could spend time with without worrying that some assassin would drive past and blow him away. We just had to worry about Shaygor and the Dragon Justice Court. Alas, they were more of a threat than assassins.

Forcing a smile, I walked over and handed Zav a two-scoop waffle cone. I sat on the opposite side of the table, turning the chair enough so the building was at my back but I could still keep an eye on him. Belatedly, it occurred to me that I didn't need to worry about people throwing knives between my shoulder blades when I was with Zav. From his position, he could see a blade coming and incinerate it. And I believed he would, but that was a lot of faith to put in someone else. I kept my back to the wall.

"What is it?" Zav gingerly held the cone, the purple ice cream too pale to match his violet eyes, but the thought made me grin anyway.

"Huckleberry Heaven. I got the same thing." I held up my single scoop. I'd gotten him a double out of some notion that men always ate more. He must have burned a lot of calories flying that massive dragon body over the mountains.

"Mine is larger."

"Yeah, guys usually prefer that."

He scrutinized the ice cream, then eyed me over the top of it. "Was that a sexual innuendo?"

"No. We haven't reached the stage of our relationship where that would be appropriate." I grinned, stuck my tongue out, and swirled it around the scoop in a gesture that most men definitely would have found sexual.

Zav watched, but I was fairly certain he was more puzzled than turned on. Maybe that elf he'd supposedly had a relationship with—Dob had mentioned it in a chatty moment—hadn't been into fellatio.

Zav tentatively stuck his tongue out and touched his ice cream. Then made a face.

"It's too sweet. Like the brown squares you gave me."

"The lavender chocolate? You actually tried it? I wondered."

"I tried it."

"That impressed, huh?" I had found it a little odd too. Not so odd that I hadn't eaten it. A woman needed chocolate after she was shot and her apartment was ravaged.

"The blood-colored beverage was better."

"I hope you weren't disappointed it wasn't *actual* blood."

He hesitated. "I do like the fresh blood of a kill, but it was not entirely unpleasant."

"You and Sindari have a lot in common."

"The Zhinevarii are not ignoble creatures. Dragons are, of course, far superior."

"Of course." I grinned and licked the ice cream normally. It was sweet, but the tartness of the berries made it good. As did having company.

I was oddly delighted to have Zav sitting across from me. Was I that starved for companionship? Companionship that could take care of himself and I didn't have to stress over?

A low whistle came from a guy ambling across the patio and looking at me. Judging by the stupid lewd grin on his face, he'd seen me tonguing my ice cream suggestively. Either that, or he was just a dick. Probably both.

"Hey, baby." He came up to the table, puffing out his chest so I couldn't miss that he and his pecs spent a lot of time in the gym. "You want to go for a stroll along the lake this evening?"

Zav rose from his seat, exuding power and almost bumping chests with the man. Before my would-be date got a good look at Zav, he lifted a hand, as if he would push him back down into his seat. But the man froze when he saw Zav's face—it had gone flinty. And that dragon aura of his must have registered for the guy, because he stumbled back even before Zav's eyes flared with violet light.

The man tripped over his feet and crashed onto the hard pavement. I dropped my face into my hand.

"You will not seek to acquire a female that is sitting in my presence."

The muscular guy scrambled to his feet but not to fight. He threw his open hands up apologetically.

"Sorry, bro. I thought you were gay."

"I am clearly not gay."

"You can't blame me for thinking that with those slippers, man." He waved at Zav's feet, but he backed away quickly.

Only when he'd scurried out to the street and out of sight did Zav sit back down. I sighed and lowered my hand. We were going to have to have a chat.

"What is *gay*?" Zav asked. "I thought cheerful and lighthearted. That is what your dictionary says."

"How *old* was the dictionary you looked at?"

A car drove by and he pointed at it. "When I first visited your world and learned your language, your people's wheeled boxes were pulled by horses."

"Uh huh. Gay means homosexual now."

Zav looked down at his slippers in thoughtful consideration. The expression made me want to laugh, not lecture him on boundaries. But I also couldn't let him think he could dictate who flirted with me.

"While you're contemplating a wardrobe change, and eating your ice cream because that's going to start melting soon, let's have a chat. By chat, I mean that I'll talk and you'll listen."

His gaze shifted from his shoes to me, his eyes narrowing. "When you *talk* at me, you never show the respect proper for a lesser species communicating with a dragon."

"I know. And I think you like it, because you haven't threatened to incinerate anything of mine since the day we met."

"I do not *like* it," he said coolly. "I tolerate it."

"Yes, why?" And why was I letting him veer away from the subject I wanted to discuss?

"You have occasionally been useful to me."

As bait. Right.

"You don't think I could be useful to you if you forced me to be a mindless drudge existing only to do your bidding?"

"Are you open to that?"

"No, I am not."

Zav leaned back in his seat. "You got my hopes up."

I grinned at him.

A melted bead of ice cream slithered off his cone and onto his hand. He frowned at it. With a tiny poof it went up in smoke.

I had better not push him. He *was* in the mood to incinerate things.

"I've been an independent person for a long time, Zav, and even though I take jobs for the government, I'm used to calling the shots and being in charge of my destiny. I've fought a lot of magical beings, and if there's one thing I've learned, it's that you're dead if you show them weakness."

"It is not weak to show respect to dragons. Elves are among the most powerful of the lesser beings, and they know to be respectful to their superiors."

"Well, I'm half human."

"Do not remind me of this taint."

"If you treated me with respect, I'd probably treat you with more."

"*Probably*."

"You're kind of fun to tease."

"Lesser beings do not *tease* dragons."

"How boring. I bet you've missed being teased your whole life and that's why you're here spending time with me."

"I am here so Shaygorthian will not read your thoughts, kill you for killing a dragon, and tattle on me to the court for withholding that information."

"So my playful teasing is just a delightful perk?"

"More a hazard of the job." Zav turned his frown toward the sky. "He is here again."

"Shaygor?"

"Yes." Zav laid the melting ice cream cone sideways on the table and stood up. "I will go answer his questions and attempt to get him to leave this world."

"Any chance it'll work?"

"It is doubtful."

I'd been afraid of that. We hadn't had our discussion about boundaries, but it would have to wait for another time.

"Do not forget to activate your charm when I am not around." Zav strode off, shifting into dragon form and flying away, before I could tell him I'd given it to Amber. Maybe I *wouldn't* tell him that.

Chapter 13

I lay in my tent, aware of Zav's presence at the edge of my senses. He was off to the east, probably curled up in the forest, or maybe on someone's rooftop, in his dragon form.

Knowing he was in the area made me feel comfortable enough to take off my armor and boots, something I rarely did when camping out on assignment, and slide into my sleeping bag. As much as I hated relying on someone else, in a world that now housed dragons, the most logical thing was to have a dragon on one's side.

There was something lonely about imagining him by himself in the forest, but I supposed it wasn't any different from me being by myself in a tent in a campground, listening to the murmured conversations of nearby families. Did dragons feel loneliness? Or were they independent creatures, not social ones like humans? He had a family, a mother at least, but how close were they? It was hard to imagine a dragon clan coming together for holiday gatherings and gossiping about the neighbors while trading pumpkin pie recipes.

My phone buzzed, a call managing to get through on my anemic cell signal. It was a local number. Who was calling me after ten? Thad? *Amber?*

"Yeah?" I answered.

"It's me calling from the house phone," my mother said.

"Hi, Mom. What's up? Did Amber and her friend make it back?"

"Yes. With an interesting story."

I waited for her to share it, curious what Amber's version had been. Though if she'd called me a gun-happy loon in combat boots, maybe I didn't want to hear about it. It was *true*, but I would prefer she play up the part where Sindari and I nobly rushed down in the nick of time to save her.

But Mom didn't expound. I couldn't remember her ever gossiping about the neighbors while sharing pumpkin pie recipes, so I wasn't sure where I'd gotten that notion about how families worked. Probably from television.

"Are they okay?" I finally asked into the silence.

"Jarred but unwounded. Before this, Amber didn't realize that her elven blood—Thad never wished me to discuss that with her, by the way—gave her the ability to sense magical beings and see dragons."

"*I've* only recently learned it gives me the ability to see dragons," I said dryly.

"She asked me a few questions about what kinds of abilities she may have inherited. I pointed out that *you* would know more about that than I." She sounded wistful.

Mom was so stoic, private, and self-reliant that it was hard to know what she felt, but I'd always gotten the impression that elves had fascinated her even before she'd met my father, and that she wished she could have left with him instead of staying on Earth. Since she didn't have a lot of ties with people here, I was surprised she hadn't. Maybe it hadn't been an option. Or maybe she'd felt compelled to stay because of *her* parents. Her mother had passed away thirty years ago, but I had vague childhood memories of an even more stoic and self-reliant grandmother.

"I don't think she wants to talk to me or have anything to do with my life," I said, half-hoping Mom would offer evidence to the contrary.

"No," she agreed.

Damn.

"It's for the best," I made myself say. "It was a mistake for me to accept this assignment. At the time, I didn't know about the dragon."

She didn't comfort me or tell me I was wrong, but I didn't expect that from her.

"I called to offer my assistance," she said. "Mine and Rocket's."

"For tracking sasquatch and goblins?"

"Yes."

I hesitated. Mom—and Rocket—probably could help, but I well remembered the werewolf fight outside of Bend. Mom could have been killed in that incident. Even though goblins were far less dangerous than werewolves, they were up to something shifty. I still didn't know whether to believe the sasquatch were real, but if they were, they should be Earth-based and not magical. That meant her bullets would protect her from them.

"Do you have your Glock with you?" I asked.

"Yes."

"Don't leave home without it, eh?"

"I don't take it to the grocery store," she said dryly, "but I planned to do some hiking while I was here. I have to be able to protect Rocket in case we run into wild animals. Or sasquatch."

She was so dead-pan that it was hard to tell if she was joking. "You haven't really seen one before, have you?"

"No. I've heard of sightings, but I chalked it up to alcohol and wishfulness."

I almost pointed out that most people would chalk up elf sightings to the same.

"I'd *like* to see one," she added.

"Judging by the smell of the clump of fur I found, you probably wouldn't."

"Humor me. I can be useful."

"I know you can. There are some two-foot-long footprints up on Cliff Way. Do you want to meet me at the house with all the broken windows in the morning? Maybe Rocket can find a trail."

"I'd like to think *I* can find that trail."

"The prints are a few days old, so I don't know how useful they'll be, but we can also look in the woods near the bike trail south of town. I saw some goblins out there this afternoon." Had it only been this afternoon? This day had gone on forever. I needed sleep.

"I'll meet you on Cliff Way in the morning. What time?"

I started to say nine, but the sun would be up at six, and I had nothing to do but read in this tent. "Seven."

"We can do earlier if you want," she said. "I never sleep anyway."

"So I inherited that from you?"

"I slept okay when I was younger. Now, I wake up at four no matter what."

Her body probably didn't make enough melatonin or something. *My problem was nightmares about all the magical beings I'd killed. Though now that Zav was back, the stupid erotic dreams would probably return. I wasn't sure which was worse. Maybe I'd ask my doctor for a supplement that turned off dreams completely. Did such a thing exist?*

"Seven. I'll bring you coffee." I had childhood memories of Mom making coffee in an old blue pot over a campfire, back when we'd lived in her converted school bus. I trusted she still enjoyed the drink.

"Black," she said firmly. "Nothing weird."

"I think, these days, it's weird to take coffee black. Do they even allow that at Starbucks?"

"Black. Goodnight. Don't get eaten by a dragon." She hung up.

It would almost be easier if Shaygor wanted to eat me. That couldn't get Zav in trouble.

Sighing, I remembered that I'd intended to warn Dimitri about Shaygor, in case the dragon went in search of witnesses to Dob's death. I sent him a text. Since he'd gone back to Bend for a landscaping gig and was staying at my mother's house, I couldn't imagine how Shaygor would find him, but the dragon had found *me* easily enough. Who knew what powers he had?

A return text came in promptly: *Thanks for the warning. Zoltan says he can make me a dragon repellent formula. I think he's joking, but it's hard to tell with him.*

You're not back up in Woodinville, are you?

Maybe Dimitri and Zoltan had become online chat buddies and were keeping abreast of each other that way.

Actually, yes. I've got my van parked behind his carriage house for now. The new owners haven't moved in yet.

What happened to your landscaping work?

I was complaining to Zoltan about how odious it was to dig holes and install artificial turf for next to no pay, and he pointed out the difficulty of being an employee after you've tasted entrepreneurship.

Does selling yard art at a farmers market one Saturday count as entrepreneurship?

Absolutely. He's helping me brainstorm ways to make a full-time income.

Speaking of money, next time you see him, ask if sasquatch fur has any value for any of his potions.

Is it okay if I call them formulas so he doesn't go ballistic?

Call them whatever you want. Just ask if it's worth it for me to continue carrying this smelly patch of fur around.

It was sitting on the bumper of the Jeep. I'd been unwilling to put it inside, and it definitely wasn't coming in the tent.

He says he doesn't want fur, but he'll take… ugh.

What?

I'm going to make him type it. It's gross.

Are you actually in the room with him?

I'm in his lab. He ordered a motor for his mechanical guard tarantula, and it finally arrived, so I'm enchanting it.

I looked at the curved ceiling of the tent and wondered what it said about me that having ice cream with a dragon wasn't the weirdest thing going on in my life.

So, he's your new best friend? Or is it more than that? Are you still wearing your cervical collar?

Greetings, my dear robber. Ugh, that was Zoltan. *I am an honorable vampire, and I do not suck the blood of friends—even those with hale and appealing veins. I much prefer to taste the lifeblood of someone who's recently been doused with dragon aura. Naturally, I look forward to your return.*

Right now, I've been doused with sasquatch stench. What are your feelings on that?

I am uninterested in the fur, but the stench is quite powerful and has magical uses. I would consider paying for fluids harvested from the anal glands.

Dear God, no wonder Dimitri hadn't been willing to text that.

I'm not harvesting that.

Are you certain? Sasquatch are quite elusive. The going rate is high. Not as high as dragon blood, of course. Can you get me any more of that?

I'm more likely to get some of that than anybody's… fluids. I couldn't bring myself to type it out either. *Are you sure sasquatch have those glands? I would have guessed they were primates and primates do not.*

It's hypothesized that they share both bear and primate ancestors. Oh, if you were to bring me an entire sasquatch to study, I would also pay for that.

Then you could harvest your own glands.

Excellent. I shall look forward to your arrival with a sasquatch strapped to the roof of your conveyance.

I didn't say I was bringing you one, but how much would you pay for it? Just out of curiosity.

I didn't seriously plan to hunt one down. Though maybe I had confirmation now that they existed and that this wasn't all a hoax perpetrated by the goblins. Sasquatch bodily fluids wouldn't be listed as an ingredient in an alchemy book if they didn't exist.

It's me again, Dimitri texted. *He's off looking up sasquatch formulas.*

Wonderful. Don't forget to have him make you that dragon repellent. Just in case. I'm hoping Zav and I can figure out a way to convince this one to leave Earth, but I'm not sure how.

I didn't go into how I believed Zav was in as much trouble as I was right now.

Chapter 14

Rocket bounded out of Mom's green Subaru and ran straight toward the back of the vandalized house on Cliff Way. I was standing in the driveway, holding Mom's coffee and reading a dragon-free epic fantasy novel on my phone. I'd been up since dawn, and the lurid dreams had won out over the nightmares, leaving me wishing this town had promising offerings for one-night stands. The odds of finding a hot unattached guy in the campground seemed low, and contemplating whether we'd go to his place or mine depressed me more than amused me.

"The tracks are in the back," I told Mom after she parked and got out.

I glanced at the passenger seat to see if anyone had come with her, but the car was empty. It wasn't as if I'd expected Amber to show an interest in tracking sasquatch, but I wouldn't have minded being surprised.

"None for you?" Mom accepted the coffee and headed around the side of the house in the direction Rocket had gone. She had her Glock in a hip holster, her hiking backpack on, and probably three days' worth of food and water.

"The selection at the bike shop was limited." I'd passed on the sweetened waters in the fridge there.

"The bike shop?"

"It's also the coffee shop. And we can get lunch there later if you're hungry."

"It's an interesting town. You can also get lunch at the hardware store."

We'd reached the tracks, and Rocket was already zipping through the rosebushes and into the woods, so I didn't comment further. By some silent communication, he seemed to know that Mom wanted him to follow the trail. Maybe she and Rocket had conversations similar to the ones I had with Sindari. But I bet Rocket never threatened to chew off her foot.

It only took us a few minutes to hike out of town. Rocket turned to stray into the trees instead of heading out onto cleared farmland. He could have outpaced us, but he kept turning back to check on us. The tree cover was sporadic this close to town, and we occasionally crossed roads and fields, but we headed generally south paralleling the lake. I thought we might end up in the same area where I'd seen the goblins the day before.

Shaygor's aura came within range of my senses, and I paused by a stout tree. When I'd woken up, Zav had been gone, or at least far enough away that I couldn't detect him. Dread sank into my gut as I realized Shaygor would be just as able to smell Mom's blood relation to me as Amber's. If she was put in danger again by being out here with me…

I drew Chopper and trotted to catch up with her, intending to tell her to find a defensible hiding spot, but as I gripped her shoulder, Zav came within my range. They were both off to the north in roughly the same area. If not for the trees, we might have seen them in the sky.

"Problem?" Mom eyed my drawn sword.

The dragons flew north and out of my range. I sheathed Chopper.

"I thought there might be, but we seem to have a fairy godmother, at least today."

Her eyebrows rose. "Fairy godmother?"

"Technically, a godfather. Judging by our conversation last night, he's not as conflicted about his gender as his slippers imply."

"Were you always this odd?"

"Yes. You just weren't paying attention."

"Huh."

We followed Rocket down a slope. Here and there, between the firs, pines, and spruce, the lake came into view. I glimpsed a couple of bicyclists on the trail and hoped Amber stayed at the house today, even if Zav was keeping Shaygor occupied.

Rocket had been following the trail without trouble, but now he paused at a jumble of boulders. He ran around it, his hackles up and his tail wagging. Was he stumped? I hadn't seen any of the big plantigrade footprints for a while, but I poked around, looking for tracks, small or large.

"There's an opening over here." Mom stood in front of the jumbled boulders with Rocket. "These rocks haven't been here that long." She waved at the pile.

It was a good thirty feet wide at the base and rose half that high. The natural boulders appeared native to the area, but there wasn't any dirt between them or weeds or trees growing up from the gaps, the way one would expect from a land formation that had been there for centuries. It reminded me of a burial cairn, a large one.

"Goblin-sized," I observed when I joined her and saw the hole she'd found. Neither of us would fit easily through it. "I don't sense anyone magical in there. And there's no way a sasquatch would have fit."

Rocket sniffed at the hole and squeezed partway in, pawing at the dirt.

"He thinks *something* is in there," Mom said.

"I see that." I wrinkled my nose, catching a faint whiff of the odious scent that had been in that house—and all over that patch of fur. It *did* seem to be coming from the hole. "Either this is a trap, or there's some way to move the boulders aside to make a larger entrance."

"Like that illusionary door covering the tunnel back in Oregon?" Mom patted the rocks around the opening.

"I sensed magic there. I don't this time."

She kept investigating. I turned a slow circle, looking through the trees in all directions. A hint of movement drew my eye, but when I focused on the spot, all I saw were towering evergreens. Maybe a pine cone had fallen. There wasn't much of a breeze, but if one of those sasquatch was out there, I had to believe I would smell it. And Rocket would detect it. Though he was preoccupied with the cave.

He succeeded in squeezing through the gap.

"Wait, Rocket." Mom lunged for his collar, but it was too late.

Loud snuffling noises came from inside but soon faded from hearing. Maybe the passage was wider in there.

"Rocket, come back," Mom said sternly, then gave me an exasperated look. "He's better trained than this. He would usually come right back."

Whatever was inside commanded his full attention.

I touched my charm necklace and summoned Sindari. Maybe he could shed some light on this.

Mom dropped to her hands and knees. "I smell an animal scent."

"I know. Me too."

"I could probably squeeze in there."

"It could be a trap," I pointed out.

"How smart are these creatures? It could be an entrance to their den."

"I haven't seen any IQ tests for sasquatch." I patted Sindari on the back after he solidified. "Goblins are as smart as we are."

"We haven't seen any goblin tracks since we left that house."

What battle have you brought me to join? Sindari swished his tail and looked at the boulders and around at the forest.

I was wondering if you sensed any goblins around.

I sense two dragons off to the north.

Can you tell what they're doing? I asked, distracted by the thought of Zav and Shaygor fighting.

No, only that they are in the same area.

Comparing penis size, maybe.

Dragons do not have external sex organs.

Comparing tail size then.

That is possible.

Sindari wandered away from the cairn, his nose in the air, and I followed him. He was looking in the same direction where I'd spotted that movement.

There's a goblin out there, up in the tree branches. I cannot see him from here, but I sense him. I think he was looking this way, but then moved farther away when I started sniffing around.

Something glinted with reflected light.

A goblin wearing glasses? I asked.

Maybe a spyglass.

Watching us then. And waiting to see if we fall for this trap. Do you think you can capture him? I couldn't sense him and remembered what Sindari had said about the other ones, that they had a way to camouflage themselves.

I will try. I'll pretend I'm going to the lake and will use my stealth to circle back to get behind him.

Good. Thank you.

A startled yelp of pain came from deep inside the cairn of rocks.

"Rocket!" Mom scurried through the opening after him.

"Mom," I whispered, "stop. I'm *positive* it's a trap. Goblins love to lay traps."

"I can't let Rocket get eaten. Rocket, come back here." She whistled, but her lips were tense with worry and the sound barely came out.

I dropped to my knees and caught her by the ankle. She was having trouble getting back there.

"Come out," I said as sternly as she'd told Rocket the same. It probably wouldn't work on her either. "I'll go in and get him. If there's magic, I'm better armed to deal with it."

I didn't think there *was* magic, or I would have sensed it, but maybe the argument would sway her.

A pained whimper floated to our ears.

"Let go of me, Val." She tried to yank her ankle out of my grip.

"No." I held on firmly. "Come back out or I'll drag you out."

She paused, and I imagined her fantasizing about stabbing me with her utility knife, but she shifted back out of the hole.

"I'll get him," I promised her, then pulled Chopper and crawled in on my hands and knees.

Rock scraped at my shoulders, and I got my braid caught under my knee. A vanity braid as Willard had once called it. We'd been discussing how people who got into a lot of fights should have short hair that an enemy couldn't grab. Right now, my enemies were my hands and knees. And a dog that liked to take matters into his own paws.

I activated my night-vision charm and could see his furry hindquarters ahead of me. He was tugging at something. Hopefully not a sasquatch tugging back at him. But the crooked passage—tunnel would have been too lofty a word—hadn't gotten any larger. There was no way a sasquatch would fit in here.

Rocket whined and didn't seem to notice me drawing closer. I couldn't see anyone in front of him. It looked like his foot was trapped by something on the ground.

"Tell him that you're coming and it'll be all right," Mom called from her belly at the entrance. "Is he hurt? Tell him I love him and it'll be all right."

"I'm sure he can hear *you*, Mom. And, with a great deal of maturity, I'm going to refrain from being bitter that you never told me you loved me and that it would be all right."

She hesitated. "You were lippier than Rocket."

"Even when I was six and afraid of the monsters under the bed?"

"There were drawers and storage bins under the bed. I made sure to use every square inch of space we had."

"That isn't the point, Mom." I reached Rocket's back end and told him he was a good boy and that I would help, but there wasn't much room to squeeze past him to see what had his leg.

"You weren't so much lippy at six as obnoxious and abrasive."

I snorted. Hadn't I used the word abrasive to describe Amber? Or maybe Sindari had. I guess that meant she was definitely my kid.

"Thanks for this honesty." I scooted up beside Rocket. Leaves and pine needles scattered the bottom of the passage, making it hard to see what had him. The way opened up ahead of him, but all I could see was more debris from the forest floor that something—or someone—had dragged in.

"I blamed myself that you didn't have a father," Mom said. "I'd never been what you would have called maternal."

"I think that runs in the family."

I was being sarcastic, but she said, "It's true. Your grandmother was even stiffer and more aloof than me. Your grandfather was a gentler soul and made me toys when I was little, but he died at work when I was only about five. He was a topper for a logging outfit."

For the first time, I sensed a hint of magic. An artifact or device, not a person. Was that what had trapped Rocket?

No, it was located deeper in the cairn. I could just make out the source, an object made from smashed soda and beer cans. I'd barely noticed it before, thinking it was garbage someone had tossed among the rocks. The urge to crawl in and investigate it came over me—that magical draw made me think of the dark-elf pleasure orbs. But this didn't put images of desires in my mind, and it didn't have the faint underlying sinister taint of the dark-elf stuff. It seemed innocent and conveyed without words that it would answer all my questions if I came and touched it.

"I bet," I muttered.

There was also something dangling from a corner of it. Another clump of sasquatch fur? If so, that would account for the smell. It was stronger farther into the cairn.

"I had a brother, too, but he also died before you were born," Mom continued. "He was a fisherman in Alaska back in the sixties. The work was as dangerous as logging, especially back then. Our family seems to be drawn to dangerous work."

"That could explain some things."

"Yes. It's in the blood. You are, as far as I know, the first assassin."

"Maybe you should have picked a less war-encouraging name for me."

"Ingrid was on the short list. It means beautiful goddess."

"Ingrid?" I mouthed it with distaste.

"But your father said *his* mother was a famous warrior among his people. And he was, uhm, adept in many areas himself."

"Please don't tell me about elven bedroom exploits." As I alternated between patting Rocket comfortingly and pushing aside leaves to find what had him trapped, I said, "I had no idea all I had to do was go hiking with you to get you to open up and talk about your family and background. I assume those were *your* parents you mentioned, not his."

An elf would probably think logging was a crime.

"I never met your father's parents. He did have a sister that I met once. She was beautiful and serene and some kind of artist or maker among his people."

"Clearly, I don't take after that side of the family." Ugh, a bear trap had Rocket. Not one purchased from a store, but something homemade out of scraps of metal, things doubtless stolen from the houses the goblins had raided. "Hang on, buddy."

His wrist was bloody, and he was not happy about the situation. I wondered if that magical artifact was what had drawn him in, making him ignore Mom's commands. That or the tuft of sasquatch fur dangling from it.

Rocket whined and laid his head on my shoulder as I gripped the teeth-filled sides of the trap and pushed them apart. As soon as he could, he jerked his paw out. In his hurry to escape the cairn, he almost knocked me over.

I let the trap snap back shut, so no other critters would be caught in it.

"Rocket!" Mom blurted when he came out. Her voice was muffled—she'd probably thrown her arms around the dog.

Maybe if I were more cuddly and affectionate, I could get hugs like that. Having soft furry ears people wanted to rub probably helped.

Sindari, I thought, reminded of someone else with soft furry ears. *Any luck out there?*

He didn't answer. Maybe that meant he'd captured the goblin and was busy dragging him over to us.

I debated between backing out of the passage and going in the rest of the way to check out the artifact. Judging by the lumpy spots under the bed of leaf litter, there were other traps waiting inside. This whole place seemed like a trap.

"Let's be smart and not fall into it this time, eh?" I scooted backward.

Before I'd gone halfway, a faint click sounded. The boulders ground and shifted above my head. Damn it, I hadn't bumped anything—I was sure of it.

Swearing, I tried to scoot backward faster, afraid the entire cairn would collapse on me.

"Look out, Val!" Mom shouted.

No kidding.

Rocks tumbled down, not on top of me but in front of the opening. Dust flooded the passage, and all outside light disappeared.

"I knew it was a trap." I thunked my head down into the pine needles.

Chapter 15

Val? Sindari spoke into my mind. *I must reluctantly inform you of a problem.*

If it's the fact that half of this cairn collapsed and blocked me in, I already know. I shifted onto my side, coughing at the dust the cave-in—no, the deliberate springing of the trap—had caused.

My chest tightened as the fine particles infiltrated my airways like the Uruk-hai invading Helm's Deep in *Lord of the Rings*. Groping in the dark, I pulled out my inhaler and took a puff.

I am positive you can deal with a few rocks, Sindari said. *My problem is that these goblins all have something similar to your cloaking charm and keep eluding me. I was almost upon this one, using my own stealth, but somehow he sensed me coming. I am ashamed of this ineptitude. It is not normal for me.*

I would tease you for it, but since my own ineptitude has me trapped under a cairn—and for the record, this is a lot *of rocks, not a few—I will forgo teasing.*

Lord Zavryd is nearby. Perhaps he can help you escape.

Oh, hell no. I refuse to need rescuing from my own stupidity. I stuffed my inhaler back into my pocket and shifted Chopper out from under fine rocks and dust that had fallen onto it—and me. *It's bad enough needing to be rescued from dragons, but since no normal person is equipped to deal with them, I can accept that. Grudgingly.*

I will return to assist you. Is your mother in trouble?

I hope not.

Someone had sprung that trap. I was positive I hadn't bumped against anything. That meant the goblin who'd eluded Sindari was out there monitoring us. Or someone else was.

Chopper was strong enough to break boulders, but I wasn't in a position to swing the blade, so I reluctantly scooted forward. Toward the bear traps.

The larger room with the artifact was still intact. Using Chopper like a broom, I scooted aside needles and revealed six more bear traps on the floor, all chained to the rocks, all unsprung. There wasn't any bait in any of them, so Rocket hadn't been lured in by food. I was positive that artifact had been the lure. The scent of the sasquatch might have brought him to this spot, but the magic had made him disobey Mom.

Curious, I let go of Chopper for a second. The pull on my mind grew even stronger. I had to know what those battered beer cans could tell me.

"Huh." I picked up Chopper again, and the pull faded.

After I'd swept aside all the bear traps, triggering them so I wouldn't accidentally spring one later, I stood up. Most of the way. The ceiling was too low for me to straighten fully. It didn't take long to look around and confirm that there weren't any other ways out or into some underground complex. The artifact was all that was here.

My curiosity almost made me poke it with Chopper's tip, to see if anything happened, but I caught myself. Touching it might trigger another rockfall, one that would crush me this time.

Val? Your mother is standing face to face with four towering furry black and brown creatures. They have two legs, long arms, and their scent matches what we found in that house. Each one is over ten feet tall.

I swore. *Do they have weapons? Claws? Are they threatening her?*

Not currently. She is pantomiming gestures, and they are looking at each other and at her. Her dog is growling at them, and they aren't coming close.

Keep an eye on the situation, please.

They're pointing for her to step aside. Several are approaching the cairn. She just pulled out her gun.

Damn it. Is she trying to protect me? I crawled back into the tunnel and stabbed between the boulders blocking the entrance, trying to find the leverage to push them aside without bringing the cairn down atop me.

I believe so. She's standing her ground and pointing her gun at them. They have paused. They seem to be communicating with each other. I will go join her to add my strength and ferocity to hers and ensure they cannot do anything to the cairn.

I'd rather have Sindari lend his strength and ferocity to digging me out, but it wasn't as if claws were great at picking up giant rocks.

A boulder ground aside three inches, but other small rocks tumbled down into the gap. This would take forever.

They're trying to communicate with hand gestures, Sindari reported. *They are pantomiming lifting boulders off the cairn. Your mother is asking her dog if she can trust them. Does she not realize that I am intelligent and wise and of far more use than some drooling canine?*

Since you can't talk to her, probably not.

"Don't start a war against greater numbers, Mom," I yelled as I went back to digging. "Or anyone *larger* than you."

You do not apply that advice to your encounters with dragons, Sindari noted.

At least someone had heard me.

I have magical weapons. That levels the playing field.

The shaggy creatures are walking forward with their hands out and open. One is pointing at the cairn and making lifting motions. I believe they want to dig you out.

If they're allies with the goblins, why would they do that? Someone wanted *me* trapped. *Someone short and green.* Unless there was another party controlling the goblins. The idea of another faction being involved made my head ache. The dust coating my eyes and throat didn't help.

I don't know, but they're adamant. Your mother is hesitantly moving off to the side while keeping her gun trained on them. They're eyeing the weapon nervously. They're also eyeing me nervously. As they should.

Don't attack them if they want to lift rocks off me, please.

I wished I could see what Sindari saw. This scenario made no sense to me.

I'm moving off to the side as well—they wouldn't come close until I did so—but I'm watching them carefully. If they start pushing the rocks down on you, I'll attack them.

I appreciate that.

Scuffs, scrapes, and grinding noises came through from above. So did a familiar stench. Apparently, it was so powerful that it could ooze through the dirt and microscopic gaps between the rocks.

A pinprick of light broke through next, not in the little passage where I was but back in the larger chamber. By the time I scooted in there, the pinprick had turned into a head-sized beam, sunlight filtering down through the gap and the forest canopy above.

As I inched closer, thinking to widen the hole further with Chopper, a big face leaned in, dimming the light. It was neither ursine nor simian but somewhere in between, with a smashed snout that reminded me of a pug. The dark brown eyes that peered in seemed more intelligent than those of a dog.

The sasquatch leaned out of sight and lifted more rocks away. When the hole was large enough, I jumped up and scrambled out, keeping Chopper in my hand in case my saviors turned into enemies.

All four of them had come to help. Nearby, Mom let out a sigh of relief and closed her eyes. The small sign that she cared warmed my heart more than I expected. It wasn't that I *didn't* think she cared, but she was as bad at sharing feelings as I was, and one could never be certain with her.

Sindari was swishing his tail and, as promised, keeping a hawk's eye on the towering sasquatch. As I trotted away from them to give them space, they started returning boulders to the cairn. Rebuilding the stack as it had been. They were precise, and it soon looked much as it had when we first walked up. One shuffled around to the front and unblocked the entrance hole.

They left the artifact inside. The ruse was back in place, other than that I'd sprung all the bear traps.

I rubbed my head. "Do they speak? Can we question them?"

I do not think they have speech as we understand it, Sindari said. *They are not magical.*

I agreed. I didn't sense auras from them.

"They were sort of pantomiming. That's it." Mom came over and gripped my shoulder. "I'm sorry. That was dumb of me. I was worried about Rocket and so shocked that he didn't come back when I called him. He's been trained." She sounded defensive. Rocket stood at her side, watching the sasquatch with the intense interest of a dog sitting at the base of a squirrel-laden tree. He didn't appear contrite, but he was obediently sticking close now. "*Well* trained," Mom continued. "Usually—"

I lifted a hand. "There was a magical artifact inside. I think it was compelling him to get closer, until he was caught in a bear trap."

"Bear trap." She knelt and lifted his leg. Blood seeped through the golden fur around his wrist. "No bear would be able to get in there."

"No, I think it was meant for people or maybe their dogs. And more as a scare tactic than a genuine attempt to incapacitate someone."

Mom frowned at me. "Scare tactic for what reason?"

"I wish we could talk to these guys, because I'd like to know. Someone has effectively isolated the town, at least for now, and it seems like a lot of the methods being used are intended more to scare than to kill." I decided not to mention that, so far, this assignment was less appealing than ones where I was shot at regularly.

Their task complete, three of the sasquatch backed away, then turned and strode into the trees. The one that had finished fixing the entrance pointed at me, then hung his head and rotated it back and forth. It wasn't quite the same as a human head shake, but that was the impression that I got. Almost an apology. Then he pointed at Mom, at the cairn, at her again, and at the cairn again, as if directing her to go back inside.

"Does he think I'm going to go get myself stuck again now that he's reset the trap?" She rested a hand on Rocket's back to ensure *he* couldn't go back in.

"I have no idea."

The sasquatch looked at me and Sindari again, then rolled his head around his broad neck a few times and strode into the woods after the others.

"Maybe it's designed to trap humans, not half-elves," Mom suggested.

"Do you really think he could tell the difference between us? These sasquatch aren't magical beings."

"I bet Rocket could, so why not? Animals have more ways than we do to sense things."

"I won't argue with that." *Sindari, do you want to follow that one? Stealthily?*

Certainly. He trotted into the woods after them, soon fading from my sight.

I'll catch up in a few. We should see if we can find out where they live and if they have any goblin allies hanging out and playing cards with them.

Goblins play Wrenches and Pliers, not cards.

Is that a game? Or do they just enjoy fun times with tools?

It's a game played with tools. Also, it rhymes in their language, so the term lends itself to poetry and songs.

Poems about tools. I guess that's not any worse than poems about fresh kills.

If you refer to the poetry of the Zhinevarii, ours is far superior. We cover far grander and momentous matter.

Like how good zebras taste?

About how much sweeter the taste of zebras is after a taxing hunt of many days to acquire them. Val, these creatures are moving quickly. You'll need to hurry after if you want me to stay within your range.

Be right there.

"Mom, why don't you go back to the house and patch up Rocket's leg?" I checked my map and, as I'd suspected, we hadn't ended up far from the lake. She could make it back in a half hour. "Check on Thad and Amber, please. They're probably fine, but you never know."

"Are you planning to go fight the sasquatch, and you want me out of the way?" She waved in the direction they had gone.

"Not *them*, but if I find out who's manipulating them, there could be a fight. I want you safe."

She grimaced and glanced at Rocket's leg. I could tell she did want to tend to his wounds, but she said, "Are you sure you won't need help?"

"I've got Sindari. He's going to orate epic poetry about noshing on zebras to me."

She squinted at me. "Did a rock fall on your head?"

"Today or when I was a kid?"

"Either."

"I'm afraid there's no logical explanation for my weirdness. Except that my work is weird." I patted her on the shoulder and trotted off after Sindari.

Chapter 16

My phone buzzed as I jogged through the trees after Sindari, who was hot on the trail of the four sasquatch. Game trails ran through the area, and here and there, the forest thinned, revealing farmlands in the distance, but the sasquatch stayed under cover.

"What's going on, Willard?" I answered, not slowing down.

The sasquatch seemed to know Sindari was on their trail and were moving quickly.

"I'm checking in on your progress," Willard said.

"I've had some leads. I'm not sure yet who's in charge of this mess."

"I've heard that the roads to Harrison have been destroyed and that the equipment that's being brought out to fix them keeps getting sabotaged."

"I've heard that too."

"Are you running?"

I didn't make a lot of noise as I ran, flowing lightly over downed logs and around trees, but maybe she could hear it in my voice. "Yes, I want to join you in your next triathlon."

"I'd call you a horrible liar, but you weren't even trying."

"Sindari and I are following some sasquatch, hopefully to their home."

"They exist then?"

"Yes, four of them dug me out of a cairn and tried to convince my mom to go in so the trap could be sprung on the right person."

"What?"

"I'm not sure, but I think they're going after humans, not magical beings, and I must count as the latter. Maybe someone conveyed to them that people who can sense magic would be able to see through their ruse and shouldn't be targeted."

"Someone? Goblins?"

"That's my guess. We've spotted a few and seen lots of prints. We haven't been able to catch any yet."

There is magic ahead, Sindari warned me. *The sasquatch are heading for it.*

Goblin magic?

I don't think so.

"There may be more here than goblins," I told Willard.

"Well, get to the bottom of it. There have been several deaths reported. Some died in Rupert's bar, and some who had visited the bar earlier in the week died later."

"People who played with that orb?"

"Mentions of it keep coming up among my informants and the people I've questioned. There are rumors of more of them popping up around Puget Sound. The Northern Pride has information, but they're not talking. They put their lawyer on the phone when I called. He's slicker than a greased pig."

"Since you're from the country, I assume you've actually handled a greased pig."

"I may have competed in a pig scramble or two in my youth. There's prize money, you know."

A faint whisper of magic crawled over my skin like a cold mist, and I slowed down.

"I'll finish here as quickly as I can," I said, "but nobody's turned up dead yet, and so far, the criminals have only broken into houses and stolen things. And bashed in inoffensive light fixtures, though that might have been inadvertent due to height and hard heads."

"What's your point?"

"Do you want me to use deadly force if I find out who's in charge?"

"No."

"Am I supposed to arrest them?"

"You sound puzzled, Val."

"I don't get sent out to arrest people. I get sent to make them dead."

Up ahead, Sindari sat waiting for me between two trees.

"Are you saying I should have sent a less assassinly agent?"

"I'm not sure what to do with a bunch of goblins if I catch them. I don't think this town even has a police department or a cell I could put them in. And I don't have anything but rope in my Jeep. No handcuffs."

"No? What if your dragon is into creative foreplay?"

"Funny, Willard."

"Catch whoever is in charge and call me. I'll arrange for some MPs to come arrest them if necessary. And finish up soon and get back here."

"You're tyrannical today, especially considering how little you're paying me for this gig."

"I thought the bonus of being in the same state as your family would be reward enough."

"Have you *met* my family?"

"Are they like you?"

"Mom is." The flintier, less funny version of me.

"So spending time with her isn't a delight?"

"What are you saying, Willard?"

"Just finish up. The next gig will pay well."

The dark elves. Great.

I hung up and stopped beside Sindari. The forest here was much darker, even though it didn't appear any denser, and blue sky was visible through the pines and firs towering over us. The sensation of mist licking at my skin hadn't diminished. If anything it was stronger.

Did you lose the trail?

No. Sindari pointed his nose toward large sasquatch footprints. The trail disappeared between one step and the next, but he didn't seem puzzled. *They went into a sanctuary, I believe. There may be traps inside, so I waited for you.*

A sanctuary?

The forest ahead appeared no different from the forest behind, at least to my eyes. A raven squawked from a branch, and a squirrel ran across the pine-needle-strewn ground. I *did* have the sense that I didn't want to keep going forward, that I should look elsewhere for a trail through the forest.

That is my guess. I've encountered them before. The elves used to make them when they visited worlds to protect their settlements from hostile native people and animals.

Sometimes, it's only an illusion to keep others from finding them, but sometimes, there are magical traps.

Elves? Would they still be here? Living with the sasquatch? I rubbed my head. *And what do I do if elves are behind this?*

I doubt they are. It's likely they had an encampment here at one point and left it, but the magical protection remains.

I hope that's all it is. I couldn't imagine why elves would be responsible for all this, but the thought of arresting one disturbed me. They were my people, even if I'd only ever met one. If I encountered more, I would want to ask them questions about the power I supposedly had, not be on the opposite side of the law from them.

I will lead the way and attempt to suss out traps. Sindari walked forward.

How good are you at sussing out elven traps?

Not as good as I am when dealing with lesser species.

Ah.

He disappeared between one blink and the next, and I gaped at the empty air. *Are you still there?*

Yes. Inside the sanctuary. Come.

Assuming he would alert me if he'd fallen into a pit trap, I followed in his footsteps.

A strange feeling came over me, like a blanket of moisture gathered all around me, but then lessened again as Sindari came into view. A thick mist made it feel like I was out on the Olympic Peninsula on a foggy morning, not in the forests of northern Idaho. Even the foliage was different, with dense groundcover, including bedewed ferns, their long fronds stretching over the damp earth. Trilliums, star flowers, and violets bloomed in the shadows. We'd entered not only a magical sanctuary but an entirely different climate zone.

The stench of the sasquatch filled the heavy air, making my stomach want to heave its contents. I tried to breathe through my mouth.

Sindari led me up to another cairn, this one more natural than the other, with moss and ferns growing up from dirt wedged between the boulders. We climbed it, and when we came out on the top, a settlement of a sort came into view.

There weren't any signs of modern civilization or even fire pits, but dozens of these cairns dotted the area, with cave openings in the fronts. Sasquatch sat inside or wandered in and out of the larger ones.

Blackberry and elderberry bushes grew cultivated at one end of the camp, and a sasquatch shorter than I—a young one?—was gathering berries into an old burlap sack. Signs of salvaged human tools were all over but nothing that looked freshly stolen from Harrison. Some of the buckets and garden hoes could have been a hundred years old. None of them had been fashioned into anything I might recognize as a goblin contraption.

I glanced at Sindari. *I don't sense any magic aside from the power of the sanctuary itself. Do you?*

No.

I'd hoped to spot some artifact or magical gizmo that was blatantly controlling the sasquatch and coercing them to go into town and wreak havoc, but there was nothing. If I arrested any of these creatures, Willard would be underwhelmed. They might be the ones scaring the townspeople, but they weren't the masterminds. No way.

I scooted away from the top of the cairn. Even though I didn't make a sound, one of the sasquatch looked in my direction. A male with ancient, deep brown eyes. He tilted his head slightly but didn't alert the others to my presence, nor did he give chase as I scrambled down the back side and trotted away with Sindari.

Maybe it would be worth staking out this sanctuary to see if they get any visitors, I said once we were outside in the brighter native forest.

As a woman of action, stakeouts were my least favorite thing, but if goblins were using these guys, they would have to come collect them at some point, right?

As a skilled and experienced hunter, I have the patience to spend days waiting for my prey if needed.

Your charm only lets you stay on Earth for six hours.

Then you'll have to take my word for my patience.

And wait out here alone. I curled a lip, envisioning a long boring day.

Perhaps Lord Zavryd will come so you don't pine with loneliness.

I'm sure a dragon lurking at the border here would make the goblins rush to visit.

I didn't have any other leads, so I did my best to hide my tracks, then climbed a tree to settle in to watch the area.

Chapter 17

My phone buzzed as I was settling into my tent, the campground much quieter tonight. I'd spent all afternoon perched in a tree, watching the borders of the hidden sasquatch community, but no goblins ever made an appearance. A couple of hikers cutting through from the lake trail to the main road had walked right past the area without noticing anything amiss. Without being aware of it, they had put a curve in their route to avoid the border of the sanctuary.

"Hi, Mom," I said, recognizing the number from the vacation house and doubting Amber was calling me to talk about boys. If she and Thad wanted to call, they had their own cell phones. My technology-disdaining mother was probably disgruntled that the phone at the house wasn't rotary.

"Hi, Val. I wanted to make sure you got back and weren't caught in another trap."

"I'm at the campground. I found an old elven sanctuary—that's what Sindari thinks it is—that the sasquatch somehow found. They make their home inside. It's probably how they've avoided notice all these years."

Years? More like decades and centuries. When I'd done a little research the night before, I'd found that people had been glimpsing sasquatch and reporting sightings since before white men had settled the area. Maybe sanctuaries like that dotted the Pacific Northwest—or the entire world—and that explained how the sasquatch had remained around but their existence unproven.

"Were there ferns inside? And lots of moss and elderberries and trilliums?"

"Yeah, it was more like the temperate rainforest than the climate here. How did you know?"

"A few months after we met, and he'd decided he trusted me, your father took me into the one his people were staying in. At the time, I didn't know it was a temporary encampment for them, that they were here studying our people and hadn't always been on Earth. They had houses built into the treetops with magical bridges connecting their decks and platforms. Even if the magic hadn't kept people out, one could have walked under the trees without ever knowing they were up there."

"Some authors and game designers will be delighted they got elves right."

"I'm sure I wasn't the only human who was ever invited to visit. The stories came from somewhere before they were in games. Was it misty?" She sounded wistful.

"Yeah. No elves though. Just extremely stinky sasquatch." I sniffed my palm and grimaced. Even though I'd scrubbed myself in the campground shower with my multiple loofahs, a faint sasquatch odor still clung to me. It was worse than dragon aura—at least dragon aura didn't smell.

"Too bad. I'm sure Eireth would be depressed to see me now that I've aged forty-some years and he probably doesn't look more than a year older, but I've missed… oh, him, yes, and their culture. It was so much more like what I prefer than what we have—especially these days. I've often regretted not going back with him. It wouldn't have worked out—his kin implied that he was expected to marry an elf and have fully elven children—but sometimes, I wonder if I might have been allowed to at least live among them and if maybe I could've earned a place in their world. A place to belong."

"Mom, have you been drinking?" I didn't mind her opening up to me, and she would tell stories if prompted, but it was unusual for her to reveal her feelings. I wondered if something was wrong. She hadn't learned she was dying, had she?

"Just one glass."

Ah ha.

"One glass of *what?*"

"It's a port that the girlfriend brought along."

It amused me that Shauna was "the girlfriend" to Mom, even after a couple of days of staying together. Did anyone actually like the woman? Besides *Thad*? I hoped he did. And that she was good to him and wasn't a gold digger. I knew Thad had his house in Edmonds paid off—a house on a large lot with a view of Puget Sound—and plenty of money from stock options from the tech outfit that had gone big before he'd left to start his own company. He seemed to be doing well with that too. And if I'd been able to dig up that information online, some girlfriend could too.

"Port is strong, Mom. You're only supposed to have a little glass of it."

"Are you lecturing me?"

"No, I'm advising." Normally, I wouldn't even advise, but I worried this was a bad time to be inebriated. Even though I hadn't sensed Shaygor for a while, and Zav occasionally flew into my range, I knew that dragon wasn't done with me. Hopefully, Amber was using my charm regularly and he didn't know where she was. I, on the other hand, was lying on my back in a completely unarmored tent.

"When did we get to the age where you're allowed to do that to me?"

"I'm not sure, but you can advise me, too, if you want."

"Really? Then you should get married, have more children, and give up being an assassin."

"I tried all that once. It didn't work."

"It's been kind of pleasant being here with Thad and Amber." No mention of *the girlfriend*. "Sometimes, you get used to being alone and don't mind it, but then when you're with others, you remember there are other ways to be."

I knew exactly what she meant. I closed my eyes, regretting that I hadn't come to visit her more often.

"It's worse after they leave," I said.

"Yes. Have you learned… Do you know of…" Mom trailed off.

What was this? She was never hesitant.

"Now that there are magical beings in the world, beings like dragons, do you know if there are any portals to other realms?"

"Like the elven world?"

"*Veleshna Var*," she murmured.

"I've seen Zav make a temporary portal. It closed behind him, and I assume it went to *his* world."

"A dragon could as easily open a portal to the elven world."

"Do you want me to ask him if he'll take you through?" I was joking and didn't expect her thoughtful silence.

"Do you think he *would*?"

"Mom, you can't leave Earth. What would you do there? They have magic. They don't need trackers."

"Retire."

"I'm sure they'd take American Express and put you up in a nice villa."

"I suppose that's…"

A crash came from up the hill, and I didn't hear the rest. I sat up, grabbed my weapons, and said, "I'll call you later, Mom."

I unzipped the tent and stepped out into the shadows, listening for more noise. It was about ten, so not too late, but full darkness had arrived. A few motor boats buzzed out on the lake, their owners not yet willing to end the day. But the noise had come from town, from the grassy park Shaygor had tried to torch.

A familiar pungent scent drifted down the hill. The sasquatch.

Glass shattered, and someone screamed.

I drew Chopper, my fist tight around the hilt as I snarled with frustration. I'd watched the sasquatch camp all day, deemed them harmless unless someone was controlling them, and left them alone. Had that been a mistake?

As I ran up the road from the campground and into town, more glass broke. Someone else screamed. A horn blared, followed by the thunderous crunch of a car crashing.

Two great shaggy black sasquatch ran along the sidewalk above the park, throwing rocks across the street. From farther down on the hill, I couldn't see what they hit, but I heard more glass shatter. They were targeting either storefront windows or cars.

"Sindari," I whispered, glad I hadn't kept him in our world for his full daily allotment of time earlier. "I need some help."

Silver mist appeared with Sindari forming inside. I didn't wait. I ran across the park, intending to drive the sasquatch out of town with my sword if I had to, but a hint of movement came from my left, along with the faint sense of something magical in use. A goblin camouflaged by a charm?

I lunged to the left and spotted a dark figure squatting atop a picnic table. I'd stepped close enough to see through his charm or whatever trinket was responsible for his stealth.

Even in the poor lighting, I could make out green skin and white hair. He wasn't facing me. His focus was on the sasquatch. The amount of shouting and glass breaking all along the street implied there were more than two of them.

The goblin gripped what looked like a platter made from folded street signs in his hands, its magic growing more discernible as I drew closer. I was about to spring and tackle him, but he glanced back, sensing me at the last second. Though startled, he leaped off the table before I landed on it.

Do I help you hunt goblins, Sindari asked from where he'd formed, *or stop the sasquatch?*

Try to scare the sasquatch out of town, I replied as I ran after the goblin.

My legs were longer, and I was on the verge of catching him, but he tucked his artifact under one arm and flung back dark pellets. They scattered across the ground like caltrops and exploded right in front of me.

I dodged to the side to avoid the brunt of them, but a few struck. Harsh, fiery pain bit into the back of my hand and my thigh.

Snarling, I sped after him again. If he got more than a few meters ahead, and still had his camouflage activated, I would lose sight of him.

Up on the street, Sindari's roar rose above all the ambient noise. The crunches, bangs, and shattering noises faded, but my goblin did not slow down. He zigzagged through the trees as fast as his short legs could carry him, hopped a chain, and ran out of the park and onto a side street.

Again, I was almost close enough to catch him when he dipped a hand into a satchel bouncing on his hip and flung something else back in my path. A paper-wrapped cylinder that reminded me of fireworks.

I leaped high in the air to sail over it and landed several feet beyond it as it hissed and smoked. I thought I'd avoided the weapon, but then it spun like a top and spat tiny projectiles. Several slammed into my calves as I ran, and I swore in pain as tiny thorns of agony burrowed in.

The goblin glanced back as he ran around the corner of a building and onto a dark street paralleling the bike trail below. The thorns stung like rattlesnake bites, but I resisted the urge to hobble to a stop, instead sprinting around the corner after the goblin. He was fading from my sight like an erratic hologram.

"Enough of this crap," I snarled and pulled out Fezzik.

Without slowing down, I took aim. I barely resisted the urge to shoot the bastard in the back of the head and chose a lower target. I squeezed the trigger, and a single bullet sped into his calf, in about the same spot where his vile metal thorns were digging into mine.

He flew forward and hit face-first on the pavement, the magical platter flying out of his hands and clattering down the street.

I had a hunch it was more valuable than he was—if this was the artifact camouflaging all the goblins, then taking it from them would put an end to how much trouble they could create—so I leaped over him and ran to pluck it up. It hit a boulder, bounced into the air, and almost went over the edge of a steep slope. But I jumped and grasped it, landing on the boulder myself and catching my balance. A stiff wind would have knocked me over the side, but I recovered and dropped back onto the pavement, wincing as fresh pain shot up my legs.

More roars came from the main street, but a large building blocked my view of Sindari and the sasquatch. I started back to collect the goblin but halted. He'd disappeared.

"That was fast," I muttered, running back to the spot where he'd fallen.

That had been a hard fall, and he had a bullet in his leg, so I wouldn't have guessed he could run off so quickly. Maybe I could get Sindari down here to track him by the trail of blood. I needed a goblin to question. Badly.

Before I could call Sindari, a thump came from above me. The goblin was being pulled up the side of the building on a rope by two more goblins crouching on the flat rooftop. They were both hazy, right at the edge of my range to see through the influence of their magical camouflage.

Was the platter still protecting them? The welded mashup of signs, everything from *No Trespassing* to *Curves Ahead*, was warm in my hand and radiated magic.

I pointed Fezzik, intending to shoot the rope, not the goblin being pulled up, but one of the rooftop goblins drew as fast as an Old West gunslinger and pointed something at me. A stick? No. Whatever it was also radiated magic. A wand, maybe, if that was a shaman.

The tip glowed red and pointed right between my eyes.

I didn't know if it was something like a gun that he could fire, but his yellow eyes were hard, his expression confident that he could do some damage. I hadn't taken my armored vest off for the day, but he wasn't aiming at my chest. And there wasn't anything nearby for me to duck behind.

Since he was holding his fire, waiting to see what I would do, I didn't shoot. I hadn't intended to kill the dangling goblin anyway. So far, they hadn't hurt anyone, just vandalized the town. It was a crime, but as Willard had reinforced, they shouldn't be killed for it. Just arrested. Somehow.

I lowered Fezzik. The shaman lowered his wand. He and the other goblin pulled their buddy up and leaned back out of sight. Back under their spell of camouflage.

Sindari? I headed back for the park, wincing at the pain in my calves with every step and hoping I wouldn't find piles of bodies, not when I'd essentially let that goblin go. *Those were wonderfully resonant roars. Were they effective?*

All sounds of vandalism had stopped, though I heard a car drive through, tires crunching on glass, and someone was shouting angrily from the direction of the town tavern.

My magnificent and fearsome roars did scare the sasquatch. I also nipped at a few of their calves.

Calves are a trendy target tonight.

What do you mean?

Nothing. I doubted Sindari could help me pull the thorns out of my own calves. Later, I would spend an hour with a camp lantern and the pliers on my multi-tool, but first, I had to check on the damage. *Is anybody wounded?*

A man who drove a car into a telephone pole is groaning, but the sasquatch appear to have attacked only objects and buildings.

I suppose they're heading back to their hidden encampment now?

They fled up a street heading east and into the hills. It is likely they can get from there back to those woods.

And where did the goblins flee? I wondered.

I never sensed them. They are using magic as irritatingly effective as your cloaking charm. Even more so, because it seems to hide a great number of them at once. Either that or they all have charms. If so, they're not as rare as I thought.

Annoying when the enemy has the same advantages that you do.

Certainly so.

Whatever the artifact I'd snagged did, it apparently wasn't responsible for their camouflage. Was it what had been controlling the sasquatch?

It grew cool as I hobbled up to the main street to take in the broken glass, battered automobiles, and a door that had been ripped off its hinges and tossed onto a rooftop to hang precariously over the sidewalk. Lights flashed on a sheriff's SUV, and uniformed men were lifting their hands, trying to placate people. I spotted the mayor getting out of a car and peering around with distraught scrutiny. She looked like she had a headache—or would soon.

Someone saw Sindari walking out of an alley and shrieked and pointed. A deputy sheriff gaped at him in alarm and reached for a gun.

You might want to camouflage yourself now that you've scared away the enemy, I noted.

Sindari was heading in my direction, but he paused to look at the deputy. Then opened his fanged maw and roared. The deputy fired. Sindari anticipated the trigger squeeze and crouched low on the pavement as the gun went off. The bullet zipped over his back and into the corner of a brick building.

Sindari faded from everyone's sight but mine. Casually, he straightened and continued walking toward me.

The deputy with the gun out scanned the area, frowning at where Sindari had vanished. His gaze chanced across me. I'd put away my weapons and started walking back across the park, making my limp more pronounced. Just another victim here. No need to come over and question me. Besides, I didn't want to talk to the clueless law man. I wanted to go examine the artifact and get the projectiles out of my leg.

There were quite a few people wandering around who'd come out in the aftermath of the chaos, and the deputy didn't come after me. He holstered his weapon, checked once more for Sindari, then went back to calming scared citizens.

Let's get out of here, I told Sindari. *There's nothing more we can do tonight.*

But you acquired something. Sindari caught up with me and nosed the platter. *Is it the key to solving this problem?*

I eyed the salvaged—or stolen—signs welded together dubiously, but the platter *did* radiate magic, and this *was* the kind of detritus goblins liked to use to make artifacts. From what I'd heard, there wasn't a word for *junk* in the goblin language. Everything had value.

I certainly hope so, I thought.

Do you have a means to heal your injury? Sindari had noticed my limp.

Pliers.

The preferred tool of surgeons.

Will that be sufficient? He sounded skeptical.

As long as the thorns hadn't fully sunken into my calf…

I certainly hope so, I repeated.

Chapter 18

I sat on a bench looking out over the lake, examining my pilfered goblin artifact and eating a sandwich from the trading post. Mom had called it the hardware store, but, as I'd learned, it was a grocery store these days, with ice cream and a deli inside.

The more I considered the artifact, the more I believed it was what had allowed the goblins to control the sasquatch. There was even a tiny tuft of shaggy black fur stuck to one of the seams on the back. Did that mean I'd thwarted their plans and they wouldn't be able to use the big animals anymore? Or was this one of ten artifacts the goblins had crafted out of the county's road signs?

"If you *are* one of a kind," I murmured to it, "they'll want you back."

Maybe it could be *my* turn to lay a trap.

My phone buzzed. It was the same number that Mom had called from the night before, so I answered, assuming it would be she again.

"Hey, Mom."

The caller paused. "It's Thad."

"Oh. Is Mom okay?" I hadn't expected him to contact me again.

"She's fine. She's checking the bandages she put on Rocket's paw yesterday. And lecturing him because he went in the lake and got them soggy."

"She has more conversations with that dog than she ever had with me when I was growing up."

I'd meant the comment as a joke, but Thad said, "Maybe the dog is easier to talk to."

I doubted he'd meant it as a dig—he'd never been as quick to tease or mock as I was—but the truth of the words made them sting.

"Probably so." I strove for a casual tone. "He's definitely cuter than I am. That little head tilt and ear quirk he does could get him modeling gigs for dog-food bags."

Thad snorted. "I'm sure you could get modeling gigs, too, if you wanted."

For a second, I didn't know what to say. I hadn't been fishing for compliments. Maybe he'd realized his earlier words might be insulting and was trying to make up for it.

"I don't know. My ears really aren't soft and cute. So, what's up? It sounds like everything is okay at the house? You haven't seen any—" I stopped myself from saying dragons, since he wouldn't be able to see Zav or Shaygor unless they wanted him to, "—weird stuff?"

"No, but I've been watching the news. The county's attempts to fix the roads leading into town keep getting sabotaged. Equipment is vanishing from under the crews' noses or ceasing to work. An entire engine disappeared from a bulldozer. That's definitely weird."

"Yeah," I said, though it sounded exactly like the kind of mischief goblins were known for.

"People are starting to get antsy and want to get out of town."

"That may be the desired result." I didn't know if Mom had mentioned the sasquatch or goblins, so I didn't bring them up. I didn't have to read the local paper to know it hadn't printed anything about magical beings. The mainstream media never did.

"Uh, all right." Thad sounded confused, but he didn't ask for clarification. "I called to ask you about something. Amber has this new little trinket, and it reminds me a lot of the ones you have on that necklace you were wearing the other day."

"It is one of them. I lent it to her."

"Oh, did you? She said she saw you in town, and you gave it to her, but I was worried she'd taken it."

As if I couldn't keep a teenager from swiping things from me if she tried.

"A couple of years ago, she went through a phase where she was stealing things. Not from stores or anything major but from friends' parents and stuff. I think she was bored and upset that I wasn't around that much. I've been trying to work from home more often and it got better—or *she* got better, and I'm not catching her. I don't know. She may have grown out of it." He sounded like he was confessing, that he believed this little mishap made him a bad parent. As if *I* could judge anyone for that.

"It's fine. The charm, not the thieving. I think the police object to the latter."

"Yeah," he said glumly.

I'd meant that as a joke too. Had Sindari truly believed my abrasiveness was more witty than Amber's? Maybe he was being diplomatic. He did keep calling himself an ambassador.

"I'm sure you're doing great with her, Thad. I..." I paused, debating how much spying I should admit I did. But I'd already told him that Willard's office kept an eye on them. Maybe he would believe the government was my source for information. Was that better or worse than me being a snoop? "I know she gets good grades and works hard at her swim-team practices and does well at meets."

"She does, yes." He sounded mollified. "She insisted on sports and gave up on intellectual extracurricular activities after only one summer of robotics and programming camps, but I don't mind. The exercise is good for her, right?"

And less likely to get her beaten up than programming or robotics hobbies, yes. Though at six feet, Amber didn't have to worry about being stuffed in lockers. Maybe broom closets.

"Yes, it is. You could see if she's interested in martial arts at all. They teach integrity and perseverance and all that." And I'd feel better knowing she could take care of herself, at least against mundane humans. And a solid kick to the groin could faze even an orc.

"She hasn't shown... martial tendencies."

I had a feeling he'd almost said something else. Brutal? Violent? Thugly? Like her mom?

"She wants to enter the Miss High School America beauty pageant when she's a junior. She has her dress picked out. Three of them, actually."

"My daughter wants to enter a beauty pageant?" I stared down at my dusty combat boots. "How is that even possible?"

"I don't know. I think she just wants the dresses." His tone turned dry. "Have you ever worn a dress, Val? Because when we got married, you wore your dress greens."

"With the skirt. That's like a dress."

"I promise you it isn't."

"You wore *your* dress greens too."

"I know. We were poor then and both still serving. It made sense. Still, I'd be tickled to see you in a dress someday."

I imagined wearing my gun's thigh holster under a poofy, frilly dress and couldn't keep from curling a lip at the phone.

"I'll keep your request in mind." I almost made a joke about not caring what I wore at my own funeral, but that was a bit morbid, and he might not find it funny.

"There's another reason I called." Thad paused again.

"Oh?" Something about the leading sentence and the pause made me nervous. Or maybe it had been the dress comment. Was it weird that he would say something like that? Or was he just being friendly? We'd been friends once. And lovers. But more than ten years had dulled the feelings, at least for me. Maybe it hadn't even been the years. As horrible as it was to admit, it had been harder to walk away from Amber than from him. I'd always felt bad about that since Thad was a good guy, but I'd never felt for him the molten passion that one read about in romance novels. He'd been the good friend that I'd married because it had seemed like the smart, mature thing to do. Settle down, get out of the army, have kids, lead a normal life…

"A friend in Sandpoint invited us to come up for a few days," Thad said. "Originally, I wasn't going to drive out of the way up there, but with Harrison turning crazy, I've rethought that. If things settle down and get resolved here… Do you think they'll be resolved?"

"Yes. Because I'm going to resolve them." I was annoyed that I hadn't already.

"If that happens, we'll come back. I paid for the house for more than a week. But if things don't get resolved… Well, I'm sure you'd hoped to spend some time with Amber. I hate to leave when you've barely talked, but we found a boat service, and my friend is going to drive down to Coeur d'Alene to pick us up."

"Oh." That was my word of the day. I almost laughed because

I'd thought— Oh, I don't know what I'd thought. That he would ask me if we could get back together? What an ego. He was here with his girlfriend.

"But if you want to try to get together another time this summer or later in the year, we can. I don't want you to think that I object to you having a relationship with my—our—daughter."

No, *Amber* objected. I got that.

"Where do you live now?" he went on. "I'm sure we can arrange something."

"Ballard," I said before I could reconsider. To make sure he couldn't find me if he looked, I'd never told him I'd stayed in the area. He'd always assumed I was traveling the world on my assassination missions, and it had been safest to let him.

"*Ballard?* You're ten miles away from us, and you never said anything?"

"With traffic, it's more like twenty miles." It wasn't the time to be snarky, but my tongue never could get timing right.

"Shit, Val. What, were you afraid I'd come over for a booty call or something?"

I snorted. "People our age don't have booty calls."

"Yeah, what do they call it?"

"Unwise decisions."

This time, he snorted, but it sounded more pained than amused.

"I'm sorry, Thad. My apartment gets broken into regularly, and I've been shot at more times than I can count this year. I was always afraid you—or Amber—would get hurt if—"

"I know, I know. You gave me the spiel ten years ago."

I slumped against the hard bench, stung by his disappointment, even if I had no right to be.

"Ballard." He swore and then was quiet so long I checked to see if he'd hung up. "Well, anyway, what I was about to say is if you're going to stay here for your mission, you can stay in the house here if you want. I don't think people *our age* enjoy sleeping on the ground in tents either."

"You never did. I remember vociferous objections whenever you had to go to the field. Even though the army gave us cots."

"Cots it took a crowbar to assemble. Tech guys aren't supposed to sleep in tents. Why don't you come by the house this afternoon—we're leaving around four, so before then—and I'll give you the door code and show you the house rules the owner left for us. I will expect you not to host any wild parties. I want my damage deposit back."

"Thanks, Thad, but the campground is fine. I really don't—"

"Cool dish, lady," a teenager called from a bicycle as he pedaled past, waving at the artifact.

Wait, I'd wanted to set a trap for the goblins. If I did it here in the campground, and the goblins came with weapons and their sasquatch buddies, a lot of people could get hurt. That house Thad had rented was tucked away on a point, halfway behind a cliff and out of sight of the neighbors. If trouble showed up there, I would be the only one around to take the brunt of it. I could pitch my tent in the yard and sleep outside so the house—and Thad's damage deposit—wouldn't be in danger.

"I take it back, Thad. That's a generous offer, and I'd like to accept."

I waited to see if there would be a hint that he'd only been offering to be nice, but he responded without hesitation.

"Good. Maybe Amber will deign to talk to you."

"About beauty pageants?"

"Maybe about dresses and fashion."

"Are you trying to torture me, Thad? I'd have an easier time talking about programming and robotics."

"Been brushing up on your Python and C++, have you?"

"Yeah, I like pythons."

"Are you making an innuendo or are you interested in developing scalable web applications?"

"Wouldn't both get you excited?"

"Yeah, but especially the latter."

"You haven't changed."

"You either. See you in a few hours."

Chapter 19

A little after three, I knocked on the door to the house, my Jeep in the driveway with my tent and sleeping bag inside, and the goblin artifact stuffed into my backpack.

Mom, her luggage already packed and outside, was sitting in the sun on the dock with Amber's friend while Rocket sniffed around on the bank. Mom lifted a hand but was reading a book and didn't come over. Apparently, we'd done our bonding for the month.

Thad answered the door. "Come in. Shauna and Amber are finishing packing. We have about a half hour until our ride gets here." He waved toward the lake.

"It's a good thing you're leaving from here instead of from the marina in town." I stepped into a two-story foyer with a chandelier hanging above us. A couple of suitcases were stacked by the door, including a pink, hard-sided spinner with raised stars. No trouble finding that one on the baggage carousel. "A boat came in as I was leaving and there was a mob. People were ready to abandon their RVs to get out of Harrison." I shrugged. "Last night wasn't *that* bad. Nobody even got shot."

Thad gave me a bemused smile. "What constitutes a bad night for you?"

"Beheadings, disembowelment. Usually of people I know. If those things happen to the bad guys, it's more of a good night."

"Were you this much of a ghoul when we were married?"

"Yes."

He smirked. "Strange that I'd forgotten."

"Thad," came Shauna's voice from a landing at the top of the stairs that overlooked the foyer. She'd said his name, but she frowned down at *me*. "Can I see you for a moment?"

"Sure." Thad handed me a card with the four-digit code for the door lock on it. "Make yourself at home."

He tramped up the stairs.

Shauna gave me a frosty look as she waited. Maybe I should have asked Thad to text me the code and then waited until they were gone to come by. He'd said something about house rules though. Maybe there was a huge notebook of instructions. I didn't want to do anything to risk his damage deposit. The place probably cost a thousand dollars a night. Who knew what they charged if you forgot to clean the dishes and take out the trash?

"What is *she* doing here again?" Shauna whispered from the bedroom they'd stepped into. She hadn't shut the door.

"I told you. She's going to stay here while we're gone."

The door closed. I might have cocked an ear and heard the rest of the conversation, but I didn't want to listen to them argue, especially not about me.

Since Amber had some elven blood, I could sense her aura, the same way I could with Nin and Dimitri. She was in the living room, putting away a laptop and a handheld gaming device, so I wandered in. Maybe I should have gone outside to hang out with Mom, but this might be my last chance to see Amber, so I felt I should take another stab at saying something.

Amber turned as I walked in, opening her mouth, but closed it when she saw me. "I thought you were Myung-sook."

"If that's your friend, she's outside playing with her phone."

"She's probably texting Heath." Amber rolled her eyes. "She misses him so much. What *I* miss is when we used to go places and nobody was blathering about boyfriends all the time."

"Does that mean you're not into guys yet?"

"They're fine, but that doesn't mean you have to lose your mind and become a different person because of them." Another eye roll.

I decided that answered my question in the affirmative but didn't say anything. I'd rolled my eyes through high school drama, too, but I'd always thought that was because Mom had homeschooled me for so long that I had a low tolerance for normal human young-person behavior. Maybe it was in the genes.

A door slammed upstairs.

"Shauna doesn't like you," Amber informed me with odd relish.

"No? There's a club she can join back in Seattle. The dues are steep, but I hear they forgo them if you try to kill me at least once monthly."

"You are so weird."

"That is not an untrue statement." Standing there, I decided that maybe I'd made the right decision to leave Thad and Amber and take my weird life with me. The fact that she was more or less a typical teenager, with nothing more significant on her mind than boys, sports, and school, was a relief.

"She said you look like a model. I think that's the main objection." Amber looked me up and down. "I said a model for a gun magazine, maybe, but she didn't get it."

"Unless I take Chopper and Fezzik off, only people with at least a quarter blood from a magical being can see them. Your kids, if you have children, will be down to an eighth elven blood, and that's usually too diluted to gain any attributes. They'll be normal."

"Fezzik?"

I tapped the gun in its holster. "It's from *The Princess Bride*."

"I *know* that." Another eye roll. Did her pupils ever get stuck back there?

"Oh? It's from before you were born."

"No kidding. But it's a classic. Like *Back to the Future* and *Goonies*."

Wonderful. Movies from my childhood were classics. Right up there with *Casablanca*. Though at least we'd had color in the eighties.

"You should have named it the Dread Pirate Roberts."

"I did consider it, but that's a mouthful. It's also something of a brute-force weapon. Fezzik seemed appropriate."

"You're not looking for an evil dude with six fingers who killed your father, are you?"

I couldn't tell from her expression if she was mocking me or hoped that was the case. "I believe my father is still alive and living in another realm." Saying *on another planet* seemed more kooky somehow, as if I also believed in UFOs full of green aliens who abducted women from

Earth for breeding purposes. "I did once kill a zombie with nine digits on one hand. He kept adding extras to stave off his leprous tendencies. It's difficult being undead."

She said something—probably how weird I was again—but a dragon came into range of my senses, and I barely heard her. It was Zav, which should have relieved me, given the alternative, but he was arrowing straight for the house.

To warn me of trouble? To accuse me of trouble? I hadn't killed any criminals he'd been assigned to hunt lately.

"I'll be back in a minute." I headed to the foyer, wanting to speak with him outside and without witnesses, but he came in fast.

He opened the door in human form and strode into the foyer, his robe swishing around his feet, feet that clacked on the tiles because they were now clad in… Were those cowboy boots? With… peacock feathers?

I barely noticed his powerful aura and the familiar tingle that ran over my skin. I was too busy staring at the boots.

"Zav." I recovered, lifted my gaze to his, and held up a hand. "You can't just walk into people's houses."

"I am Lord Zavryd'nokquetal. I go where I wish."

"No, you don't." I smiled into the living room at a gaping Amber and clasped Zav's hand to lead him out before Thad came down.

Zav seemed startled by the handclasp. I pretended not to notice that his skin was warm and pleasant—or the little zing of electricity that shot up my arm. He let me lead him out onto the porch, where I pointed at the doorbell.

"When you go visiting, you press that first and wait to be invited in. You can't presume that humans want you in their house."

"You cannot presume that a dragon wishes you to hold his hand." Zav withdrew it from my grip.

He didn't wipe it off, as if I'd contaminated him with cooties, but I couldn't help but feel stung.

"Look, you pressed your forehead against mine last month, and I'm pretty sure you were contemplating kissing me. I think that entitles me to a hand-holding if I wish it."

Zav gazed at me with his violet eyes, his strong jaw tight. I expected him to deny that he'd contemplated anything kiss-related.

What he said was, "We have battled together, and I would like to believe your intentions are honorable, but I do not trust you so close to me."

My mouth fell open. "What? Why? I'm just a mongrel—your own words—so it's not like I could do anything to you even if I wanted to." Admittedly, I'd sliced open a couple of dragon toes this summer, and Dob was dead, but that had been due to an extenuating circumstance. Zav had grievously wounded Dob beforehand, and he'd been lying helpless in the river.

What did Zav even think I could do to him? Poison him or stab him with some horrific dragon-slaying artifact? If I had such a thing, I wouldn't be hacking at toes with Chopper.

For a long moment, it didn't look like Zav would explain. His jaw remained tight, his face carved in stone.

Then he spoke quietly. "I cannot read your thoughts, and I have been betrayed and almost killed before by a lesser being."

There was a story I wanted, but he'd only reluctantly admitted as much as he had. I doubted he would tell me the rest. But the little he'd given me made a couple of our past encounters make more sense. Like the time I'd reached for his shoulder to brush off a leaf and he'd grabbed my wrist to stop me. I'd definitely gotten the vibe that he'd been suspicious of my intent.

"I don't have any plans to betray you," I said, holding his gaze. "Just get rid of the dragon threats to Earth."

His eyes narrowed, and I realized he might think I meant him. Earth would be better off without *any* overpowered dragons around, but I'd been thinking of Shaygor and anyone else who came here to cause trouble for humans.

I opened my mouth to explain that but grew aware that Thad had come downstairs. He stood in the foyer, and Amber was leaning out of the doorway to the living room. They were both staring at us. Amber was gaping at Zav, and Thad was glowering suspiciously at him.

Zav and I were chest to chest, less than a foot apart, and though he was only a few inches taller and didn't exactly tower over me, he did radiate that power. Even mundane people sensed it to some extent and saw him as a threat.

"Are you all right?" Thad asked me, taking a few steps closer, his fingers curling into a fist. "Who is this? What's he doing here?"

Thad was the most unlikely bruiser out there, but he genuinely looked like he planned to step in and protect me if needed. That would not go well.

I lifted a hand, palm outward toward him, intending to explain, but Zav spoke first.

"I am Lord Zavryd'nokquetal. I am here to ensure that Val is not arrested by the inquisitor from the Dragon Justice Court. I am also here to inform her that a pack of goblins is spying on this house from up on the hill."

Even though I'd been hoping the goblins would come for their artifact, I barely heard his second sentence. Something about the way he said the first made me certain that a new development had come along.

"Is he on drugs?" Thad asked me.

"Probably not. I don't think he'd know where to get them."

Amber hurried into the foyer and grabbed Thad's hand. "Don't bother him, Dad. He's something scary."

She looked at me, eyes seeming to ask if she was right, and I nodded. She ought to be able to sense that Zav's aura was as powerful as Shaygor's had been, and she'd had the opportunity to sense Shaygor up close. Too close.

Thad scoffed, but the disbelief didn't quite reach his eyes. I kept my hand up in case he had some delusion of rushing to my rescue in a manly and misguided manner.

"Thad, Amber, this is Zav. He's a—"

"*Lord* Zavryd'nokquetal," Zav interrupted coolly.

"They're not going to be able to pronounce that any more than I can," I muttered.

"Your species is linguistically challenged."

"Yes, it is." I waved to Thad and Amber to finish my introduction. "He's a dragon from a place I also can't pronounce." Had Zav even told me the name of his world? I couldn't remember, but I was positive my statement was true. "He has the ability to shape-shift into different forms, such as this one. I hadn't realized he could change his shoes, but apparently, he can."

Zav squinted at me. I suspected he was underwhelmed by my introduction.

"He's here on Earth collecting criminals who have fled to our world to escape the Dragon Justice Court." There, that was true and not even snarky.

I waited for Amber to comment again on how weird I was—or how weird my acquaintances were—but she tried to tug Thad out of the foyer instead.

Scowling, he rooted his feet to the floor.

"Uh, Zav." I wasn't sure I should finish the introduction, since it wasn't going superbly, but I wanted to make sure he knew this was my family and—hopefully—that they were to be protected, not hurt or threatened. "This is my daughter, Amber, and my ex-husband, Thad."

Zav had been indifferent to them before, but now, he turned his attention on them. Mostly on Thad. He skimmed over Amber—he'd probably already known she was my daughter, the same way Shaygor had detected it—and looked Thad up and down. Dismissively.

"That is your mate?" Zav stepped closer to me, his chest brushing the back of my shoulder as he faced Thad.

"He *was* my mate. We're divorced."

Remembering his overreaction to the guy who'd hit on me at the ice cream parlor, I turned and planted my hand on his chest. Unbidden, the memory of our kiss-and-grope session in the water-treatment plant jumped into my mind. His chest was as hard and muscled under his robe as it had been then, and he didn't budge when I tried to push him back.

Thad was Mr. Nice Guy and also Mr. Mellow Guy. He rarely got angry, but now, his face flushed red, both hands clenched at his sides. Since Zav wouldn't move, I stepped away from him, though it annoyed me that he wouldn't respect my wishes—and my space—and step back on his own.

"Zav, I'll talk to you later," I told him. "I appreciate you coming to warn me, but I have to learn about the house rules."

And if I only had a few minutes to spend with my family before they left, I wanted to spend it with Amber discussing six-fingered men, not trying to break up a staring contest. Now, I wished I hadn't let myself be distracted from having a discussion with Zav about boundaries. I wasn't sure what his deal was, since he'd told me numerous times he wasn't attracted to me, but I wasn't going to let him loom over my shoulder like a jealous lover every time I spoke to a man.

"It'll only take a few minutes," I added, since he was still standing there glaring at Thad. "Then I'll come find you and listen to everything you have to say. I promise."

"You would prioritize speaking to that one over me?" His glare left no doubt that he meant Thad, not Amber.

"Yes, I would. Maybe you can enjoy a walk on the trail while you wait. Or fishing in the lake. Or, look, there's a porch swing and a hot tub on the deck. Knock yourself out." I stepped back into the house and closed the door in his face.

Almost immediately, I worried he would throw a dragon temper tantrum and make it burst into flames. Fearing for Thad's damage deposit, I almost opened it again, but as I reached for the knob, I sensed Zav stepping back. He paused at the top of the steps—maybe he was checking out the hot tub—then strode toward the driveway. Through a window beside the door, I saw him change into dragon form and fly toward a hilltop.

"Do dragons use hot tubs?" Amber's tone was less dry and sarcastic and more awed.

"*No*," Thad said firmly, then stalked into the kitchen.

I was tempted to ignore him and discuss dragons, or whatever she wished, with Amber, but Thad made a noisy show of yanking open drawers until he found a pen. He grabbed a piece of paper hanging from a fridge magnet and wrote something on the bottom. Then he stalked back to me and thrust the page at me.

House rules, it read across the top. In a tidy font, a list of requests for the renter went down the page. Take the garbage out before leaving, no pets on the furniture, air conditioning to be turned off at departure… and a new addition in Thad's execrable handwriting. *No dragons in the hot tub!*

"I suppose the homeowners won't object to that addendum," I said calmly.

"He's not coming back, is he?" Thad asked.

Given that I sensed Zav loitering on a cliff top less than a half a mile away, he probably was.

"It's fine. If he does, it's work-related." Or saving-my-life related. I wanted to know what Shaygor was up to and if I needed to watch out while I was trying to spring a trap to get a goblin.

"*Work*-related." Thad frowned at me. "That… *man*—" despite his addition to the house rules, he seemed unwilling to admit that Zav might be a dragon, "—was standing by you like some creepy, possessive boyfriend. He wanted to kick my ass."

"It's more likely that he would light your ass on fire."

Amber nodded, definitely a believer after her encounter with Shaygor.

"Val—"

"I get it, Thad. It's fine. When have you known me *not* to be able to take care of myself when it comes to guys? Or anything?" I wouldn't point out that numerous dragons had proved they could immobilize me and compel me to do their bidding. He didn't need to know about that.

His shoulders slumped, some of the tension finally leaving his body. "Never."

"But thank you for still caring." I rested a hand on his shoulder and smiled at him.

He managed a forced smile back. "Always."

A thump came from the landing upstairs as Shauna maneuvered out a second suitcase that matched the pink-stars one by the door. She glared icily down at me. I lowered my hand and gave Thad a punch that I hoped looked more manly than flirty.

"Amber, can I talk with you for a minute before you go?" I touched my necklace, hoping she would accept the request if she believed it was about the charm I'd given her.

Amber glanced at Shauna's frosty face. "Yeah."

She grabbed her own suitcase and her laptop bag and walked out onto the porch with me, looking warily around for Zav.

"He's over there." I pointed to the tree-filled hills, though I could only sense him, not see him.

"He didn't leave completely?"

"No. I need to talk to him, but I wanted to say goodbye to you guys first." I heard harsh whispers coming from the foyer and closed the door on them. "Especially to you. I'm less enamored with the girlfriend."

I shouldn't have said that. It wasn't mature or adult-like.

But when Amber snorted in agreement and said, "Tell me about it," I felt a twinge of pleasure at having something in common with her.

"Do you want your charm back?" She dug it out of her pocket.

If they'd been heading straight back to Seattle, I might have said yes, but Sandpoint was only about eighty miles to the north. Shaygor might be able to track her down at that distance. And if Zav, who I knew was the only reason Shaygor hadn't come after me again, stayed here with me... Shaygor would be free to go after Amber.

"Eventually, yes, but I'd like you to keep it for now, until you're back in Seattle and I'm positive the dragon that attacked you is gone and back in his world." However I would achieve that.

"Are you more vulnerable without it?" Amber surprised me with the question.

I wouldn't have expected her to care enough to ask. "Yes, but I have a weapon that can hurt a dragon." I waved toward Chopper's hilt. "And Zav is watching out for me."

"The scary guy in the robe? He's way more..." She flexed her hand in the air, groping for a word. "Strong-feeling than anyone else I've met. Sometimes, I get a weird feeling and can guess when people have power, but there was no mistaking it with him. He was really intense."

"I know."

"And he seemed to be, like, staking a claim on you."

I shook my head. "He's another dragon. They don't understand Earth women. Or Earth in general. But we're... kind of stuck working together right now."

"He sounds super dependable then."

"Not much is dependable in my life. I'm used to it. Keep the charm for now. I'll come get it back when there aren't any more vengeful dragons around."

"Are you sure? I think you're in more trouble than you're telling me, and I'm leaving so those dragons shouldn't care about me anymore, right?"

"I hope not, but I can't be positive. Take it. I'd rather not worry."

Her brow wrinkled. Maybe she didn't believe I worried. Why would she?

"Take it." I nodded as encouragingly as I could and stepped back.

Amber looked dubiously at the charm in her hand but grabbed her luggage and walked out to the dock. I hoped she wouldn't lose it along the way. Getting it off the bottom of the lake would not be easy.

The rumble of a motor drifted across the water. Mom put away her book and helped Thad and Shauna arrange the luggage on the dock. Amber went over to talk to her friend. I hung back, leaning against a column on the porch. I wasn't a part of their group.

As they climbed into the boat, I walked around to the back of the house, not wanting to watch them leave. Zav had mentioned goblins spying on the property—or spying on *me*, more likely. That artifact was strong enough that they would be able to sense it in my backpack from a ways off.

Which was exactly what I wanted. I had several hours of daylight left. It was time to set some traps.

Chapter 20

I pitched my tent on the lawn and set a few trip wires and traps around the house, what I could fashion out of the rope and limited gear in the Jeep. Amber and Thad and the boat that had picked them up were long gone when my trap-setting took me close to the dock, and I sensed a magical trinket. A familiar magical trinket.

My cloaking charm rested on top of a post, not dropped but placed carefully where I would find it. I gazed to the north in the direction my family had gone. By now, they were in a car heading up to Sandpoint. Shaking my head, I threaded the charm back onto my leather thong.

I did my best not to worry as I finished setting up, the artifact in my backpack. I wouldn't risk setting it down and letting it out of my sight. It was time to capture a goblin or two and get some answers.

But would they come with Zav lurking in the hills? If his aura was noticeable to me, it would be to the goblins too.

I wished I could speak telepathically with him—he could hear me when he was paying attention, but that wasn't the same as me being able to reach out—so I could get his update on Shaygor. And tell him to fly off to the north or stifle his aura somehow. But I'd have to find an elf to teach me how to use my power.

"Someday," I murmured.

As the sun set, I turned off all the lights in and around the house, everything except a couple of nightlights inside and dim solar-powered lamps around the deck that refused to be turned off. I slipped into my sleeping bag in my tent to wait.

Zav, perched on a nearby hilltop, emanated power like another giant nightlight. Or lighthouse.

Will you go away, please? I tried to project the thought in his direction.

Not surprisingly, I didn't get an answer. A moment later, I sensed him spring into the air. Maybe he'd heard me and would fly north to keep an eye on the town.

But he flew toward the house. I groaned, sat up, and opened my tent flap.

There are traps out there, I thought. *Be careful if you land.*

He landed in the yard. *As if puny mongrel traps would be strong enough to vex me.*

I'm less worried about your vexation status and more about having to redo them. I'm trying to capture goblins.

His great black head came into view—almost came through the opening of the tent—violet eyes glowing softly in the dark as he gazed in at me.

When you have acquired your goblins, you will leave this place and return with me to locate the dark elves?

As long as I can get answers from them and figure out how to keep them from terrorizing this town with their sasquatch allies. Or magically compelled minions, as the case may be. If you want to speed things along, you could go capture a couple for me.

I sensed them when I first arrived, but they are hidden to me now. They have something akin to your cloaking charm.

I know. Guess I'm back to doing it the old-fashioned way then. Capturing one with a trap.

These are meager traps. I do not think you will be successful.

Thanks so much for your honesty.

I am always honest. His eyes closed. *Almost always.*

Except when you're trying to save others from the Dragon Justice Court? I could sense his discomfort, even emotional pain, at the choice he'd made, and couldn't help but feel guilty.

I should not have been dishonest. Zav opened his eyes again. *But I did not—do not—wish to see you standing before the court and being condemned to punishment.*

Thank you. I don't want to see that either.

You did not understand the law of dragons, and I know you were defending yourself from Dobsaurin.

Yes, I was. He was an asshole. He deserved what he got.

Zav's unwavering gaze discomfited me, and I resisted the urge to squirm.

Do you believe all dragons deserve that fate? he asked.

Just the ones who come to Earth and start killing people. This is our world and has nothing to do with your court.

All worlds fall under the jurisdiction of the Dragon Justice Court. We flew the skies and hunted here before your people evolved into your present forms.

Are you sure? I'm pretty sure dragon bones aren't in the fossil record.

Dragons did not die here. They hunted.

Well, I'm trying to hunt some goblins, and I think your big aura is going to keep them from coming down to get this artifact. Will you take a nice flight around the lake for a while?

I spoke again to Shaygorthian today. He has made it clear that he will capture you at the first opportunity.

Capture or question? Had something changed?

Both. You wounded him when you fought. Now that he realizes you have a weapon capable of harming dragons, he has started to suspect you played a role in his son's death. He returned for a time to our world to do a secondary investigation of Dobsaurin's body.

My gut twisted. *Did he find anything?*

He did not tell me, but it is possible he unearthed my tampering. When he returned, he was more angry than before, and he promised retribution. Then he flew off to a mountaintop, but he is not far away. I can still sense him.

I thought of Amber and worried anew. I needed to wrap up this mission and get out of here.

I have been contemplating an option to protect you from the court, but it is not an appealing solution, especially not when I am in this form. Zav's tone turned dry. *When I am in human form, it seems less unappealing.*

What was he talking about? *I'd love to hear about it in the morning. After I get my goblins. Could you move out of their range for a while? I'm trying to lure them down here.*

How?

By getting rid of the powerful dragon standing next to my tent.

A powerful dragon could assist you with capturing them. And then you can return to the city and assist me in finding the dark-elf scientists.

Yes, yes. I'll do that as soon as I'm done here.

It is not only I that they fear but the Ruin Bringer. They may not come down when you have those weapons on. They are cowardly.

I *was* wearing my gear as I lay on my sleeping bag, everything from ammo pouches to armor to gun to sword.

So I need to appear more helpless?

Likely. Perhaps you should activate your charm but leave the artifact out in the open nearby.

I don't think they're dumb enough to fall for that. They'd see it was a trap.

Perhaps.

But they'll know I'm helpless when I fall asleep. Which I was pretending to do when you came.

I can diminish my aura so they can't tell I'm a dragon.

You don't think the tail and fangs would give that away, aura regardless?

I would do it after *changing forms.* His tone grew dry again. Maybe he found my situation with the goblins amusing.

Well, come back in human form if you want, but maybe you could just wait a few miles away and keep an eye on Shaygor so he doesn't come after me tonight. I would appreciate that.

Hm. Zav backed away from the tent.

I leaned out in time to see him spring into the air and fly away. This time, he sailed off over the water and out of my range.

I settled back onto my sleeping bag to feign sleep while worrying about being dragged before the Dragon Justice Court.

Chapter 21

Hours passed, and the goblins didn't come. Now and then, one would wander away from whatever artifact was keeping the group camouflaged, and I would sense him for a moment, so I knew they were still there. But they kept their distance.

I yawned, almost falling asleep in truth, and made myself sit up. This wasn't working. Maybe, as Zav had suggested, I needed to appear more helpless. By taking off my weapons? If they were next to me, I could still easily grab them. Maybe…

An idea popped into my mind, and I snorted. I wouldn't have considered it at the busy campground, not that I'd seen anything as luxurious as a hot tub there.

Taking the backpack, I picked my way past my trip wires to the house's deck. The hot tub overlooked the lake and the blanket of stars above it. A few houselights were visible on the far side, but they were too far away for anyone to see me getting naked.

I opened the lid on the hot tub, wrinkling my nose at the bromine smell, then removed my weapons and my clothes and set them on a bench built against the deck railing. The backpack went down next to the pile. There were towel hooks closer that I could have used, but if the goblins believed my gear was within my reach, they wouldn't come. I would have to keep a close eye on that pile, though, or the camouflaged goblins could make off with everything, my weapons included.

Standing naked on the deck, it was hard not to feel vulnerable and second-guess this choice, but I shook my head and slipped into the hot water. I ignored the buttons on the side for turning on the jets, since the motor would be loud, and I wanted to hear the goblins coming—or at least hear them rustling in my gear.

I draped my arms over the side, leaned my head back, and closed my eyes to slits. *All right, goblins,* I thought. *I'm helpless. I can't attack you from here. Now's your chance.*

"This is how you will lure them in?" Zav's skeptical voice came from beside the hot tub.

I swore and lurched to my feet before realizing that would show off my spectacular nudity from the waist up. Folding my arms over my breasts, I sank back down so that the water lapped at my shoulders. The solar lamps on the deck posts allowed me to see Zav in his robe, his chiseled face turned toward me.

"What are you doing here? I didn't sense you coming."

"No." He sounded pleased. "I am masking my aura."

"Good for you."

He'd been looking at my face, but his gaze drifted downward. I couldn't tell if he was trying to check me out or curious about this large box full of water. Probably the latter, but I reached over to hit the button to turn on the jets so the bubbles would obscure me. I wasn't the self-conscious type, but I'd already been feeling vulnerable without my weapons, and something about a dragon ogling me was disconcerting. Actually, if he *had* been ogling me, it would have struck me as normal, but his scrutiny was always faintly puzzled, like I was an unexpected and flummoxing outcome in a science experiment.

Instead of hitting the button for the jets, I managed to turn on the underwater lights, putting my nudity on full display.

Zav's eyebrows rose. He was still looking at me—with the lights, I'd practically invited him to. "What is this contraption for? Bathing?"

"Relaxation."

"Relaxation?"

"Yeah, soothing aching muscles." I stood up and leaned over, giving up on hiding my boobs or anything else, and found the right button. When I thumbed it, the jets flared to life, creating strong bubbles on the surface. I sank down onto one of the seats, hiding myself beneath the froth. A jet pummeled hot water against my back. "Do dragons not get sore muscles?"

His head was tilted as he regarded the burbling water, and I decided he'd definitely been checking out the "contraption" and not me. "Rarely, but I ached a great deal after my battles with Dobsaurin."

"I don't doubt it."

"I have healed since then, but I am curious, so I will try it."

He peeled his robe off before I could object, and I found myself gaping at another shifter who opted for a sculpted fitness-model alter ego. Why didn't anyone ever turn into an aging human with a dad bod?

I did my best not to peep as he carefully hung his robe on a hook, then bent over, his naked back and ass all I could see from inside the tub. He held the position long enough, shifting left and right slightly, that I grew curious. Unless he was doing some pre-relaxation stretches, it was odd.

"Is there a problem?" I pushed myself over to his side of the tub and peered over the edge at him.

"This new footwear is difficult." The robe had come off in a quick swoop, but he was struggling with the cowboy boots. His back flexed and shifted, nicely highlighting his strong muscles, as he stood on one foot and tugged at the other.

"What happened to your slippers?"

"That male that attempted to *skylitha* you in town implied there is a human cultural implication that slippers denote same-sex mating preferences."

"*Skylitha?*" I could have sat back and looked away from his boot problem, but it was hard not to want to check out a guy that nicely proportioned, even a dragon-guy, and he wasn't paying attention, so it wasn't like he would know.

"I do not know the human word. Court or woo is inadequate. It is when a male or female has lustful thoughts about another and wishes to mate as soon as possible."

"And you're sure that was his plan for me?"

"Yes. I may have a hard time reading *your* mind without extensive probing, but human vermin couldn't hide their thoughts from the lice that infest their hair."

"Gross."

"When I am in this world, when I change into a human form, I will wear footwear that makes it clear that I—" Zav tugged, growling but getting the boot halfway off with this effort, "—am not—" another tug finally removed the first boot, "—gay."

He stood straight, holding the boot aloft in triumph, and I got a good look at his front half, which included verification that he had indeed made himself anatomically correct. And suitable for nude modeling and any other nude activity a human could want to engage in. I admit to looking a little longer than intended, and he caught my perusal.

Blushing, I looked away and pointed toward the bench. "People usually sit down to take off boots that tight. And sometimes they own bootjacks."

Zav sat down without commenting on my gawk, and I gazed out at the lake, only watching him out of the corner of my eye. After a few more seconds of straining, he tugged the second boot off.

"This footwear is ridiculous." He thumped it down on the bench.

"It's hard work to be a manly man."

He squinted over at me.

"Why didn't you just use your magic?" It crossed my mind that he might deliberately be putting on a show for me, muscles rippling in the ambient lighting of the hot tub, but that seemed a touch disingenuous for my straightforward, honest dragon. And since he hadn't announced any intent to *skylitha* me, why would he?

"I am joining your ruse to make the goblins believe we are helpless. They had crept closer when I arrived. I walked on foot in human form down the trail so they would not recognize me as a powerful predator."

The powerful predator rubbed his heels. The idiotic boots had probably given him blisters during his walk, and if he wasn't using his magic, he couldn't heal them.

Sympathetic, I patted the side of the tub. "Come satisfy your curiosity then."

As he walked over, the light gleaming on his defined chest, I scooted back to make room for him. There was no way we were sharing a bench. If he had been into me, I wouldn't have invited temptation in, but I was positive he would sit there and be confused about the appeal of a hot tub and then get out. Maybe we could calmly have that discussion on boundaries while we waited for the goblins.

I looked away when he climbed over the edge, everything on display and highlighted against the dark backdrop of the lake.

"This water smells of chemicals. I fail to see how dousing oneself in them is relaxing."

"The bubbles make it therapeutic for your muscles. Sit down and find a jet to lean against."

Zav looked at me on my side of the hot tub, as if wondering if he should join me. I pointed to the opposite bench.

He sat down, but then sprang up as if something had bitten him, and I got a face full of dragon penis.

"Zav," I protested. "What are you doing?"

His head was craned over his shoulder. "A strong gust of water shot up my cloaca."

"I promise that you don't have one of those as a human. Unless you're not as anatomically correct as you think you are."

He shot me a dark look, as if he thought I'd played a trick on him.

"You sat on one of the jets. They're for massaging your muscles."

Judging by the way he rubbed his butt, he'd gotten more of an enema than a massage. I couldn't blame him for being offended.

"Here, sit down." I patted the bench beside me to make sure there weren't any jets on it—he must have sat on a lounging seat designed to massage calves—then pulled him down.

He let me, fortunately putting his lower half under the surface, and settled beside me. Sort of. He felt the jets pushing at his back and kept adjusting himself. It was amusing seeing all the goofy facial expressions on someone who usually wore a hard mask that was either full of arrogance and indignation or simply difficult to read.

Finally finding an acceptable position, he looked at me, his shoulder brushing mine. The touch sent an electric tingle along my nerves, and my thought that this might not be a good idea returned. Though the goblins probably *would* believe we were suitably distracted now.

His expression had returned to its usual, harder masked mien, and I had no idea what he was thinking. But I steeled myself for the conversation we needed to have.

"You are not attracted to me, right?" I asked.

He blinked. That must not have been the topic he expected me to bring up.

"Correct," he said.

"And you don't want to *skylitha* me, right?"

"Correct."

"And I'm not attracted to you and don't want to *skylitha* you."

His eyebrows drifted upward. "You do not?"

"Of course not. You're arrogant, you've tried to use me, and you wanted to kill me the first time we met."

"But it would be a great honor for you to have a dragon mate. Many males and females from lesser species attempt to get dragons to shape-shift into their form so they can seduce them."

"That's not going to happen here. That kiss was Dob *making* me try to seduce you. I assume you know that." I hoped he believed that, anyway. If he were human, he wouldn't, not after catching me peeping at him.

He gazed at me now, his face only a few inches from mine, as if he were trying to discern the truth. Maybe he couldn't believe that some mongrel Earthling girl wouldn't want him.

"Why do you bring up this subject?" he asked.

"Because you got huffy when that guy hit on me. You don't have the right to get in the way of any relationships I may want to pursue with men, simply because you're in the area. I don't know why you would care, anyway, unless you've been lying to me and you're having secret fantasies about getting horizontal with me."

"It is improper and a sign of disrespect for another male to attempt to *skylitha* a female who is with me. It would not matter if you were my sister, my offspring, or my mate. A male dragon is a warrior, trained from birth to use magic and fight when necessary to defend the females in the clan. They are the rulers among our kind. Many are very powerful and capable fighters themselves, but it is our role to protect them and keep the peace, if that is their wish, or fly into war, if that is their wish."

Huh, a matriarchal society? I believed what he was telling me, but it was hard for me to grasp that his behavior hadn't been more possessive than protective. Maybe that was my human way of interpreting things and it couldn't be applied to him, but...

"You got huffy when I was talking to Thad, too, and I know he doesn't want to *skylitha* with me."

"That is incorrect. He had sexual desire for you."

"No, you're wrong. We've been divorced a long time, and he has a new girlfriend."

"As I said, I can see the thoughts of humans, of the men around you.

They do not *all* desire you, but many do." He smirked. "Those who don't mind a challenging female with a tongue as sharp as her sword."

"You'd think that would cut things down a lot."

I should have been dwelling on what the revelation about Thad meant, but I was busy being aware of Zav looking at me, of his face so close to mine, of the way his eyes gleamed, even when they didn't light up, when he smiled. Or smirked. His humor—he'd promised me once that dragons had senses of humor—was on display, and it made him more appealing. It would be easy to shift over and kiss him, but there wasn't another dragon around for me to blame it on this time. And I wasn't going to give in to his assumption that all *lesser* species wanted to seduce dragons. Please.

"I guess it's good that *you* don't feel that way," I said. "How embarrassing would it be for you to be caught in bed with some mongrel from Earth?"

"Dragons do not care what other dragons do for meaningless recreation." He shifted his arm out of the water and rested it on the edge behind me, his chest turning more fully toward me. A faint furrow creased the skin between his eyebrows. "My kin would not approve if I chose a *mate* from a lesser species. That would be cause for familial embarrassment."

"I bet. Those lesser species from the wrong side of the tracks. A plague to families throughout the galaxy." I thought about moving away from him and his arm. I also thought about scooting closer. If I slipped into his lap, I'd find out for sure if he was attracted to me. Right now, his lips were saying one thing and his eyes were saying something else. He wasn't looking away from me, though his gaze occasionally dipped to my mouth or my chest—funny how boobs tended to float in bubbling water—and I felt like a mouse in the hawk's sights.

"Is that something you've contemplated before? Dob said something about an elf."

Zav hadn't been moving much, but he froze at that. A long frosty moment passed, and I got a chill even in the hot water.

"It was not his place to do so," Zav said.

"What happened?"

Would he tell me? I shifted toward him, attempting to look curious and guileless. Which I truly was.

For the first time, he turned his gaze toward the distant lake instead of me. "I was sent as an ambassador to the home world of the elves and lived several moons among them in their form. The king's eldest daughter spent much time with me, showing me around, teaching me elven ways, and flirting with me. More than that. She seduced me. I believed she desired me and had no reason to suspect anything malicious, but as with you, and with many of the more powerful elves, I could not read her surface thoughts. And I had no reason to force my way deep into her mind. I was attracted to her and cared for her, inasmuch as one can a lesser species."

I snorted. "You're not exactly the material of romance novels, you know."

"So you've told me before. Because I lack money."

"Trust me, that's not the only reason."

He frowned at me. "I did not think you would bring your blade into this place of relaxation."

I glanced toward the bench—the forgotten bench—and was relieved to find my gear still there, but then I realized he was referring to my tongue, not Chopper.

"Sorry, but it's your arrogance that brings out my *blade*. I can't resist the urge to let you know that the galaxy doesn't revolve around you."

"You are a strange female."

"Yes, I am."

"Other beings take the greatness of dragons for granted."

"How lovely for them. What happened with the princess that you cared for inasmuch as one can a lesser species?"

Zav shook his head, and I feared I'd put him on the defensive. I wasn't good at quiet, vulnerable moments with guys—or anyone—and even if he was being his arrogant self, I regretted pointing it out. I wanted to hear the rest of the story. Maybe this had to do with why he didn't trust me.

"Did the elf princess betray you?" I lifted my arm and rested it next to his—only because I was getting warm in the hot water.

"Yes." His gaze shifted toward the lake again, his eyes unfocused. "She almost succeeded in assassinating me. It was not our first night together. I would have been more on guard if it were. But we were a few weeks into an invigorating relationship."

"Invigorating?" I mouthed but did not say aloud.

"I'd even spoken of her to my mother and brother. Perhaps unwisely since they both counseled me to stick to my kind. They were right." His mouth twisted. "She drugged me at dinner one night, putting something that affects elves in a beverage not dissimilar to what was in those bottles you gave me." He turned a sharp eye toward me.

Hell, how was I supposed to have known someone had poisoned him with wine once?

"Since I was in elven form, I was somewhat susceptible to what affects them. I believe she thought I was completely susceptible. We proceeded to have sex and as I dozed off, she planted a small device on my chest and turned on its magic. It had the power to stop a heart instantly. Even a dragon heart. My kind are feared throughout the Cosmic Realms, and lesser beings have put great effort into creating artifacts that can harm us, even kill us. Many of them want to end our rule and get rid of us forever."

His voice had turned understandably cold, and my earlier humor evaporated as a tendril of fear wound through me. What if he believed I might be in on some plan like that? Or that I might one day be tempted by an entreaty from one of his enemies?

But I felt affronted on his behalf that this female elf had feigned feelings for him only to get close enough to kill him. I reached up to touch the back of his head, not sure if I meant it as an apology or a soothing gesture, but I was lousy with words when it came to comforting people. So I stroked his soft, short curly hair, the strands damp from the spray of the water.

He didn't pull away. He continued his story, barely seeming to notice. "She almost succeeded. I was not as sleepy as she believed, and I knocked the device away in time. Elsewhere among the Realms, other elves had been taking part in similar schemes. It was the eve of war, one they believed they could win if they took out key warriors among the dragons. They had no chance. Even though other elves succeeded in killing a few dragons with their vile assassinations, their people were divided. Not all of them wanted war with us—the smart ones knew better than to upset the natural order of the universe—and we persevered. We defeated those who stood against us, and we backed another elven family to rule over their kind. But there were losses. Among them, one of my brothers. It was a beautiful siren who seduced him, manipulated and paid to do so by one of the elf insurgents. She succeeded at the assassination. *That* is why I do not trust those whose minds I cannot read."

His eyes were intense when they turned again toward me, and he lifted his hand to capture my wrist. He moved my hand from his hair, bringing it down between us.

I'd meant to comfort him, not make him suspicious of me, but maybe that wasn't something he would ever accept from a *lesser* being. And I was way lesser. Not even a full-blooded elf but some wandering elf's by-blow.

This was about him, not me, but I couldn't help feeling a twinge of indignation. "Fine by me, but know this, Zav. If I ever decide we're enemies, I'll come after you openly and with my sword, not with some wussy seduction routine and magical gizmo."

"You would be foolish to challenge a dragon face to face."

"I think we've established that I'm no genius." I hadn't meant that to come out quite so… self-derogatory, and I grimaced.

He chuckled and rubbed his thumb across the back of my hand. That little gesture shouldn't have sent a jolt of pleasure through me, but it did. Only my own dignity, what remained of it, kept me from scooting closer.

Why did he stay so close and ooze animal magnetism at me when he wanted nothing to do with me?

"It would also be foolish of me to allow myself to be attracted to an elf again. Even a half-elf." He was still holding my wrist, still tracing the tendons of my hand with his thumb.

"Then it's good that you aren't. Keeps things simpler that way, right?"

"Yes."

Why didn't I believe my honest dragon? I peered frankly into his eyes, as if I could read *his* mind.

It wasn't a good idea. I wouldn't have guessed I would be as attracted to him when he was dampening down his dragon aura and I didn't feel the usual tingle of his power crackling over my flesh. But those eyes of his were still appealing, and it was hard to forget that he was risking his reputation and maybe his family's standing to protect me from his peers. Why would he do that? We'd fought together, yes, and maybe bonded in a way, but I wasn't one of his kind. Surely, I'd been more of a pest to him than a loyal ally.

That made me feel like a heel and want to apologize to him for giving him a hard time. He was putting his assignment on hold to be here in another state with me, keeping Shaygor away. His family wouldn't approve, and if Shaygor was paying attention, he might figure out the truth.

I needed to get out of this hot tub now before I did something stupid. Something that would make him suspicious of me, since anything potentially bordering on seduction would ignite alarms in his head. That whole incident with Dob in the water plant must have brought bad memories flooding back for him.

I started to scoot back, deciding we would have to figure out another way to lure in the goblins, but his grip tightened on my wrist. For the first time that night, his eyes flared with inner light, and a hint of his aura seeped out, that familiar aching tingle raising goosebumps as it sped along my nerves.

The arm that had been on the edge came around my shoulders, drawing me back close to him.

"Stay," he growled. I couldn't tell if there was a magical compulsion in the command, but it sent a thrill of desire through me, and I longed to obey.

My heart pounded in my chest and my voice was on the squeaky side when I asked, "Whatcha doing?"

"Being foolish."

He pulled me into his lap, crushing my breasts against his chest and pressing his mouth to mine. Molten fire roared through my veins, and I flung my arms around him. Sane thoughts scattered from my mind, and all I could think about was how good this felt—and that he'd been lying to me earlier. He might not *want* to be attracted to me, but his body clearly was. Bodies didn't lie. And as he kissed me, his hands roaming my naked flesh, I knew he'd never believe me again if I tried to pretend that I wasn't attracted to him. To hell with it. We could figure things out in the morning.

No sooner had I made the decision than Zav turned his face away from mine. I protested, nipping at his ear and hoping to draw him back.

Goblins, he spoke into my mind.

Damn it, my trap. I shoved my libido aside and scrambled out of the water. The bench was close enough for me to see the green three-foot-tall figure pulling the artifact out of my backpack. I lunged for him, but he was faster. He leaped over the deck railing and sprinted across the dark lawn.

Chapter 22

The bottoms of my feet were as wet as the rest of me, and I slipped on the deck as I tried to spring over the railing and after the goblin. I managed to catch myself before going down and muscled my way over and into the yard. But the goblin hadn't hit any of my traps and was already fading from my sight, using whatever camouflage magic he had activated.

"No," I snarled, then swore as I sprinted after him, furious with myself for having been distracted.

The goblin jerked to a halt as if he'd been clotheslined. He pitched backward, the artifact falling from his hands. Magical power wrapped around him, lifting him into the air.

The goblin shook his shaggy white head and called into the darkness. I didn't have my translation charm activated and didn't know what he said, but it sounded like a cry for help.

Zav strode into the yard, as naked as I was, his aura no longer diminished. The goblin's pleas for help grew weaker. I doubted any of his buddies would risk a dragon's ire to come help him, but I went back and grabbed Chopper just in case.

As I drew even with Zav, he gave me a look somewhere between exasperation and chagrin. Because we'd almost been outwitted by a goblin? No, we'd almost outwitted ourselves and the goblin had taken advantage.

"We should probably keep our clothes on in the future," I said.

"Yes," he said firmly, almost vehemently.

Even if I had proof now that Zav was attracted to me, it didn't mean he wanted to be—if his story was true, he *absolutely* didn't want to be—and I wasn't going to try to change that. I didn't want to be attracted to him either. I'd almost lost my goblin because of hormones. I *definitely* wasn't a genius.

Something brushed my shoulder, and I jumped. My clothes were dangling behind me, with Fezzik and the backpack right beside them. Zav really wanted me clothed.

"I will watch your prisoner," he said. "Dress."

"Yes, master. Right away." I grabbed my underwear.

He frowned. Probably because I was disrespecting his dragon ass again. I sighed and tried to put my disgruntlement aside. He'd told me a painful story—not just about him almost being assassinated but about a brother he'd lost—and I didn't want him to regret sharing things with me.

"I'm sorry." I tugged my shirt over my head. "But I'm going to need you to dress, too, so I'm not overcome by your masculine handsomeness."

"Your tongue is sharp even in apologies," he noted quietly.

"I know. It was honed to a razor's edge a long time ago."

The robe and boots floated over, but he let the latter clunk to the ground. "Need I put those vile things back on?"

More magic flared, healing magic this time, and the blisters on his feet disappeared, but the distasteful look he gave the boots did not.

"No. I'm not the one who told you to try them in the first place. If you want to be manly, just get some black high-tops. Or brown loafers. But nothing with tassels or we'll be back to where we started."

"High-tops." He donned his robe, fastening a seam hidden neatly in the silver trim.

The goblin was floating horizontally three feet above the grass, his head dangling back as he stared at us. If he understood English, I couldn't imagine what he thought of this conversation.

"You may question him," Zav said when I finished dressing. He sounded relieved. "If you need me to compel him to answer truthfully, I will do so."

"Uh, we'll start with the old-fashioned way."

"Torture implements?"

The goblin's eyebrows flew up.

"Yeah, I keep a complete set in my camping backpack next to my collapsible bowl and foldable cutlery."

Zav nodded, and I don't think he got that I was joking. What did dragons think of humans anyway? Besides that we were vermin?

"I'm Val," I said, walking up to the goblin. I drew Chopper, murmured the Dwarven word I'd learned to make it glow blue, and leaned the blade against a nearby landscaping boulder. The sword's light shone on the goblin's face, making his fear clear. "What's your name?"

"Gondo," he whispered, demonstrating that he understood English, but then saying a few more words in his own language.

After activating my translation charm, I continued. "I have a few questions for you, Gondo. Your people have been terrorizing the townsfolk here, and I was sent to put a stop to it. Want to make things easy on yourself and tell me why you've been taking out roads and smashing up people's houses?"

"You have a dragon for a mate," he breathed.

"We're not mates. We're…" I spread my hand toward Zav. Would he find it presumptuous if I said we were allies? He merely lifted his eyebrows, as if wondering how I would designate us. "We're working together this month."

Gondo glanced toward the hot tub, and I blushed. Damn it, fearsome assassins did *not* blush when interrogating enemies.

"It is not fair," Gondo said. "Work Leader Nogna didn't say anything about dragons. She said this would be easy."

"What exactly would be easy?"

Gondo shook his head and flailed, trying uselessly to escape the magic that held him aloft. He did manage to flip himself over, but that only made him dangle facedown with nothing but grass and my boots to look at.

"Will you be punished if you tell me?" I squatted down so I could see his face and rested my elbows on my thighs.

"No, but I'll be the weak link in the chain, the one who failed the labor party. Sunga said we should postpone our activities until you left and give up the artifact, but we can't control them without the *yub-yun*." He waved toward the artifact.

"Control who? The sasquatch?"

"The shy furry ones."

"The sasquatch." The damage they'd left in that house wouldn't lead people to think the sasquatch were shy, but if the goblins had been controlling them…

"It was their idea, but they weren't willing to go near humans or break anything on their own."

"Wait, the sasquatch clan had an idea? They can, uh, think independently? And make plans?" I glanced at Zav, wondering if he was reading the goblin's thoughts and could verify this.

But his gaze was focused on the sky to the north, and he didn't look over. If the goblin hadn't remained suspended in the air, I would have thought he wasn't paying attention at all.

"They're smart enough to make plans," Gondo said. "Smart enough to have not appreciated us finding and encroaching on their magically protected territory, but they're peaceful. They didn't want to make war with us. And we're not warriors either. We just want a safe place to live and raise our children. We—"

"Shaygorthian has left this area." Zav turned to face me. "He will not answer me. I do not know what he is up to, but it likely has to do with you."

"Which way did he go?"

Not north, I urged silently. Not north. The cloaking charm suddenly weighed heavily on my necklace.

"He flew across the lake toward the northwest. He may be returning to your city."

Seattle was west from our location, not northwest, but I hoped Zav was right. Maybe Shaygor wanted to investigate the place where Dob had died. So long as he didn't head up to Sandpoint to look for Amber.

"He may attempt to question your allies about the night of the battle. I will follow him and learn where he is going." Zav looked at the goblin. "Can you detain and question that one on your own?"

"Yes. He's being a reasonable goblin thus far."

"There are others out there. Be wary."

"I can handle some goblins. Thank you. You be wary of Shaygor."

"Yes." Zav shifted form and took off, the wind from the flapping of his wings enough to toss my damp braid around.

Sensing his magic leaving, I summoned Sindari and grabbed Chopper, resting the blade on the goblin's collarbone. Instead of dropping to the ground, Gondo floated down and had time to settle himself on his feet. He crouched, glancing toward the dark woods across the trail, and I tapped the sword against his shoulder to remind him it was there.

When Sindari formed, his head higher than the goblin's, my captive's shoulders sank, and he seemed to give up the idea of escape, at least for now.

More goblins? Sindari asked, prowling around to sit behind Gondo, more incentive for him to stay put. *Their world must have become extra unappealing of late.*

Maybe due to an influx of dragons.

Possible.

"You wanted a place to raise your kids, Gondo," I said. "Were you thinking of the town of Harrison, by chance?"

He shook his shaggy white-haired head. "Not at first. We wanted to live in the forests here. Our shamans sensed old magic that elves had created and left in place long ago, and we thought we might hide and build our community there, but the sasquatch were already making their homes in the mists. They were friendly to us and let us stay for a time, but they made it clear there was not room for both of us. Our work leaders knew of the nearby town and thought… what if we could convince the humans to leave and claim the place for goblins? Our shamans studied the elven mists protecting the sasquatch and thought they could weave something similar around the town to make visitors forget about it with time. It would be difficult—though so much easier if we knew a dragon." He gazed longingly in the direction Zav had flown. "He could easily hide an entire city from humans. But the humans would have to leave first. Nobody would be fooled if they were living there. We thought if they were scared and chose to go, the town could be forgotten. Especially if there were no roads remaining to it. It has been difficult for us to achieve our goals. With a dragon ally, it would be so simple."

I'd never seen anyone look longingly after Zav before. "Aren't dragons the reason you had to leave your world?"

"Not that dragon. He is Stormforge Clan, yes? His kind have never preyed on goblins. They are indifferent to goblins, but in realms full of beings who would exploit us, force us aside, or hunt us outright—as if we are dumb animals—indifference isn't that bad. Most of us would be pleased by indifference."

"I get that you're trying to find a place you can stay in this world, but you can't take over a human town. And you can't—" I grabbed the artifact and held it up, "—use magical devices to control an entire species of animal or race of people, whatever they are."

Gondo pouted, green lips turned out.

"That *is* what this is for, isn't it? And why you came back to get it? Without it, you can't force the sasquatch to do your bidding."

"Nobody is afraid of goblins. We needed their help."

"Well, you're not getting this back."

He lifted a hand toward it and stepped forward. Sindari growled, and Gondo halted.

"Our shamans spent many moons making the *yub-yun* and instilling it with power. You have no right to take it."

"I do if you're using it to control beings in my world."

"Nobody has been hurt."

"Millions of dollars in property damage has been done."

"You still have no right to steal our artifact." Gondo lifted his chin. "Or has the Ruin Bringer no honor? Did you steal that dwarven sword you carry? It is also not from this world."

I didn't like the turn of this conversation.

Sindari gazed at me over the goblin's head without commenting. He didn't agree, did he? I didn't want to bully the goblins who'd spent their whole lives, if not their entire evolution as a species, being bullied, but I couldn't give the artifact back and let them continue with their plan.

"I suppose throwing it in the lake won't work," I muttered.

It wasn't like I wanted to take the thing back and put it on my wall for the next home intruder to steal.

Perhaps you should consult your employer, Sindari suggested.

It's almost midnight. She's probably asleep under her cat.

I have seen you contact her during off hours before.

These are off, off hours.

But he had a point. Willard was more of a diplomat than I—who wasn't?—and she *had* said to call about this.

I dug out my phone. Gondo threw a few more glances into the

woods. I couldn't hear or detect anyone out there, but that had been the case with the goblins this entire time. For all I knew, there were a hundred of them out there watching us.

"The only socially acceptable reason to call at this hour," Willard answered groggily, "is to announce a birth or death. Are you dead, Val?"

"No."

I was debating how to fit the artifact problem into one of those two categories when she spoke again.

"I would also allow you to wake me at this hour to announce a wedding," Willard said. "Are you getting married?"

"Who would I marry?"

"I thought you were making progress with your dragon."

"You've got this elaborate fantasy concocted, and I have no idea where it's coming from." I pointedly did not look toward the hot tub or bring up the case of wine I'd given Zav.

"Hm. What do you want then?"

I explained the goblin problem and asked what I should do with Gondo and the artifact.

"Are you actually calling me for advice instead of running in with guns blazing and mowing down enemies?"

"These goblins aren't exactly the hardened murderers you usually send me after." At least I didn't think so. I caught Gondo's gaze and narrowed my eyes at him. "Have you killed anyone during your schemes and shenanigans?"

"No." He lifted his hands innocently.

"Have the sasquatch you're controlling killed anyone?"

"No."

"Would you tell me if you were lying?"

He opened his mouth to answer promptly but surprised me by pausing to consider his response. "No," he finally said.

That actually made me inclined to trust him, but that didn't solve my problem.

"Can't you just tell them to knock it off?" Willard asked.

"And give them back their artifact?" I asked.

She hesitated. "That's probably not a good idea."

"So we're stealing it."

"Confiscating it."

"In the name of a government and legal system that doesn't recognize them as citizens or even people?"

"You've changed, Val."

"My therapist brought up some interesting points. And my mom suggested I should try helping magical beings instead of always shooting them." The goblin looked hopeful, or maybe that was his scheming expression, so I scowled, putting on a tough face, and added, "*Sometimes*, you have to shoot them. But maybe not always."

"What do you want from me?" Willard sounded tired.

"Maybe you should come out here. You could host a meeting. Talk to the goblins and figure out... something. Right now, they're difficult to find, but maybe they would talk to someone who isn't the Ruin Bringer and who can offer them some solutions."

"What solutions can I offer them? I'm just a soldier."

"If nothing else, you can draw them a map to Canada. There are a lot more forests up there."

Willard snorted. "*You* could do that."

"You're a neutral third party." Sensing her objection, I added, "If you come out, I'll tell you about the hot tub."

"What hot tub?"

"The hot tub where I was naked with Zav." I pointed the phone at Gondo. "It's true, isn't it?"

Gondo's face screwed up, his bulbous nose twitching. Maybe he didn't know if he wanted the unknown-to-him Willard to come out. "I'm not certain. I thought it was earnest mating, but then you captured me. You may have been faking."

"Fake mating?" Willard must have heard him well enough. "How does that work?"

"You'll have to come here to find out."

"I'll see what I can push around tomorrow. You better have some goblins for me to talk to when I get there."

"I'll work on it."

"I'll bring a swimming suit for this hot tub."

"You're not expecting a dragon in it, are you?"

"No, that's your dragon. But feel free to find me a hunky man."

"I'll see what I can do." I'd mostly seen flabby tourists so far in town, unless she would consider the Yosemite Sam cowboy desirable.

I hung up and looked at Gondo, wondering how I could talk him into bringing the rest of his goblin buddies out to meet with Willard.

"*I* am hunky." He puffed out his chest.

"Uh, sure you are."

"Human females are interesting. They are tall and often their biologically intriguing parts are—" he grinned mischievously and made cupping motions with his hands, "—larger."

"If you hit on Willard, she'll smack you into Canada. Which, come to think of it, might solve all our problems."

"What is Canada?"

Zav speaking telepathically interrupted my answer. *He is not flying toward your city. He is going north toward a small town on another lake.*

My humor evaporated. *Sandpoint?*

I do not know the names of your cities. There is a large mountain near it.

Sandpoint. My daughter was taken there. He might be after her. Would he be able to track her by scent?

By magic, perhaps. When he saw her before, he may have used his power to mark her.

Shit, Zav. I'm going to drive up there. If you can keep him from getting her… I'd really appreciate it.

How long will it take you to drive?

I scowled. Even if the roads hadn't been jacked up, the route wasn't direct. It would have taken close to two hours. *A while,* I admitted. *But I'll be there as soon as I can.*

Sindari whirled to face the darkness, and Gondo lunged, almost escaping. I sprang and grabbed him by the scruff of the neck, raising Chopper threateningly. Dozens and dozens of goblins crept across the trail and into the yard. They were armed with bows and magical artifacts that they held up toward me like a priest might hold crosses toward a vampire.

I stared bleakly at them. I did not need this grief now. All I wanted was to toss Gondo aside, jump in the car, and get on the road. But dozens of goblins now stood between me and my vehicle, and they didn't look like they were in the mood to negotiate.

Chapter 23

Do we attack them? Sindari sounded more uncertain than daunted as he eyed the dozens of armed goblins. Not much daunted him.

I don't know. They're criminals, but they're petty criminals, as far as we know, not murderers and rapists.

If they murder you, I shall ruthlessly slay them.

Thank you.

Light flared in the driveway, and a goblin with a blowtorch stepped forward and hurled a burning brand. The flames danced with far more vigor than would have been possible on normal wood, and I sensed magic as it sailed toward me.

His—no, that was a female goblin—aim was good, and it would have hit me in the face, but I knocked it aside with Chopper. It landed on the lawn, the grass damp enough that it didn't burn. But the brand didn't smolder and go out. It flared even brighter, flames reaching up higher than my waist. I didn't take my eyes off the goblins.

Gondo surged forward, trying again to escape, but I tightened my grip on the back of his shirt and kept him from taking more than a step. I didn't want to negotiate by using a hostage, but he—and the artifact—might be the only reason they weren't yet attacking.

"Who's your work leader?" I called.

More brands came flying out of the night. These weren't directed at me. They landed all around the yard, including on the dock.

Thinking of Thad's damage deposit, I asked Sindari to watch Gondo and ran over to kick the brand into the water. It sizzled as it hit, then floated and kept burning. Handy magic.

Goblins didn't need light to see, so they were sending me a message. That they could burn this place down?

When I returned, Sindari had flattened Gondo—I assumed the goblin had tried to escape again—and was using a front paw to keep him pressed facedown into the grass. The rest of the goblins had crept closer, several stepping off the driveway and into the yard.

Sindari growled and crouched as if he would spring. Maybe he would.

"Who's your leader?" I asked again. "*My* leader is coming out to talk to you all in the morning, so if we could put this meeting on pause until then, that would be great." Even better if they would let me get to my Jeep so I could find Amber before it was too late.

"The Mythic Murderer is an enemy of all magical beings," an older female goblin called, "and now you steal our valuable artifact and capture one of our workers." She lifted her arms like a preacher in a movie, bracelets jangling on her wrists—or were those bicycle chains decorated with bottlecaps?

"So you're the work leader?"

"I am Work Leader Nogna."

"Good to know. Your people have been terrorizing this town and using innocent animals to scare the inhabitants. FYI, I'm not the bad guy here."

Gondo squirmed and cried out dramatically.

I swatted Sindari on the flank. *Less pressure, please.*

The pressure is minimal, and my claws are retracted. He's being dramatic.

Of course we had to capture a thespian goblin.

"Let's talk about what you're trying to accomplish," I said, focusing on Nogna. Instead of a bow or blowtorch, she wore a tool bag slung across her chest. Maybe that was a sign of importance among the goblins. Bows for minions, wrenches for power players.

Two of the goblins stepped in front of her, as if my attention itself was a threat, and fired bows. I tensed, prepared to spring behind the nearby boulder, but with all the fires, there was enough light to calculate the trajectories of their arrows. They plunked into the grass, one to Sindari's side, one to my side.

He growled again, muscles coiling as he readied himself to attack.

"Wait," I whispered.

If one of those arrows sailed directly toward us, I would agree with attacking—and I'd run for cover and take out Fezzik. But so far, the goblins were shooting warning shots.

"My tiger is losing his patience," I called. "Negotiate with us, Nogna, or get off the lawn and go back to where you came from."

"*Work Leader* Nogna," one of the bowmen growled.

"Yeah, yeah."

"Give Gondo the artifact and release him, and we'll spare your life," Nogna said.

"That's not how it works." Since Sindari had Gondo, I didn't need my hands free, so I pulled out Fezzik, putting the big pistol in my left hand. I kept Chopper in my right. I'd trained hard to be ambidextrous with the weapons and would have no problem putting both to use on the goblins if necessary. "I don't cave to threats, and when I get backed into a corner, I fight like a banshee."

A few of the goblins glanced backward, toward the wooded slope and the road beyond. The headlights of a car—multiple cars—flickered through the trees as the vehicles turned down the driveway.

The goblins scattered off the pavement. A few of them looked at the dark trail as an escape option.

"Do we run?" one of the goblins asked in his own language.

"We can't leave Gondo."

More cars turned down the driveway. Big SUVs were in the lead, a couple of them with racks of lights on the top. County law enforcement? How had the townsfolk figured out the goblins were here? Ah, there was a fire truck too. Someone must have seen the burning brands from a house on one of the other points.

Gondo squirmed again, but Sindari didn't release him.

The SUVs stopped, and grim-faced deputies stepped out in full body armor. The sheriff looked at me, but most of the men spread out, pointing firearms at the goblins.

"Are these the freaks that have been terrorizing our town?" the sheriff demanded.

"Apparently," I said, choosing my words carefully, "they're looking for a new place to live."

I was surprised the local authorities had figured out the goblin connection and weren't blaming the sasquatch—or *just* the sasquatch—but they'd had longer to dig into things than I had.

"Not *our* place." The sheriff waved his men forward, and more jumped out of vehicles—vehicles now blocking the driveway and my escape from this place. "Disarm them, and if they resist, *shoot* them."

The goblins backed away from them as more firearms came to bear. They might have scattered into the trees, if they'd been willing to risk running across the trail and past the SUVs and officers, but they glanced at Gondo and the artifact, as if they wouldn't go without them.

One unwise goblin fired a bow at one of the vehicles. The arrow sank into a tire. One of the deputies fired at him. He sprang to the side, but I heard the round pierce flesh, and the goblin groaned, dropping his bow in the grass.

All the other goblins scattered down the bank toward the water or under the deck of the house. Some even flung themselves between the legs of a few men and under their SUVs.

A tingle of magic touched my nerves, and I sensed them disappearing from sight, all except a few who were close enough for me to see. If I could see them, the authorities could too.

"Get them," snarled the sheriff.

"Wait." I sheathed my weapons and walked toward the men with my hands up. Hopefully, not like a six-foot-tall ambulatory target. "I'm not sure what brought you over here, but I'm already in the process of arresting them."

The sheriff squinted suspiciously at me. "Who are you? Didn't I see you at the attack in town last night?"

"I'm Val Thorvald. I work for the army, the special operations office in Seattle that handles all things and beings magical." I held up a finger, dug into the pocket with my credit-card holder, and very quickly showed them my military ID. Never mind that it was a veteran's ID and got me little more than discounts at the movie theater. The lighting was poor, and I snapped the case shut before they could see much.

"This isn't Seattle."

"Careful," one of the men in back whispered, one with a hint of magical blood. "She's got a sword."

"I don't see any sword," another said.

"And a gun."

The men around him shook their heads.

"Also, you guys know that's a big-ass tiger over there in the shadows, right?"

"I think that's a dog."

"That's *not* a dog."

"This isn't Seattle," I agreed, ignoring the chatter in the back, "but we've been researching these goblins for some time." I'd been out here a whole three days. "We believe they're related to a clan in our area, out near Duvall, that's been causing trouble." I silently apologized to the Duvall goblins—they'd caused only minimal trouble and been preyed on by a dragon. "If this clan is related to the other, I'm going to arrest them and deal with them the way we deal with all troublemaking magical beings."

"By shooting them?"

"Exactly so." I thought that would be more likely to move them than talk of slapping them on the wrists and recruiting them as informants, which was more Willard's MO for thieves and vandals. Granted, these guys were doing more vandalism than usual, but... "I can deal with them—I was *about* to deal with them—and get them out of your hair, so your people can rebuild your town and the roads into it without trouble."

I sure hoped I could do that. Or, more precisely, that Willard could. If not, we'd have a lot to answer for when vandalism started up again. But I thought Willard could find a place to relocate these goblins, somewhere less inhabited. If they were willing to stick around and listen to her offer.

"You got someone I can call who has a *real* military ID?" the sheriff asked.

"As a matter of fact, I do." I carefully dug out my phone, pulled up Willard's contact information, and walked over to show it to him. She was already awake, so what was one more call tonight?

He jumped when I was close enough that he could see through the magic that hid my weapons from mundane humans. "Shit, you *do* have a sword."

"And a gun," the man in the back repeated.

"What kind of loon runs around with a sword?"

"One who needs a magical weapon that can kill vampires, werewolves, wyverns, rocs, and other beings who occasionally get the urge to prey on humans. Here's her number."

Thankfully, the sheriff didn't refute the existence of any of those beings. I would be shocked if the county authorities here hadn't encountered any—and they were looking at goblins, including one peering out from between the tires next to us. The goblin who'd been shot had crawled across the lawn and disappeared near the water.

I shifted from foot to foot, looking to the northern sky and worrying about Amber, as the man called Willard. This was taking too long, and even if it worked and they left me alone, what was I supposed to do with these goblins? There was no way I would stay here all night holding them instead of going to check on my daughter.

"Are you *sure* we can't just shoot them, Colonel? They're not human." The sheriff had moved away from me to make the call. It sounded like he got a lecture in response. He rolled his eyes several times.

Would he accept her as someone with authority over the magical and back off? It wasn't as if there was anything official on the books. The Seattle Police Department usually handed off magical problems to her office—with glee—and she had connections in the neighboring states and British Columbia, but I had no idea if she had any authority out here.

"If they're not gone by tomorrow night, or if anything else happens to our town, it's going to be open season on those freaks."

Willard's response was terse, and she hung up first. The sheriff pocketed his phone and glowered at me.

"I have something of theirs that they want back," I said. "They'll deal with me."

"Your boss said she's driving over and will be here in six hours."

Willard wouldn't be happy about making that drive in the middle of the night. She'd probably planned to wait until morning and catch a flight to Spokane. Still, I would be glad to hand the goblins off to her sooner.

"We'll get everything straightened out then." Not that I planned to stick around. With luck, I might find Amber and get back before Willard arrived, but I couldn't count on that.

"You better. I wasn't joking. If I see these short green freaks messing up our roads or towns again, I'm going to shoot without asking questions."

I shrugged as if I didn't care. "It's your county."

"*Thank* you for noticing that. You want us to leave some men?"

I was about to say no, but it wasn't as if I'd truly had things under control when they'd arrived. "Maybe on the road up there. I'm going to round them up with my tiger, but if any stragglers get away…"

That was more for the sake of the goblin listening from under the SUV—I hoped it was one of their leaders and that he or she wasn't positive their camouflage was working well.

"Fine. Don't screw this up."

"Your pinpoint advice is noted," I said dryly.

The sheriff looked like he wanted to argue with me, or maybe deliver a nice lecture, but I sensed that he and his people didn't *really* want to deal with the goblins. They'd probably been trying to round them up for the last week with no luck.

"Mount up," he ordered his men, like some wrangler in a cowboy movie.

When the SUV next to me drove away, there was no sign of the goblin that had been hiding under it. I walked back to Sindari, glad he still had Gondo and that I still had the artifact in my backpack. Maybe that would be enough to bring the goblins back out.

That man called me a dog, Sindari said. *Are humans blind?*

"We like to put strange things into categories that we can understand."

You have *tigers in this world, albeit puny, dumb ones. And did you call me strange?*

The tigers here are orange and don't hang out on people's lawns. A couple of goblins came up from the bank, and I sheathed Chopper to appear less intimidating.

Because of my current location, I'm flummoxing?

Humans need a lot of context to label things.

How odd that your species has become the dominant force on this world.

Tell me about it. Not for the first time, I wondered how much education his people received. He'd once joked about math teachers with me, so I assumed they had something akin to our school system, but there had to be a limit to how complex of problems they could solve without writing anything down.

Questions for another time. I waved to the goblins, trying to encourage them all to come over.

My Jeep was no longer blocked in, so I could leave as soon as I figured out how to get these guys to stick around for Willard. Capturing them, tying them up, and putting them in the kitchen was unlikely to work. Goblins were as good at escaping from traps as they were at setting them up. And there was probably a house rule about tying people up on the property.

Since only a handful of them had appeared, and they were eyeing each other warily, I pulled out the artifact. Time to be blunt.

"If you want this back, I'm going to need some cooperation. My boss is coming out to talk to your leaders and hopefully find you someplace where you can live that doesn't involve chasing citizens out of their own town."

They regarded each other with some interest. Nogna and her bicycle-chain bracelets were visible in the back.

"But you need to agree to stick around until she gets here. It'll be about six hours. Around dawn," I added, realizing none of them wore watches or carried cell phones. "If you work things out with her, I'll give this back to you."

"And will you give us Gondo back?" Nogna asked.

"If you agree to stay here tonight, yes." I hadn't planned on taking him up to Sandpoint, but they didn't need to know that.

A male I recognized as the shaman who'd helped the goblin escape the night before appeared, trotting out of the darkness, and ran up to whisper something to Nogna. Hopefully not that I was heinous and couldn't be trusted because I'd shot his buddy. He'd filled my calves with thorns first.

"I see. I had wondered about that." Nogna considered me.

I shifted my weight, fingered my car keys, and silently urged her to agree to my terms.

"You assisted goblins to the west not long ago." It didn't sound like a question.

"The ones being chased by hunters?" I hadn't had any other dealings with goblins recently. "Yes."

"We will accept your word that you will return our artifact to us if we wait to speak to your work leader. We will wait tonight in that structure." She pointed to the house, and I envisioned goblins all over the place, raiding the pantry, lounging on the furniture, and watching Nick at Nite.

But I was in too much of a hurry to object. I would have to offer to pay Thad for any damage they caused.

"I agree." I waved for Sindari to release Gondo.

As soon as he lifted his paw, the goblin rolled away, leaped to his feet, and stumbled to his leader's side.

I was already heading toward my Jeep, but I halted and stared in horror. Someone's wayward arrow stuck out of the front tire, and it was half-deflated.

Chapter 24

There was a spare tire on the back of the Jeep, but I snarled at this new delay and furiously ripped out the arrow and snapped it in half. As I opened the back door to hunt for the jack, Zav's aura came onto my radar.

Why was he coming back? I thought he'd been going after Shaygor.

What happened? I blurted in my mind, though I doubted he was paying attention to my thoughts yet.

The goblins must have sensed him coming, too, because they hurried into the house, slamming the door behind them. They weren't camouflaged now, and I saw at least three dozen green bodies disappearing inside. That damage deposit was in serious trouble.

I came to retrieve you, Zav replied calmly, then added more sternly, *You are not wearing your cloaking charm.*

Because I've been negotiating with goblins. Where's Shaygor? He flew north? I thought you'd try to stop him.

I will do so, but you will come assist me. Your offspring will fear me as much as Shaygorthian if I attempt to interact with her, and you have been helpful in the past.

So helpful. Maybe he can compel me to attack you the way Dob did. Despite the words, I dismissed Sindari, promising to call him back when it was time to battle Shaygor, and ran out into the yard to wait for Zav to land. As long as he was here, I wouldn't object to a ride, since he could get me there much faster than I could drive, but I worried that nobody was up there now, preventing Shaygor from hunting down my family.

You resisted Dobsaurin's compulsion, Zav said.

Not the first time. I had been nothing but a liability to him in that water-treatment plant, and I hated it.

You resisted it when he commanded you to kill me. Zav's dark form soared into view over the trees, and he landed in front of me. *Perhaps you found that more deplorable than the first compulsion.*

His violet eyes glowed softly—the amusement I thought I saw in them was surely my imagination.

I'm not going to respond to that, I decided.

Because you cannot object. Kissing me is undeniably more appealing than killing me.

I was just more pissed the second time. That's why I was able to resist him.

You were pissed because the second time, he did not order you to do something appealing.

Kissing you is not appealing.

He used his power to levitate me up to his back. I wanted to find Amber, not have this conversation, but since he was in the process of taking me to her, I couldn't complain.

Many females believe it is.

I'm not like many females.

This is notably true. But nobody was compelling you to kiss me in the water box. Therefore, it must be an appealing activity.

You kissed me in the hot tub. I was just being polite and going along with it.

Yes, I've often noticed how polite and respectful of dragons you are. Who would have thought Zav could make his telepathic tone so dry and sarcastic?

His powerful muscles bunched, and he sprang into the air. I flattened myself to his back, not trusting that he wouldn't lose his concentration when we did this and I would fall off.

You still haven't installed seatbelts or a saddle, I see. Maybe I could divert him from his current line of questioning.

He didn't get as affronted as he had the first time I'd brought that up. *I am still not a lowly horse or a mindless human conveyance.*

I'd die as soon as I hit the ground if I fell off, so it's a moderate concern for me.

I will not let you fall. This time, his tone was utterly serious and sincere.

I appreciated the sentiment, but it was hard for me to believe he couldn't be distracted if another dragon swooped in to do battle with him. Best not to think about it.

Tangled Truths

As we soared across the lake and toward the dark forests and farms north of it, I pulled out my phone to call Thad. I hoped nothing had happened and that he would be bewildered by my late-night contact.

But he didn't answer. Dread dropped a boulder in my stomach.

"Nothing to worry about yet," I muttered, frowning at the display. Maybe I'd dialed the wrong number. No, it was right. Maybe Thad had his phone in airplane mode for sleep.

When the phone dropped me into voice mail, I hung up and dialed again. On the fourth ring, Thad answered.

"Sorry, Val. I was on the other line." He sounded tense, a little breathless.

A second dread boulder slammed down onto the first. "With who?"

"The police here in Sandpoint. Amber disappeared out of the back yard. They were hanging out around the fire pit. Her friend saw everything and said some guy in green ran out of the woods and grabbed her."

Some guy in green. More like a dragon-masquerading-as-an-elf in green. Why hadn't Amber kept my charm?

"Your mother and the dog went after them. It just happened maybe ten minutes ago."

I swore. The only thing worse than Amber being killed would be my mother *and* Amber being killed.

"The police are on the way, but we're not right in town, so I don't know how long it will take." He sounded like he was pacing and pulling his hair out. "Max's house is by the ski resort and backs up to the woods."

"Wonderful." What a perfectly easy place for a kidnapping. There would be thousands of acres of nothing up there and probably few people around this time of year.

I laid my hand on Zav's scales, abruptly glad he'd come back for me. If I'd had to add a drive up a windy mountain road in the dark, it would have taken me even longer to arrive.

"I better go out there and catch up with your mother to help," Thad said.

"No," I said more sternly than I intended. I didn't need *him* getting killed too. "I'm on my way. *I'll* help. This is what I'm trained to do, and Mom and Rocket are trained to find people in the woods." Not that I *wanted* her to find them. Shaygor could kill Mom and Rocket with a thought. "Nobody else should be risking themselves out there."

With Thad's meager wilderness skills, he could fall into a ravine in the dark even if he never encountered Shaygor.

"What's your address?" I asked.

He gave it to me, and I plugged it into the phone, but he added, "I *have* to help, Val."

"You are helping. Wait for the police. I'll be there soon."

"I can't. Max has guns. He's getting them out of his safe. We're going after this guy."

I groaned into Zav's scales. "He's not a *guy*."

Thad hung up.

I jammed my phone into my pocket. *Shaygor has my daughter,* I thought. *He may get my mother too.*

I heard. We will be there soon.

Do you need the address to the house? Or for me to direct you? I supposed he wouldn't have a GPS navigator built into his brain, or care a whit for how houses were addressed on Earth.

I have no need for a mong— for you to direct me. I am a dragon. I can find another dragon.

Still thinking of me as some worthless mongrel, huh?

You are not worthless. But you are not a dragon.

We can't all be perfect.

No.

I closed my eyes. We were flying over city lights. Coeur d'Alene? I wanted to urge him to go faster, but this was already a much faster alternative than if I'd been forced to drive.

Besides, we needed a plan. Just showing up wouldn't work if he had Amber as a hostage. I *hoped* he had her as a hostage and that he hadn't dragged her out into the woods to kill her. But why would he? It was the information in my head that he wanted. Maybe he planned to trade her for access to my mind. The access that would condemn me—and reveal Zav as a liar.

Hm. Zav thought into my mind.

Was he listening to me mulling? *What?*

He must know that I am coming. He has diminished his aura, similar to what I did when we lured the goblins into coming to the water box.

Does that mean you can't sense him?

Not at this time. I will be able to when I get close. It is unlikely he has an artifact to help hide him, the way Dobsaurin did, because until now, I've had no difficulty locating him.

Because until now, he didn't care if you knew where he was. Now, he's doing something nefarious, and the bastard knows it.

He likely believes the law is justifying what he does. He is not a blatant rule-breaker as his son was. Though I do believe he would lie if he succeeded in killing me here.

Is he going to try to do that?

We will find out.

Can you sense Amber?

Not yet. He may also be cloaking her. I am going to travel to your mother's location. If she is within a few miles of Shaygorthian, I will be able to sense him, no matter how much he masks his aura.

How can you sense my mother? She doesn't have any magical blood.

Another cluster of city lights came into view below, a town hugging another large body of water. Sandpoint on Lake Pend Oreille? It had to be. I could see Schweitzer Mountain to the north, a few white patches of snow still clinging to the peak.

She shares your blood.

I wasn't sure that was an answer, but Zav flew over the city and arrowed down toward scattered lights on the mountainside. I'd never been to the area and wasn't familiar with it, but the lights had to represent the ski resort and nearby vacation homes. He was on the right track.

Greetings, mongrel, Shaygor purred into my mind. *You are not riding the conveyance I expected, but I cannot pretend surprise.*

I know you have my daughter, asshole. Since Sindari wasn't there to advise me to be circumspect around dragons, I felt no compulsion against cursing at Shaygor.

A dragon wouldn't let anyone but a mate ride him. This proves what I suspected before, that you have value to him... and that you may be hiding his secrets.

We're not mates. Why did you take my daughter? She hasn't done anything to you or any other dragons. Or anyone at all.

Actually, she clawed at me and scratched my cheek when I wasn't paying attention.

Good for Amber. That's not a crime, not when you're in the middle of kidnapping her.

It is a crime to assault a dragon. She is being punished.

What? I sat bolt straight, my fists clenching.

I will refrain from punishing her further, and even let her go, if you come to me. Without your faithful dragon lover. Willingly give me your thoughts, and I will have no need to keep her—or stay in this stinking cesspit of a world.

He's my ride. I can't get there without him.

Have him drop you off and leave the area. If he does not, we will attack him for obstructing justice, and, unfortunately, your offspring might be grievously injured in the battle.

I shook with anger at the threat and the admission that he'd already punished her. What had that bastard done to my daughter? Though I wanted to rage at him and pound my fists, I groped for a rational response. I had to learn as much as I could.

What do you mean we?

I mean we.

Abruptly, I sensed powerful auras on the mountaintop. Not only the familiar aura of Shaygor, but unfamiliar auras of two other dragons.

Zav had been beelining toward the treed mountainside off to the west of the parking lots and buildings of the ski resort, but he banked hard and flew parallel instead of landing.

We have a problem, he told me.

I know. Did you hear Shaygor's demands?

Yes. I was going to ignore them, but he's brought allies.

Allies loyal to him and against you?

I believe that is the definition of allies, yes, but your dictionaries change often, so I cannot be certain.

I wasn't in the mood for jokes. *Is my mother down there?*

Yes. I can smell her. She's climbing the mountain with the dog, about a mile from a clearing where the dragons are waiting with your daughter.

Is Amber alive? I trembled at the idea that I might be too late, but if she wasn't alive... I'd be a fool to do what Shaygor wanted. I'd be a fool to do it anyway, but what choice did I have? Zav might have bested Shaygor in a fight, but he couldn't take on three dragons at once.

She is, yes.

Drop me off near my mother. I'll go in alone to face Shaygor.

To what end? Your sword will not allow you victory against three dragons. They will hold you captive while he reads your thoughts, as he started to do on the road before I showed up.

I know. I wasn't delusional enough to believe I could avoid that fate.

Then he will learn that you were the one to deliver the death blow. And he will have witnesses to learn it alongside him and take the news back to the Dragon Justice Court. He will also take you back for punishment. Or he will ask them to look the other way while he kills you. Zav truly sounded aggrieved.

It touched me that he would care if I died, but better me than Amber. With luck, I could talk them into letting her go, and then… maybe somehow, I could escape while they were trying to read my mind.

I want to appear to be complying with them, I said, *but if you were to hurl some distraction at them while they're scouring my mind, I promise I'll do my best to get away.*

How will you get away from three dragons? Zav demanded, frustration in his tone.

I doubted he'd expected to find Shaygor here with allies.

I have my cloaking charm. Assuming Shaygor didn't take it right off the bat. *I'm more worried about how Amber and Mom will get away.* I would have to lead the dragons away from them… somehow.

Zav landed in a long gap between the trees—a chairlift track, the cables and posts stretching up the mountainside. I slid off his back and into waist-high grass.

This is unacceptable, Val, Zav told me. *I will go confront them and tell them what I must. Your mother is nearby. Wait with her. One way or another, I will convince them to free your offspring.*

Zav, don't. I have to appear to do what they want, or they'll hurt her. Or worse. I need you to fly off so they'll believe you're not going to help. But then make a distraction. Please.

Without answering, he sprang into the air, wings flapping as he sailed up and over the trees.

"Shit."

Chapter 25

Barks came from the trees fifty yards up the slope.

"Hello, Rocket." I ran in that direction. I could sense Shaygor and the two other dragons farther up the mountain, and it looked like the dog had been heading the right way. "Is Mom with you?"

"Val?" came her call from near one of the lift posts. "Someone has Amber."

"I know. We're going to get her." I hurried to catch up with her.

Since she had no magical blood, Mom was harder for me to detect than the dragons, but she stepped out of the shadows and surprised me with a quick hug.

"Rocket is on his trail."

"I'm sure." I pointed up the mountain. "They're that way."

"They?"

We took off at as quick a pace as we could manage in the dark. The ground under the lift was cleared of trees and brush, but there was no trail, and we couldn't sprint up the slope like I wanted.

As we drew near, the power emanating from the three dragons made me want to run in the other direction. Rocket whined and slowed his pace.

The clearing Zav had mentioned came into view ahead, loose shale covering the ground and the rocky bowl of the mountainside rising behind it. A few patches of lingering snow dotted the area. My senses told me the dragons were waiting in the open on the slope. I could barely pick out Amber among them, her aura like that of a candle burning next to three suns.

Mom drew her Glock and surged ahead, but I caught her arm.

"Stay here in the trees. I'm going to get Amber, one way or another, and I'll send her back to you. Then you take her and get off this mountain. All the way off, not just back to Thad's friend's house. Go back to Seattle with them. And then hide."

"But the man—"

"It was a dragon, Mom. A shape-shifted dragon, and he's got two buddies waiting up there." I gripped her shoulder. "I'll handle it. Stay here."

Mom swore. She'd thought she was tracking a normal kidnapper. If only that were true.

"Stay," I repeated, then drew Chopper and summoned Sindari.

I thought about camouflaging myself, but the dragons knew I was here. Besides, if I tried to sneak up on them, they might hurt Amber. I did, however, pause to remove my camouflage charm from my necklace and slip it into my pocket.

Usually, I relish it when you call me forth to do battle, Sindari said after he solidified next to me. *But you do know that three dragons are waiting ahead, don't you?*

I do. Jaw clenched with determination, I strode toward that unappealing fate.

I assume you have a plan?

I'm going to trade myself for Amber.

That's an anemic plan.

You're so diplomatic. Most people would call it a shitty plan.

I save my references to excrement for when they're truly needed.

I'm guessing that'll be in about five minutes.

Maybe three.

Yeah.

We came out of the trees, and all three dragons came into view. Shaygor, the silver dragon, was in the center, and two gold dragons flanked him. Someday, I would ask Zav if the colors denoted anything, but today, I didn't care. Amber lay crumpled on the rocky ground in front of Shaygor.

I ground my teeth in loathing as I strode toward them. They had no right to involve her in this.

Zav, either obeying my wishes or planning something of his own, felt distant to me, as if he'd flown partway down the mountain. I was both relieved and terrified to face these guys alone. But at least Shaygor couldn't accuse me of disobeying his orders.

The two gold dragons looked at each other over Shaygor's back, their eyes glowing green. They radiated so much power that fear threatened to bubble up and make me flee back down the mountainside. I kept my gaze on Amber and did not slow my pace.

You have come to let me read your thoughts, Shaygor spoke into my mind, the words perfectly understandable without my translation charm.

You and your bodyguards, I guess.

The gold dragons flexed their wings, like birds ruffling their feathers. Maybe they were monitoring my thoughts and did not approve of my snark. Like I cared.

These are my cousins. They will witness this event and report to the Dragon Justice Court.

I stopped downhill from them, the trees within a hundred yards behind me. It didn't make sense to put myself right in their reach, especially when I still had negotiating to do.

Let Amber go, and then I'll let you read my mind.

Come and let us scour your thoughts, and then we'll release her.

"That's not how it's going to work." I glared defiantly up at them.

You do not have a choice, human. Shaygor's yellow eyes flared with light, their glow eerie against the night backdrop. His dark form loomed large against the mountain behind him.

Magical energy flowed from him and wrapped around me, then lifted me into the air. I brandished Chopper, but there was no point. I couldn't reach him to use my blade.

Sindari, try to get Amber while they're distracted by me. Please.

I will. He crouched on the ground. So far, they either hadn't detected him or were ignoring him.

Take her back to my mother, and then usher them down the mountain as far as you can.

I will. If they take you to the Dragon Justice Court, summon me there. I will do my best to speak for you.

I couldn't imagine these guys letting me keep my charms if they arrested me—or whatever they called it—but I told him I would.

With my feet dangling in the air, I was maneuvered toward the dragons, their glowing eyes the only lights on the dark mountainside. As surreptitiously as I could, I slipped my cloaking charm out of my pocket.

"Val?" Amber called uncertainly as I was levitated into her view.

She was on her back, bound by magic and unable to escape, and the pain in her voice stabbed a dagger into my heart. Since she was right in front of Shaygor, I hoped he would bring me close to her. I was counting on it. There hadn't been time to come up with a *real* plan—like finding someone to sell me a case of magically enhanced grenades.

Shaygor maneuvered me closer, keeping me ten feet off the ground. As I floated closer to Amber—I was within a few feet—I carefully tossed the camouflage charm down to her. In the dark, she wouldn't see it, and I didn't know how much she could move, but it bounced off her sternum. She had to *feel* it.

Out of the corner of my eye, I saw it land on the shale near her hand. I was careful not to look at her, to draw attention to what I'd done. Hopefully, the dragons would consider the magic of my charms too insignificant to notice. Hopefully, they were focused on me and preparing to peel away the layers of my mind.

The power holding me aloft wrapped around me so tightly that my body ached and it was hard to breathe. I wore my armor, held my sword, had my gun, had my tiger... and still I could do nothing to fight this fate. How was I supposed to distract the dragons enough for Sindari to sneak in and take Amber away? Had she noticed the charm hit her and would she grab it if the power locking her into place faded?

The charms on my thong slipped around to the back of my neck, dangling in the air. I envisioned the lock-picking one in my mind, remembering how it had allowed me to break a dark elf's magical bond once. But it had never worked on the dragons. Their magic was too strong.

Now, I will see all that your mind holds, mongrel, Shaygor said. *This time, there will be no interruptions. My cousins will see to it.*

"You're going to be in for a boring show," I managed to get out, my jaw almost too immobile to form words. "There are a lot of years of washing my hair, shaving my legs, and binge-watching *Deadliest Catch* floating around in there. You dragons might be into that. You like fishing, don't you?"

Pressure pushed at my mind, like a finger prodding at a gelatin dessert before breaking through.

"Though maybe dragons, being so serious most of the time, are more into guilty pleasures. *Real Housewives, The Bachelor. Cupcake Wars?*"

"Val," Amber whispered, staring up at me. Had she managed to shift her hand slightly to grab the charm? It was hard to tell. "What are you doing?"

"Trying to rescue you."

"Well, you suck at it."

"I know. Sorry. Assassinations are more my forte."

I gritted my teeth, trying to deny the dragon access to my mind, but mental talons scraped deep, sifting through my thoughts, trying to force me to think about the night of Dob's death.

"I'd be okay with you assassinating them," Amber said.

Her voice sounded distant. I was too focused on blocking the dragon to respond, to think about anything else. No, that wouldn't work. He'd almost broken through before. I had to try something else, had to get them to release Amber, or at least move them away from her so Sindari could fetch her.

"Wait," I blurted. "Stop. It hurts. I'll tell you everything, make it easy on you. Just promise me you'll protect me from Zav."

The pressure lessened, and I felt an inkling of curiosity.

What has he done? Shaygor asked. *Forced you to take him as a lover?*

No, he's the only dragon who hasn't been an asshole, I thought, but I didn't form the words in my mind where he could see them. It surprised me that Zav's enemies would think so poorly of him.

"He's spoken to me of his political plans. I'll share them with you and tell you everything that happened the night Dob died."

He has political plans? That was one of the gold dragons speaking for the first time. *I thought he was his mother's mindless toady.*

"I've heard a lot in my time as his, uh, lover." Maybe I should have spoken those words in my mind, because Amber gaped up at me in horror. "He warned me that he'd kill me if I spilled the beans, but if you can protect me…"

She is lying, the second gold dragon spoke telepathically. *Zavryd'nokquetal would not threaten even the lowliest vermin. He is irritating and obnoxious to come up against, but he is honorable. Don't let her fool you, Shaygorthian.*

Whoever this guy was, I didn't like him. I focused on my lock-picking charm, trying to pour my energy into it to break the dragon's bonds around me. Even if I could only get free for a second, that might distract them enough to loosen their magical grip on Amber. Then she could grab the charm and use it to get out of here.

I believe you are right. Shaygor's eyes flared brighter, and the pressure returned to my mind. *She is lying, as she has lied to me from the beginning. Finally, I shall find out the truth.*

Acute pain stabbed into my brain, and all thoughts of drawing upon magic rushed out of my head. All I could think about was the agony. And that I hated dragons.

Shaygor forced me to relive the night under the house, the battle with the shifters and facing off against Dob.

She fought against my son that night, Shaygor said, speaking to the others, not me, acting like a brain surgeon discussing what he was doing for the sake of a camera. *She presumed to fight against a dragon. And then Zavryd'nokquetal arrived. He attacked Dobsaurin without provocation.*

Without provocation? Dob had been *killing* me.

He will be punished, Shaygor said. *He should be killed.*

Yes, one of the gold dragons agreed. *If he killed one of our own, the punishment will be steep. Even his own mother won't be able to stop us. If she does, she'll bury herself among those who vote on the court.*

Our family will finally be able to rise up and officially take power, Shaygor said.

"No," I snarled, frustrated with their stupid politics and that Zav could be killed because of me. Enough hiding. I had to own up to the truth. I didn't regret killing that asshole anyway. "Zav always obeys your stupid pompous laws. He didn't kill Dob. *I did!*"

What? all three of them cried at once.

Then they *all* dove into my mind, tearing thoughts away, learning everything of that night. The pain was so intense that I would have collapsed to the ground if their power hadn't kept me aloft. In that moment, I prayed for death. This was too much, so much worse than simply dying.

The pain and pressure vanished from my mind. I tumbled to the ground, almost landing on Amber as Shaygor and the gold dragons spun around.

Zav, his black form like the fist of Death streaking in across the night sky, plummeted toward the three dragons. I grabbed Amber—she was sitting up, the charm clenched in her hand—and tugged her to her feet. Zav slammed into Shaygor like a wrecking ball, and the two dragons almost flattened us as they rolled past, tails, wings, and limbs entwined, fangs snapping at each other.

My head throbbed with pain, but I scrambled down the slope with Amber, determined to get her out of danger. I pushed her toward the trees where I'd left Mom. Sindari ran over to join us.

"Use the charm to hide," I whispered to her, aware that Zav would only be able to strike at one dragon at a time. "Go find Mom and Rocket. Sindari will protect you."

She grabbed my arm. "What about you?"

"I have to help Zav."

"*How?*"

I had no idea, but I couldn't abandon him, not when he was risking so much to help me. In attacking his fellow dragons, including one appointed as an inquisitor by his Justice Court, he might have turned himself into a criminal. He might end up getting that loathsome punishment and rehabilitation himself. What if they changed his personality? Turned him into another ass like Dobsaurin?

As Shaygor and Zav parted, both on the ground now, both turning to face each other, the gold dragons roared and sprang at Zav. The air crackled with energy as he launched a magical attack at them. It struck them like a wall, making them pause, but when he was focused on them, Shaygor charged in, fangs snapping toward Zav's throat.

"Go." I pushed Amber again. "Get my mom and get off the mountain, and then drive back to Seattle tonight."

She looked like she wanted to argue more, but a glance at the insane battle raging twenty yards away must have changed her mind. She clenched her fist around the charm and ran down the slope, disappearing before my eyes as its power cloaked her. Sindari ran right behind her, though he glanced back, eyes meeting mine, and I knew he wanted to stay and help me.

Orange fire lit the night sky, casting weird shadows among the trees. Roars, grunts, and angry screeches silenced the sounds of all wildlife on the mountain.

With Chopper in hand, I rushed up the slope toward Zav. All three dragons had gathered around him. He was still on his feet, hurling power with his mind even as he lashed out with fang and claw at anyone who got close.

Before I could get close enough to strike, an invisible blast of power slammed into me. None of the dragons had been looking at me, but I was hurled twenty feet into the air. I twisted, maneuvering so I came down on my feet, then rolled to keep from breaking any bones.

One of the gold dragons had also been hurled back by that blast, but he simply took to the air, flapping his wings instead of landing. He flew up, banked, and dove toward Zav's back. Zav was busy facing off against the other two.

"Look out!" I yelled at him, not that he could do anything even if he knew of the attack coming.

I yanked Fezzik from its holder and sprayed bullets at the gold dragon. They bounced off a magical shield, as I'd expected they would, but he looked at me and adjusted his target. His green eyes flared brightly as he dove toward me.

There was nothing to hide behind, the ski slope cleared of boulders long ago, and the trees were too far away. I crouched, facing him like an idiot. An idiot with no other options.

He opened his maw as he descended, fire preceding his dive. I ran to the side as flames blasted the shale on the ground, rocks snapping under the heat. My fire-protection charm kept me from suffering the same fate, but the blast of heat turned my skin pink.

The dragon came through the flames, jaws snapping at my head. I shifted my body out of his reach as I whipped Chopper up to meet those fangs. I connected with his mouth, the blade clanking as it sank into scale and flesh, but a wing swept in from the side and knocked me back.

Only by a near-impossible feat of agility did I manage to keep my feet under me. Which was good because he landed, his neck swinging to the side, his maw coming in for another attack. Dark blood dripped from the side of his mouth, but he wasn't seriously injured.

I sprinted, not away from him but away from his neck and head. His tail lay ahead of me, flexed out a few feet above the ground. I rushed toward it as his maw followed me, his jaws snapping at the spot where I'd just been. Springing, I landed on the curving, flexing, balance beam of a tail. In a move I couldn't have replicated in saner moments, I ran up it onto his back, his scales as slick as ice under my boots. Or maybe that was his magical shield.

The dragon spun in a circle, bucking to throw me into the air. I went up but somersaulted and jabbed outward with Chopper as I came back down, trying to plunge my blade into him like a mountaineer burying his pick in the rocks.

Fearing my sword would bounce off, I cried, "*Eravekt*," the only command for it I knew, and dumped all of my will—all of my *power*—into that thrust.

Chopper flared intensely blue and sank through the shield and into dragon flesh.

My foe stiffened and cried out in startled pain and rage. Unlike with Dob, my sword had stabbed into his back to one side of his spine, not hitting a vital target. But I was shocked the blade had entered at all. I gripped the hilt with both hands to stay on as the dragon bucked and writhed, trying to knock me off, roaring in fury. Only thanks to my grip on the hilt of the embedded sword did I stay on. But then a spearhead of magical power slammed into my chest like a battering ram.

Chopper was torn from the dragon's flesh, and I flew backward, unable to do anything except slam down onto the ground. The power had hit me right in the solar plexus, and my muscles spasmed. I couldn't breathe, and a magical weight crushed down on me from above, keeping me from rolling over and jumping to my feet.

The gold dragon stalked toward me, my death blazing in his eyes.

Chapter 26

As I struggled to rise, to at least get off my back so I could face my death head on, the gold dragon stalked straight at me. His magic held me down. I couldn't move. Even as I tried to will Chopper's power to free me, or my own power, I knew it wouldn't work. The dragon wouldn't underestimate me again.

His great maw yawned open, orange fire roiling up from the back of his throat. If I couldn't move and it hit me straight on… even my charm wouldn't save me.

A shadow came in from the side, and something black landed atop me, blocking my view of the gold dragon.

Zav.

Blood dripped down his sides and splashed the rocks to either side of me, but he crouched, powerful leg muscles rippling under his sleek scales, and he breathed fire at the gold dragon even as the gold targeted him. The flames *should* have targeted me, but Zav blocked them with his body.

Heat and dancing flames scorched the ground to either side of him, shale blasting apart and striking my face and hands.

Distracted by Zav, the gold dragon no longer held me down with his magic. My chest muscles were still spasming from the blow to my solar plexus, but I managed to suck in a few wheezing breaths as I rolled to my hands and knees and then into a crouch. Zav was so large that I could almost stand straight under his belly.

But what could I do from under there with fire blasting down all around him? He was my shield, and I feared the sacrifice would cost him, that he could only withstand so much fire. This entire *battle* would cost him, even if we somehow beat the odds and won.

The gold dragon's fire halted. Zav's fire also halted, and darkness returned to the mountainside. I sensed the two other dragons farther up the slope, one injured and lying on his side and the other facing us. But he didn't advance. All of the dragons had stopped moving.

Since their auras were so powerful, it took me a moment to sort through all the magic that I sensed to realize that a portal had opened. I scooted to the edge of Zav's body, reaching up to rest a hand on his scales to try to convey that I appreciated his help, and saw the glowing silvery pane floating vertically in the air. The portal was huge, large enough for a dragon to fly through. Maybe someone was calling back the inquisitor and his cursed allies. Dare I hope?

Three more dragons flew out of the portal. I groaned. Had this many dragons ever been on Earth at once? Was all this because of me? Because I'd killed Dob?

Two of the new dragons were black, but I had no idea if that denoted a relationship to Zav. The third was a striking lilac that, under other circumstances, I would have admired.

Zav's wings drooped.

"Are we even more screwed now?" I asked.

That is my mother, my sister, and Shaygorthian's brother. They are all on the Dragon Justice Court.

"I'm not sure that answers my question."

The arrival of two of Zav's kin seemed to suggest that he had reinforcements, but Shaygor and his relatives outnumbered them. And I didn't know if Zav's mother and sister were here to help him... or to punish him for his role in Dob's death.

You think this is some lawless frontier where our rules and regulations will not be enforced? one of the black dragons boomed into my mind—into all of our minds, judging by the shuffling feet of the dragons. Only Zav stood immobile, still over me, still protecting me.

The voice sounded female and old and confident. I guessed this was Zav's mother.

We came to collect this mongrel who admits to having killed Dobsaurin, Shaygor replied. *This is not breaking any regulations.*

You were trying to kill her, the mother said.

Had Zav been communicating with her somehow from across the galaxy? Or did dragon magic allow them to look into what was happening on other worlds? How else could she know? Maybe she had the power to read the minds of other dragons.

She deserves that fate, Shaygor said. *And our laws were never meant to protect verminous human criminals.*

Our laws are for all.

The mother looked at me, violet eyes similar to but harder than Zav's pinning me.

I stepped out from under him, Chopper in hand, and held my head up. I wouldn't cower or hide behind someone else in front of her.

And, she continued, *this one is not fully human. Did you smell her blood?*

So, she's some elf's illegitimate child. It doesn't mean she didn't commit a crime.

She is King Eireth's offspring.

I blinked. My mom had slept with a king? If she'd known that part of the story, she'd failed to mention it. But would it matter at all to these dragons?

So, she's King Eireth's illegitimate mongrel child, one of the gold dragons said. *What does it matter? He wisely abandoned her on this backward scab of a world.*

If you let her go after she killed Dobsaurin, you yourself will be violating our rules and regulations. Shaygor looked at his colleagues, speaking to them as much as to her, and I sensed him scheming, maneuvering politically to try to take advantage of the situation.

Zav growled low in his throat. I wasn't sure any of the others would hear it. He wasn't talking much, but he was listening and doubtless had opinions.

This is true. Zav's mother looked from me to him. *If she truly slew Dobsaurin, she must be taken for punishment and rehabilitation. Not—* she looked pointedly at Shaygor, *—to be killed.*

I grimaced. Death sounded more appealing than what Zav had described.

She is unaware of our laws, Zav said. *This entire world is. They are ignorant of dragons.*

Maybe the Dragon Justice Court should establish a presence here to educate and train them, one of the gold dragons said.

Who would volunteer to rule over billions of mouthy vermin? Shaygor stared at me with cold intense eyes. *I care only about exacting justice upon my son's killer.*

Whatever happened, if I managed to survive to see another day, I would have an enemy for life. That was nothing new, but it wasn't as if I could defend myself against a dragon.

Justice is for all in the Cosmic Realms, Zav's mother said. *Ignorance of the law is not an excuse.*

Funny, we had that saying too. Maybe someone had originally gotten it from an arrogant visiting dragon.

She will learn dragon law as part of her rehabilitation. Zav's mother, the larger of the two black dragons, walked down the hill toward me.

If a dragon could look smug, Shaygor did. I was surprised he wasn't arguing harder to have me killed, but maybe he knew the truth, that their punishment and rehabilitation was worse than death.

Zav turned to stand beside me and face his mother, his dragonly shoulder much higher than but still next to mine.

Step aside, son, his mother said. *I will take her. Our family is not above the law. Our family, with so many eyes upon it, must uphold the law even more than others.*

And I always have, Zav replied. *But she was only defending herself against Dobsaurin, who not only tried to kill her but also came to this world specifically because he believed he could kill me and get away with it. He is the one who broke the law first.*

That may be true, and our official inquisitor will have to determine it, but that does not make it acceptable to kill a dragon. You knew this. That is why you did not try to land a killing blow. His mother looked to Shaygor and the other dragons, as if she was making a point. *Am I right, Zavryd?*

I did not try to land a killing blow, though it almost cost me my life. Dobsaurin attempted to compel Val—King Eireth's daughter—to strike a killing blow against me when I was down and dazed. He thought to use her to circumvent the law. Like the coward he was.

Do not speak ill of the dead! Shaygor stood straight, expanding his wings to their fullest. *My son was not a coward. No dragon in my family is a coward.*

The golds and the black dragon who had yet to speak shifted over to stand next to him, leaving Zav's mom and the lilac dragon—his sister?—standing alone and facing us.

"Maybe you shouldn't aggravate them," I whispered.

Had Sindari been here, he also would have offered that advice.

Step aside, Zavryd, his mother said firmly. *However it happened, the half-elf has slain a dragon. We will uphold the law.*

No. This is not the right thing, Queen Zynesshara.

I guessed he wasn't allowed to call her Mom.

The law is the law. One dragon cannot decide to change it.

Shale stirred behind me as Zav's tail shifted to encircle me, as if he could pull me close and protect me. I appreciated the gesture, but I'd already screwed things up for him and didn't want to be the source of a rift between him and his family.

Do not turn this into a battle, my son. Not over something so minor as this. Already, tensions are high among dragon-kind. You know this. Do not be the spark that ignites the wildfire.

I stepped around the tip of Zav's tail, touching it gently in case… in case I didn't see him again. "I'll go. I don't want to spark anything."

No! Zav boomed, and an image flashed into my mind of me running down into the forest while he dealt with his family. It had a touch of a compulsion to it, and I knew it was what he wanted, not a reflection of my own wishes. *You were not at fault,* he added, almost growling the telepathic words. *I will not let them take you.*

His mother paused, her eyes narrowed as she regarded us. Ugh, was she going to guess that we had feelings for each other? Everyone was quick to assume that—or at least that I was Zav's mate—but she hadn't suggested it. Yet.

She helped me in battle, as she has assisted me several times now, Zav stated to all the dragons. *I will not return this favor by handing her over to the court.*

I grimaced. He'd done more favors for me than I had for him. He didn't owe me anything. It wasn't that I wanted to stand in that court, but I didn't want to screw up his life.

She is loyal to me, Zav said.

When had he decided that? The other day, he hadn't trusted me fully. But I wouldn't dispute him. When it came to dragons, he was the one I would least be willing to cross.

I will not allow any of you to take her, Zav added.

You cannot stop us, Shaygor said, bolstered by the allies standing close to him.

They were an intimidating sight. As powerful as Zav was, he hadn't been winning his battle against them.

I do not have to because I will cite an even older law, from the time of the first dragons. Zav's serpentine neck rose, lifting his head to his greatest height. *I claim Tlavar'vareous for this female.*

He did what? That was the first word that hadn't automatically translated into my mind.

Zavryd, no, his sister warned, jerking her head up and speaking for the first time.

His mother's eyes narrowed even more, their violet light glowing brighter. *Do not be emotional, my son.*

One of the golds spoke in a sneering tone, *You, of all dragons, know that neither elves nor humans feel loyalty to us. All the lesser beings resent us for our power and have plotted for ages to see us gone.*

This is not true, Zav said. *Many are loyal to dragons. To* some *dragons.*

The gold dragon hissed at him.

I claim Tlavar'vareous for this female, Val Thorvald, Zav repeated. *If you strike at her, it will be a challenge to me, and you will have to fight me in open battle. Where you die. Within the confines of this ancient ritual is the last place a dragon may kill another dragon without repercussion. In a duel, one on one.* Zav looked Shaygor and each of his allies in the eyes. *Will any of you challenge me in this manner? Shaygorthian was not brave enough to face me without his kin here to hold me down.*

Several of the dragons growled and glared, but nobody challenged him, at least not this night.

If she is your female, then you are responsible for her actions and will be legally responsible for her punishments, Shaygor pointed out.

Er, *his* female? What had just happened?

I will be responsible for her future actions, yes, Zav agreed. *But I cannot be held responsible for what she did before I claimed her. And you may not now punish or kill her since she is under my protection. Only if I die can you take action against her.*

I didn't like this talk of claiming and being his female, but the way the enemy dragons were shifting their weight, ruffling their wings, and fuming made me realize he'd found some loophole in their laws.

Do not make this mistake again, his mother warned him, her words soft in my mind, her eyes on Zav. *Do not risk ruining your reputation—losing your life—for some female from a lesser species. Do you not remember the elf princess?*

Tangled Truths

Of course I do. But it is my mistake to make again if it is one. Zav looked down at me, and I feared he saw horror in my eyes rather than gratitude.

I am disappointed. His mother's voice grew louder again, the words for all, perhaps, instead of only Zav and me. *Tlavar'vareous is a personal matter and is your right to claim as a dragon lord of noble standing. This inquisition shall end, and Shaygorthian will not remove your female from your side, but if she commits any further crimes, you will be responsible for them. If she earns punishment, you will take it.*

I understand.

The others were still growling and fuming, as if Zav had gotten away with something. Or I had.

I rubbed my face, terrified that this would be as bad as if they'd killed me. Oh, I didn't want to die, but every time I accepted an assignment to assassinate a magical being, wouldn't I be breaking one of their laws? This was insane.

Finish it then, his mother said. *Make it official.*

The sister was swinging her head on her long neck, reminding me more of a pendulum than a head shake, but I could tell it was a sign of disagreement.

Zav shifted his tail again, sliding it around my waist as a wing came down to rest on my shoulders. The air glowed golden around him and tendrils of power formed, visible to my eyes as well as my senses. They curled around me and flowed into me, imparting euphoric energy that made me want to run sprints around the mountain. I felt power such as I'd never known, the magic of a dragon coursing through my veins. Zav's eyes glowed as he looked down at me, the magic flowing between us. The intimacy of the shared moment was both alien and scary yet familiar and appealing, and I found myself stepping close to him, resting my body against his leg, leaning my forehead into him as his wing covered my back.

What are you doing? I whispered in my mind.

Marking you so other dragons will know you're mine and under my protection.

I almost pointed out that I was my own person, and there was no way I would acknowledge that he had any claim over me, but with the mother and the others looking on—and maybe listening to my thoughts—I kept my mental mouth shut. *Later,* I could object.

The magic faded, the golden light gradually disappearing, but I tingled in the aftermath of the magic, even more than I usually did from standing next to him. If being marked meant I was going to tingle for the rest of my life, that might be problematic. It felt good, but it would be distracting.

Zav lowered his wing and faced his mother. I realized I'd been rubbing my cheek against his leg and flushed with embarrassment. Tingling apparently made a girl forget her surroundings—and the creepers watching on.

It is done, his mother said, sounding very reluctant. The look she gave me was not friendly. Her next words, I suspected, were only for me. *It is now your duty to serve him and obey him. If you betray him or cause the family to be disgraced, I will personally bite off your head, the laws be damned.*

I managed to clamp down on the sarcastic retort that wanted to come out—Sindari would have been proud.

My son, do not return home until you've apprehended those dark elves. And the rest of the criminals you've been so casual about finding. The next time you appear in the Dragon Justice Court, I need for you to be victorious and the champion of all those who were wronged. You know what's at stake if we don't maintain our majority status.

I know. I will, my queen. Zav bowed his head.

The portal formed in the air again. One by one, the dragons flew through it until Zav and I were alone on the mountainside.

Chapter 27

Zav shifted into his human form, and I now stood looking at his face rather than a meaty dragon forelimb. A breeze stirred the hem of his robe and riffled through his short black hair. His grave face was impossible to read.

"We have to talk," I said.

"I thought those would be the first words out of your mouth."

"That was a ruse, right? To get them off both our asses? Because your mom thinks I'm going to serve and obey you now, and we both know that's not happening."

Zav's violet eyes glowed faintly in the dark night. "It was not a ruse—if it had been, it would not have worked. I claimed you in front of many witnesses, and you are magically marked now. Other dragons and the more powerful of the lesser beings will recognize it. It may give you some protection. It may make you more likely to be targeted for manipulation and plots against me and my family. I admit I haven't fully considered all of the ramifications yet. It was…" He spread a hand, palm toward the sky. "All I could think of to keep them from taking you."

"I do appreciate that, but *Zav*." I couldn't keep the anguish out of my tone, the upset snarl of emotion out of my tight throat. "I don't want *you* to get in trouble now for things I do. You know what my job is and why I do it."

He stepped forward, chest brushing mine and lifting an arm to offer a hug. A part of me wanted to step back, to demand he figure out a way to undo this before it got us both in trouble—*more* trouble—but my body had other thoughts in mind. I found myself leaning into him, accepting the hug and returning it, resting my face against his shoulder. He had very likely just saved my life, at great risk to his own. I wasn't sure why he'd done it when I'd given him grief the whole time I'd known him, but I owed him something now. There was no way I would serve and obey him—gag—but I didn't want him to regret putting himself at risk to keep me alive.

Zav shifted his arm from merely wrapping around my back to rubbing the back of my head with his fingers. That felt amazing, but then he ruined it by saying, "I will provide you with a book detailing all of the dragon laws."

"Is that book as long as it sounds?"

"It is substantial. I will give you time to read it thoroughly and then quiz you."

"Homework? My punishment for helping you in a fight is homework?"

"You *did* help me," he said, his voice lowering into a pleased growl that sent a shiver down my spine. "But I am worried that you are getting more proficient at sticking that sword into dragons."

I almost joked that he had better watch out, but then I remembered the elf princess and his well-founded fear of someone seducing him and assassinating him.

"Only some dragons." I kissed him on the cheek to let him know he wasn't one of them. I didn't mean to, but my lips lingered on his warm skin, as I enjoyed the feel of my chest and body pressed against his. I grew more aware of his power wrapping around me, the alluring pull of his magic—of *him*.

His fingers stilled where he'd been rubbing my scalp, and without mind-reading skills, I knew we were both thinking about the hot tub. I drew back so I could see his strong face, his intent eyes, his perfect mouth. He looked at my lips, and his own parted. My heart raced and I leaned closer again.

"Up there!" came a cry from down the hill. "He's got her!"

Zav and I sprang apart.

Was that *Thad*? I groaned.

But maybe his arrival was saving me. I shouldn't have fallen into Zav's arms after he'd claimed me as his mate, making him think that I was going to *be* that. No way. If it kept the Dragon Justice Court off my back, fine, but there would be no obeying or serving or any of that crap.

"Shoot him!" a man yelled.

"No!" I shouted, stepping in front of Zav and raising my hands. It was out of instinct and, I decided a half a second later, stupid, because he could stop bullets more easily than I could. "This is my dragon ally. The bad-guy dragons have left."

"Bad guy?" Zav murmured, sounding unconcerned about the threat of gunfire. "You do know that large female was my mother, right?"

"Yes, I gathered that."

"I wasn't sure how much she was sharing with you."

"All of it, I think."

"Hm."

"Maybe we can have a discussion later about this elf king I'm supposedly descended from." *Directly* descended from.

"I will have to research that. King Eireth is the elf who took over after the failed rebellion I told you about."

After the old king was ousted for conspiring against the dragons? If all that had happened after Mom had her elven dalliance, then this was recent history for the long-lived Zav. No wonder he was twitchy about people reaching for his neck. Or kissing him.

Rocket came bounding out of the trees, followed at a more majestic pace by Sindari. He'd presumably escorted Mom and Rocket to the end of the mile-range he could be from his charm and then waited to make sure they got away. Or maybe they'd encountered Thad and his friend coming to search for them.

"Dragon ally?" Thad asked skeptically as he, his buddy, and Mom walked out after their four-legged guides.

Flashlight beams sliced across the rocky mountainside, one shining in my face for a moment. Zav grunted, and I remembered his displeasure with my phone's flashlight app. Chopper was still glowing from when I'd called out the illumination command—I needed to learn if the sword had more useful commands—so I held it aloft, hoping they would put away their flashlights.

"Isn't that the man who came to the house and glowered at me?" Thad stopped several feet away, eyeing Zav, me, and my sword.

Everyone was eyeing that sword, even Rocket, though he was also sniffing the air liberally. The dragon-scented air. But thanks to the light, everyone could see that the dragons were gone. Chopper's illumination command must override its built-in camouflage.

"He's good at glowering, yes," I told Thad, "but he's still an ally."

"I am more than an ally," Zav stated, his chin up, his shoulder brushing mine. "I have claimed Val as my *Tlavar'vareous sha*."

"Your what?" Thad's hand tightened on the rifle his buddy had unwisely given him.

Before Zav could clarify, I reached over and placed my hand over his mouth. "We're also pen pals."

His eyes flared with violet light—and indignation. I lowered my hand, reminding myself not to be too presumptuous with him, though at this point, I didn't think he would lash out at me in anger. Instead, he'd probably put a lot of handwritten addendums into that book on dragon laws.

"Is Amber okay?" I'd assumed she was with them and camouflaged, but she hadn't yet spoken up. My heart almost stopped as I realized she might not have found them.

"I'm here," Amber said from behind my mother.

She appeared as she eased closer, her arm extended, the charm on her palm. She was also eyeing Zav warily and didn't get too close. As the only one among them who could sense his aura, she had the clearest idea of what he truly was, of the power that came with a dragon.

Bringing him to family dinners was going to be out; I could tell. Not that I planned to attend those any time soon. This whole trip had only reinforced what I'd known all along. Thad and Amber and Mom would all be safer if I had no contact with them. I accepted the charm with glumness and didn't speak as I threaded it back on my thong.

I am pleased your offspring is no longer so wary around me. Sindari was sitting and watching everything calmly.

Probably because you're not blocking her exit from the bathroom this time.

She has learned that I am here to help. The canine is less enamored with me.

Why?

He peed on a tree and I placed my mark over it. It is important for the mountain wildlife to know that Sindari of Del'noth was here.

You don't think it's important for them to know Rocket was here?

That simple creature? Certainly not.

"This isn't the guy who kidnapped you?" Thad's buddy asked.

"No," Amber said. "He's the guy Shauna said is hot."

There was enough light to see Thad's eyebrows fly up. Amber hadn't said it snidely or jokingly, more as a simple statement of truth, but I had a feeling it was part of her ongoing conscious or unconscious attempt to sabotage that relationship. Well, that was Thad's issue to deal with, though I felt guilty sending him back with a teenage daughter and no co-parent to help work things out.

"I am capable of producing flames of more than two thousand degrees Fahrenheit," Zav stated.

Everyone looked at him.

Zav looked at me. "Fahrenheit? Is this not your word for measuring temperature?" He asked it in the same way he'd asked me if his definition of gay was correct.

"Yes, but she wasn't talking about that kind of hot. But don't look it up. Your ego is already gargantuan." I raised my voice so everyone would hear. "Zav won't be a problem. The other dragons are gone, at least for now, but you should head back home, and I... should go back to not showing up at your doorstep."

Mom shook her head grimly. She'd probably liked having the family together, sort of, for a couple of days. This was for the best though. She could continue to do things with them. I would be the only odd woman out. Odd. That was me.

"Now that the threat here is gone," I added, "I have to go back and help Willard deal with those goblins."

"You found them?" Mom asked.

"They came to the house looking for me." No need to mention I'd been baiting a trap.

"The house?" Thad frowned. "The house I rented and am responsible for?"

Remembering the goblins tramping inside and peering out the windows, I lifted a placating hand. "I'm going back there. I'll make sure they didn't do any damage."

"This vacation isn't going at all how I'd planned," Thad said.

He, his buddy, and Mom turned and headed back down the hill with Rocket.

"Can I talk to you a minute, uh, Val?" Amber asked.

She didn't know what to call me. I didn't know what to ask her to call me. Val was fine.

"Yes." I took a few steps forward, assuming she wanted to speak in private.

Zav walked forward with me.

I stopped and put a hand on his chest. I almost asked him to meet me back in Seattle in a couple of days but remembered I needed a ride—a flight—back to the house, where I would likely spend the night sweeping and mopping goblin detritus until Willard showed up.

"Give us a couple of minutes, will you? Your aura intimidates those who can sense it."

"It does not intimidate you." Zav smiled slightly, as if that pleased him.

"Yeah, but we've discussed how I'm special."

"You vex dragons."

"That's what makes me special. And trust me, your aura is problematic for me too. Apparently, it lingers. I've tried to scrub it off, but full-blooded magical beings keep saying they can sense it on me."

"Scrub it off?" Zav tilted his head, forehead creasing in puzzlement. "That will not work, not now. As I informed you, I have magically marked you so other beings will know you're mine."

Something we were going to have to discuss. Once dragons stopped being interested in reading my mind, I expected him to *un*-mark me.

"I guess I might as well toss my loofah collection in the lake then."

"Yes." Zav nodded once firmly, but then lifted a finger, the puzzled expression returning. "I am not familiar with that word."

"You can look it up the next time you're perusing one of our dictionaries." I patted him on the shoulder, held up a hand to encourage him to stay put, and joined Amber farther down the slope.

"Your life is really weird," she said without preamble.

"I think we established that earlier. Are you all right?" I looked her up and down by the blue light of the sword. "The dragon leader said he hurt you."

"He did, but it doesn't hurt anymore." She shrugged. "I'll be okay, but I don't want to see any more dragons ever again."

"I keep saying that, too, but I don't think I'll be that lucky." I glanced at Zav.

He'd moved over to stand beside Sindari. Maybe they were chatting about how confusing Earth terminology was.

Amber lowered her voice. "They won't kidnap me again, will they?"

"I don't think so. They left, and the situation should be resolved for the time being."

Never mind that the resolution was going to put a serious crimp in my dating life, should I actually have plans to pursue male companionship. It wasn't something I usually had time for, but knowing Zav might show up and loom behind me at any dinner date I tried to arrange abruptly made me feel that my freedom was being impinged. It wasn't as if I could date *him*. Even if he didn't have baggage, he was too alien, arrogant, and dragonly to seriously consider as a mate. I hoped I could avoid being stupid and having sex with him now that I knew he was into me. Or at least his human biological bits were. But he'd agreed our kiss had been a mistake. As long as we both kept our clothes on, we should be fine. Absolutely no more hot tubs.

"Thad has my number," I said. "Let me know if anyone magical comes and bothers you, dragon or otherwise."

Amber hesitated, studying the shale between our feet. "Can I have your number?"

I bit my lip, torn between wanting to have a relationship with her—this was the first hint that she might be vaguely interested in that—and knowing I should avoid any further contact with her.

"Yes." It might not have been wise, but that's what I said.

On the dark mountainside under the stars, we exchanged phone numbers.

"Thanks." She looked at me, as if wondering if we were supposed to hug, then gave a choppy wave and ran off. Mom and Rocket were waiting by the tree line.

I returned the wave more slowly and solemnly, then walked toward Sindari and Zav, ready to go back and help Willard deal with the goblins.

A thought occurred to me before I reached them. I held up a finger and pulled out my phone.

"Uh, yeah?" Amber answered. "What'd you think? I gave you a prank number?"

"No. I need to talk to your grandmother for a minute, and I didn't want to distract your dad when he's holding a gun."

Amber snorted. "Good idea."

"Yes, Val?" Mom asked when she took hold of the phone.

"Remember when we were talking about abandoned elven sanctuaries? And you said you'd been to one before my father's people left? Do you think there's any chance that it's *still* abandoned? With all the magic guiding people away from this one, it seemed like it was chance that even the sasquatch stumbled across it."

"I wouldn't know, but it's possible."

"Do you remember where it was?"

"Of course. I went there often. Out past Granite Falls, on the way, sort of, to the hiking trails in the area."

"Sort of as in ten miles away from an actual road?"

"Only five or six. Let me see if I can put a pin in this phone's map and send it to you."

"Thank you."

I hung up and said, "My mom is remarkably adept with technology for someone who doesn't have any of her own."

"Your technology is simple to learn compared to magic," Zav said.

"That *can't* be true. Orcs and trolls use magic, and they'd have to multiply their IQ points to come up with a positive number."

Zav looked at Sindari, and Sindari looked back at him.

"You know, because their IQs are negative numbers. Never mind." What was the saying about if you had to explain a joke…?

"The magic of lesser beings is less sophisticated," Zav said, "but dragon magic is very intricate and complex."

"Any chance elven magic can be picked up in a weekend crash course? Or that there are CliffsNotes?"

"No," Zav said, though I was positive he didn't know about CliffsNotes.

Perhaps, Sindari told me, *your mother should have fallen in love with an orc, thus to ensure your magical education would be simpler.*

"I'll ask her why she didn't consider it when she sends that pin. Everybody knows tusks are hot."

"Hot?" Zav stepped away from us to give himself room and transformed into his dragon form. *I have not yet had an opportunity to research alternative meanings of that word.*

"No need," I said as he levitated me onto his back. "Just take me back to Harrison, please. I may have a solution for the goblin problem."

Chapter 28

The night felt like it had been going on forever, but dawn was barely creeping into the eastern sky when Zav flew across Lake Coeur d'Alene, past Harrison, and toward the house on the point. A Pilatus PC-12 seaplane that hadn't been there when we'd left was snugged up to the dock, a uniformed soldier standing guard beside it. The house and landscaping lights were on, and I spotted Willard, also in uniform, gesturing as she spoke to thirty or forty goblins sitting cross-legged on the lawn.

"Huh. They actually stayed." As Zav took us over the plane to land in the grass, I noticed that the front door was open. I hoped the goblins had only napped on the couch and maybe played a few video games while they'd waited. When Zav settled low so I could slide off easily, I did so and patted him on the side, careful not to touch any of his wounds. "Thank you for the ride. Why don't you go rest somewhere, so you can heal those deep gouges?"

I was healing while I was flying. My wounds were not as grievous as others I've earned in battle. They will continue to regenerate with time. I am capable of overseeing the negotiations with the goblins.

My boss, Colonel Willard, is handling that.

A dragon would be able to command respect and acquiescence from them far more ably than a human.

By threatening to light them on fire if they don't do what you want?

No. By magically compelling them to obey my wishes.

We're going to try to do things in a way that they won't later resent. I patted him again and headed toward Willard's meeting.

They would not dare *resent a dragon. Besides, it is an honor to do the will of a dragon. As you will learn.*

Uh huh.

It must have been a breaking point in the meeting, because Willard turned away from the goblins as I approached. She rubbed her temples and glowered at me.

"Are you crabby because it's not going well or because you didn't get your beauty sleep?" I asked.

"Both."

"You couldn't sleep in the plane?" I waved to it. "How did you manage a private ride out here?"

"The local sheriff said you were being an ass, and the government is concerned about the roads that keep getting destroyed and wanted a solution put in place immediately."

"Do they know goblins are responsible?" I ignored the comment about the sheriff.

"They've heard sasquatch. They believe terrorists."

I eyed the goblins. Two were sharing a box of donuts they'd found in the kitchen. White powder smeared their fingers and chins.

"I'm certainly terrified of them."

"The problem is that there's no place for them to legally go that isn't someone else's property—or claimed by the indigenous wildlife."

"I may have a solution for that." I showed her the pin my mother had sent. "It was once an elven sanctuary and may still be protected by their old magic. We'd have to see if anyone else has stumbled onto it in the intervening years."

"In the Mt. Baker-Snoqualmie National Forest? You want to bring these goblins closer to *us?*"

"To a spot where they could make a home and not be hunted by people."

"How do you know about this place?"

"My mom used to get laid there."

Willard blinked and looked at me.

"Trust me. It's just as appalling to me that my mom once had a sex life. But it could have been worse. She could have been into orcs."

"You're an odd woman, Thorvald."

"Why does everybody say that?"

"Let me make a call and have someone go search that spot to see if it's as unclaimed as you think. Since it's the National Forest, there shouldn't be anyone living in there, but the world isn't what it once was."

"Tell me about it." I turned to look for Zav and was surprised that he wasn't where he had landed.

He'd ambled out to the dock and was curled up in a ball like a cat. A giant cat that took up the whole dock and then some, with his tail dangling off into the water.

The soldier who had been guarding Willard's exit—or maybe he was the pilot who'd stepped out for a smoke—was in the same spot, oblivious to the dragon sleeping—or regenerating his wounds, maybe—two feet in front of him. He would be in for a surprise if he tried to take a walk.

"Make sure to send someone with magical blood," I called to Willard as she made her call. "Mundane people will be diverted without noticing the place."

She waved a few fingers in acknowledgment.

The goblin work leader with the bike chain bracelets—Nogna—left the group gathered on the lawn and approached me.

"You looking for your artifact?" I'd been toting it around all night. If I'd thought about it, I might have taken it out of my pack and used the platter like a chakram.

"We would like it returned, yes," she said, "but I came over to say that I did not expect the Ruin Bringer to help goblins."

"I'm working on my image. Apparently, I'm known for brutalizing people."

"Yes." She nodded, no hint of humor in her eyes.

I grimaced.

"We appreciate your assistance. It has been difficult for us to find a place."

"I guessed that from the ad hoc sasquatch alliance." Not an alliance, I supposed, if the sasquatch had been unwillingly controlled by an artifact.

What would the goblins find to control in the Baker-Snoqualmie National Forest? Wolves? Cougars? Squirrels?

"Yes. They are kindly creatures and were amenable to helping us, inasmuch as they understood what we wanted, but they weren't interested in giving up their home."

"Understandable."

The goblin reached up and gripped my forearm, her chains clacking. "We will remember this favor, Ruin Bringer, especially if we find a new home."

"Thanks." I couldn't imagine calling upon a goblin for a favor, unless one was working in the city and could be an informant, but I pretended to be grateful.

I walked up to Willard as she ended her call. "Any luck?"

"I've got a couple of agents going out to check." She yawned and rubbed her eyes. "I'm beat. I only slept for an hour before you called me."

"You slept? Colonels lead luxurious lives."

"What were you doing while I flew out here?"

"It's a long story. I may tell you later."

"You may put it in your report like a normal government contractor who wants to be paid."

I didn't think that field trip to retrieve Amber had anything to do with my regular duties, but I shrugged. I'd share something.

"I half expected to find you in that hot tub with your feet kicked up." Willard nodded to the deck, the lid still off the hot tub. "Perhaps with a dragon. Didn't you mention that you and your hunky dragon were in it together?"

Lacking magical blood, Willard wasn't aware of Zav sleeping on the dock.

"Briefly," I said. "We were putting on a ruse to lure in the goblins."

"They get excited by naked humans and dragons?"

"Who doesn't?"

"Did *you* get excited?" She raised her eyebrows in curiosity. "By a naked dragon? I assume he took on a human form."

"Of course he did. Dragons don't fit in hot tubs as they are."

"They're big, are they?" Her eyes crinkled.

"Well endowed, yes. From what I've observed, shifters always take the form of fit and handsome individuals. Which is weird if you ask me. Pudgy balding people would fit into society better."

"But wouldn't be as exciting to look at in the hot tub," Willard said.

"Probably not."

"Did you do anything other than look?"

My cheeks flamed with heat at the memory of being naked in the bubbling water with Zav. And of the kiss we'd shared.

"A lady doesn't smooch and tell, Willard. You know that."

"I'm wondering what month I should put into my planner for the wedding."

"Dragons don't get married." They just claimed women as their own. I grimaced.

Fortunately, Willard let the subject drop in favor of a new one. "If your sanctuary pans out, I need you to get these goblins back to Washington."

"Me?" I touched my chest.

"You. Consider it the final item on the checklist you need to complete in order to get paid for this mission."

"You're making me nostalgic for gigs where all I had to do was lop off the heads of bad guys."

"Not all problems can be solved with violence."

"Yes, but those problems are for *you*. Colonel Diplomat Willard."

"Uh huh. Find a trailer, Val."

I thought of the RVs in the campground but supposed I couldn't liberate one of those.

Her eyes glinted. "Or a dragon."

"I don't think he'd be willing to transport thirty goblins on his back."

"Thirty-six. I counted."

"Of course you did."

Thirty-six goblins wouldn't fit in my Jeep. And a bus couldn't make it over the washed-out roads. My head was already hurting from the logistics of this problem.

"You can handle it." Willard patted me on the shoulder. "And good work on this mission. I know you prefer shooting people to solving mysteries. But now that I've seen you do that, you know what that means."

"You'll give me more missions like this?"

"Bingo."

❖❖❖❖

Sindari sat in the front passenger seat of the Jeep and growled over his shoulder whenever one of the six goblins riding in the back jostled either of us. I could have fit another goblin or two in Sindari's seat if I'd left him in his realm, but I'd wanted sane company for the ride home. Besides, the other thirty goblins hadn't seemed to mind being packed into the U-Haul trailer I was pulling. All they had requested was that we stop halfway back so they could have a bio break. I planned to do that alongside the highway on an abandoned road, not at a public rest stop, though it would be amusing to see people's reactions as green goblins streamed all over the place.

How many more hours will this trip last? Sindari asked.

Uh, we've barely turned onto the interstate, so probably about six. I thought the answer instead of replying out loud, though the goblins probably wouldn't have spied on us. They were busy building extensions on the oh-shit handles back there, so they would have something to grab if the ride got rough. I'd told them the interstate was smooth all the way home and that the only iffy spot had been when we'd crossed the road that *they'd* washed out, but they didn't believe me.

Sindari turned a glum expression on me. *I missed the entire dragon battle while escorting your offspring down the mountain, and when you bring me back into your world, it is to babysit goblins.*

The dragon battle was nuts. You're lucky you missed it.

I remembered how many cuts and deep claw marks I'd seen on Zav's flanks as I'd ridden him back to Harrison. When he'd been in human form, with the dark of night around us, they hadn't been as noticeable. Once again, he'd taken a lot of damage to protect me. I would have to think of a suitable gift to give him as a thank-you. He didn't like sweets, and wine reminded him of the drink the elf chick had used to drug him, so I'd try something else. Maybe a nice quarter of beef from the butcher shop. Or a charcuterie board. Did dragons like cheese?

Lord Zavryd said you sank your sword into the back of one of his enemies.

He spoke to you?

While you were talking to your daughter, yes. He seemed impressed by your warrior prowess, especially given the limitations placed on you by your human half.

It's been a difficult handicap to overcome, but I've persevered.

My phone buzzed. It was Willard, already back in Seattle, most likely. She'd had a certain glee in her eyes when she'd informed me that Corporal

Clarke had located the sanctuary and found the spot unclaimed, but that the seaplane she'd ridden out in didn't have room for extra passengers. That meant it was up to me to transport all of the goblins to their new home.

I didn't want to pull over, so I reluctantly let the call run through the Jeep's speakers, so everybody could listen to what I hoped would be a short conversation. She probably wanted to check and make sure I'd gotten my green passengers all loaded up.

"Back home already, Willard?" I answered.

"Back in the office. I have a visitor."

"On a Sunday?"

"On a Sunday."

"Is there a reason you're telling me about it?" I couldn't imagine who I had been in contact with lately that would have gone to her office. Neither Nin nor Dimitri knew where it was. Zoltan, with his internet expertise, could have found out easily enough, but even if he was hoping for sasquatch gland secretions, he wouldn't have gone out in daylight.

"It's about you. A guy in a robe and slippers is demanding that I assign you to work with him to apprehend the two dark-elf scientists, as well as every other criminal on a long list he's showing me. Also, I need to run all of your future assignments through him to ensure you will not be assassinating magical beings in violation of the Laws of the Cosmic Realms put in place and enforced by the Dragon Justice Court."

It was rare that I didn't know what to say, but I didn't know what to say.

A resounding thud came over the phone, like something thumping against wood.

"What was that?" I couldn't imagine Zav pushing Willard around to get his way, but it had sounded ominous.

"He put a copy of a book on my desk. The legs wobbled under its weight."

"That is a complete set of the Laws of the Cosmic Realms as decreed by the Dragon Justice Court, modern era," came Zav's voice from somewhere in the room. "I was thoughtful and made two copies, one for you and one for my *Tlavar'vareous sha*."

"Your what?" Willard asked.

"It means pen pal," I blurted.

"I have claimed Val Thorvald for my mate," Zav stated.

I wanted to drop my face in my hand, but I couldn't do that while driving. A bevy of goblin whispers started up in the back. They were speaking in their own language, and I decided I didn't want to activate my translation charm.

"Does that mean there won't be a wedding?" Willard didn't sound nearly as stunned as she should have. "Because I was looking forward to seeing Thorvald in a dress."

"I'd make you my maid of honor and get a dress for you too, Willard."

"It is inconsequential whether our union is recognized by Earth governments," Zav stated. "Only that other dragons recognize her as mine and leave discipline and punishment to me."

"Discipline and punishment? Is that as kinky as it sounds?"

"*Willard!* Don't encourage him."

"I can't help myself. I'm fascinated, though I am rather shocked you would agree to being disciplined by anyone."

"I didn't agree to any of this. He *claimed* me without asking first."

"I claimed her to save her from being hauled before the Dragon Justice Court by my irate enemies and kin," Zav said.

"Both your enemies *and* kin were irate with Val?" Willard asked. "I suppose I should be surprised, but I'm not."

"Tell him to go away," I told her. "And that he can't boss you around. You have to stand up to him, no matter how powerful his aura is."

"I told him I'd already assigned you to finding the dark-elf scientists and that we would discuss the rest after you've accomplished that. And after my office has gone over this, ah, *robust* tome."

"You're not actually going to *read* it, are you?"

"Are you kidding? I'm going to have my intelligence gatherers scrutinize it with an electron microscope. Do you know how long I've been scrounging data from unreliable informants that I've had to blackmail, bribe, and brutalize for facts on the magical beings popping up on Earth? Not to mention the interplanetary politics that we've been ignorant of for the entire existence of mankind."

"Are you allowed to brutalize informants?"

"Just the orcs. They kind of like it."

"Only when someone hot does it."

"Are you saying I'm not hot, Thorvald?"

"I'm sure you're fine to guys who like that muscular, firm type."

"That's a lot of guys. Trust me."

"Hot," came Zav's voice in the background. "Definition 2-b-2 in your Merriam-Webster dictionary lists that as sexy. As in 'that guy she's dating is really *hot*.'"

I groaned. "I told him not to look that up."

I looked at Sindari.

Dragons are not known for obedience, he commented.

"Did Thorvald call you that?" Willard sounded highly amused.

I still couldn't believe Zav had gone to her office.

"No," I said. "Thad's girlfriend apparently did."

"Your dragon did choose an attractive human form," Willard said. "I usually prefer my guys darker, but I'd take him to bed."

I hoped she was messing with me and not truly flirting with Zav. That would have been surreal and also horrific on a lot of levels.

"I have claimed Val because we have battled together several times and she has stood at my side," Zav stated. "She also prongs dragons with her sword. Few other females from lesser species would be worth considering."

"Your dragon just dissed me, Thorvald."

"He disses me too." I kept my voice neutral and definitely not smug at Zav's words. I didn't *want* a dragon, and this was only going to be trouble going forward. I could tell.

"While he's disciplining you?"

"Don't sound so fascinated."

"It's hard not to. You know you're one of my more entertaining contractors, right? With all this going on, there's no need for me to read novels or tune into television."

"You're the most interesting boss I've ever had, Willard."

"It's a mutual love-fest around here. Hurry back. Your dragon is waiting for you to prong someone new."

THE END

CONNECT WITH THE AUTHOR

Have a comment? Question? Just want to say hi? Find me online at:
http://www.lindsayburoker.com
http://www.facebook.com/LindsayBuroker
http://twitter.com/GoblinWriter
Thanks for reading!

Printed in Great Britain
by Amazon